Hidden Ability

Book One of the Crown Saga

By Aldus Baker

DEDICATION

For my wife and children.

Thank you for your love, understanding, support and being at the center of all good things.

And, thank you to the other best people in the world, my readers.

CONTENTS

ACKNOWLEDGEMENTS

My gratitude and thanks to the people that have encouraged me by both example and valuable assistance, especially to:

My #1 beta reader and the best wife in the world, Tina, for still loving me after trying to help me.

Pete Carter for his imparting to me the basics of book cover design and being helpful and encouraging in general.

Simon Whistler who, though he doesn't even know it, provided vital inspiration and information with his *Rocking Self Publishing Podcast.*

Prologue

Scrub oak and evergreens gave way to brush and grass where Krenis dismounted and rushed to the overlook. As he had feared, the carriage had heedlessly entered the narrow way and been forced to a halt by a barricade of logs and stones. Arrows rained down on the carriage. The driver struggled to back the horses away from the barrier in a worthy attempt to escape the trap. An arrow struck the driver's right arm. The man howled in pain and shouted curses at his frightened and confused team.

The bowman had abandoned his seat next to the carriage driver. He appeared to be using the horses and carriage to shield him from the enemy archers. Krenis spotted two of them on the far hillside. The sound of a bow gave away a third archer on the slope below him.

Krenis loaded a lead ball into his sling and sent it flying. The deadly projectile struck the helmet of the archer below him with the heavy thud of a hammer on an anvil. The man tumbled forward and rolled down the hillside like a rag doll.

The defending bowman lay crumpled on the ground now. A carriage horse screamed in pain. The driver fought for control of his team with both sets of reins wrapped around the fist of his good left hand while he continued to curse and plead with his horses.

Krenis spun the sling again. A second ball slammed into an enemy archer standing on the far hillside with sufficient force to penetrate his leather jerkin and put him down. Krenis released a third to similar good effect and the final archer collapsed.

Four men in ring mail armor bounded over the logs and stones of the makeshift barricade and ran toward the carriage with weapons raised. Their bellowed cries of attack echoed off the walls of the deep slender cut through which the roadway passed.

The carriage door sprang open. A very large angry man wielding a broadsword leapt out. The four attackers hesitated. Perhaps they expected help from the incapacitated archers. Krenis watched Lern swing his broadsword in a wide arc. The big swordsman disparaged the hesitating assailants by claiming they were spineless pathetic weaklings and the sons of goats. Lern loudly insisted any swine herd had more honor and smelled better than the four of them. One enemy charged toward Lern screaming threats as he brandished his war axe. The other three followed their companion's example.

Krenis smiled to himself as he left the overlook and returned to his horse. The ring mailed attackers had already lost. Lern was an expert at enraging his adversaries and then carving them up with his broadsword while they were too angry to think. Krenis wished he could stay and watch the fun, but it was not to be.

Captain Erida and his lancers would arrive soon. By now they must have routed the diversionary riders who had drawn them away from the carriage and sent it fleeing into the trap. Krenis could not afford to let Erida discover him. King Tamaron's orders had been clear. "Protect my son and remain hidden," he had said.

Even though Krenis and the lancers shared the same mission, he could not approach them. He almost laughed as he thought about the puzzle the three dead archers would make for Captain Erida. He pictured Erida in his House Mar plate mail of Black and Green; the captain wore a scowl while trying to determine the meaning of the three bodies. He would know someone had helped him, but not who, which Krenis believed was for the best. The last time he and Erida met, it had been difficult to avoid killing the man.

Δ

Krenis traveled a twisted and confusing route to keep Captain Erida's men from picking up his trail. He would have preferred to know who the attackers were but he could not approach any of the fallen enemies without risking contact with the king's lancers. He had managed to obey orders and remain unseen. He was not going to waste that success by being careless once he had the time to be careful.

As he rode, Krenis thought about his visions, especially the one from only an hour before. He had been lying flat on his stomach as he kept watch over the party. They moved along a more open section of road that ran through the Sand Hills.

Two lightly armored young riders wearing the royal Black and Green rode at the end of the short procession. They fed on a steady diet of dust kicked up by the carriage and horses in front of them.

The carriage driver sat on his high seat and gave his attention to his team and the road ahead. Next to the driver sat a bowman, his short bow unstrung in his lap and a quiver strapped to the side of his seat. The archer probably had the best eyes among them. Krenis made a point to stay out of his line of sight.

Beyond the carriage were four more lancers, also in Black and Green. Captain Erida rode in front on the right. Lieutenant Burk rode beside him on the left. Both men kept a careful watch and sat a saddle like the veterans they were. Behind Erida and Burk rode two lancers more experienced than the dust eaters at the rear. They carried their light lances well, the tailing ends deftly rested upon the rumps of their horses, the points angled out and forward of their mounts' heads.

Krenis had been wondering why the king sent him. Was the escort of six royal lancers and the large broad-shouldered sword master Lern not enough? How much protection did one wet nurse and a two-month-old baby prince need? In that moment the vision took him. Instead of watching the procession of lancers and carriage from his concealed position on a hilltop, he stood among them. He moved surrounded by the smell of dust mingled with horses and men. He heard horses' hooves striking hard packed earth accompanied by the creek and groan of the carriage suspension as it negotiated the rough ground. He saw the carriage and each lancer in his place. He perceived the contrast of sunlight and shadow, the heat of the road and the voices of the riders conversing.

Krenis ghosted unseen within the group of travelers. Ahead was a lightly forested area through which the carriage and lancer escort would soon pass. With a shift of his attention, Krenis moved there. He stood within the spot fully surrounded by woodlands.

He opened himself to the experience of this new place. Sunlight speared through the crowns of trees and struck the shadowed foliage lining the roadside. Bird song mixed with the furtive animal sounds in the undergrowth. A horse whinnied followed by a man's muttered curse. Krenis looked closer at the shadows and perceived the essence of the ten mounted brigands hidden in the woods.

He pulled away from the vision, a sure way to confuse himself, but speed mattered most now. When his real surroundings became clear, Krenis found himself sprinting down the back side of the hill to the draw where he had left Boy. He grabbed the horse's reins, leapt into the saddle and spurred Boy to a gallop in the hope of beating the travelers to the woods and spoiling the brigand's ambush.

As it often happened, what the vision revealed to him changed by the time he could react to it. Once he and Boy came galloping out of the hills and onto the road, the brigands had already attacked.

Krenis watched the six lancers wheel their mounts about to form a line. Each lancer took up his light lance in his right hand and his saber in his left. They were going to spur their horses forward and together charge the oncoming brigand riders. It would be something to see the six defenders come crashing into the ten attacking riders.

But he could not remain. Separated from the lancers, the carriage bounced along the roadway as it fled the oncoming battle. Only the bowman remained to defend it. Krenis believed as certain as daybreak that this was part of the enemy's plan. The brigands from the woods were not meant to overpower the lancers and capture or kill the prince. They were merely the hounds that drove the hart to the hunters by setting the carriage running.

Under orders to remain hidden and not wishing to be trapped with the carriage, Krenis spurred Boy back into the hills. He rode parallel to the road and headed for the choke point, the section of road that passed through a narrow cut between two hills. It was the most natural place to set up an ambush.

There had been no trouble when the lancers and carriage came through it earlier. But men could have followed along behind and blocked the road after the carriage passed. Then all they had to do was wait for the brigands to emerge from the woods and send the carriage fleeing back to them.

When Krenis reached the overlook above the choke point, that was precisely what had happened. The carriage was under attack and the ambush would have succeeded if he had not been there. *Kings and their secret plans within plans.*

King Tamaron must not have told anyone about Krenis or those he did tell were as loyal as Krenis himself. It was clear the ambushers had not expected a lone white haired kingsman with a sling.

It took Krenis until after dark to work his way back to a concealed position where he could check on the party again. When daylight returned Krenis did not see the bowman. The driver now sat next to one of the junior lancers who drove the carriage. Lern looked no worse for wear. The wet nurse tended to the baby and both looked to be well. *Jalan Mar. You won't get to use that name for long, little prince.*

There were seven new horses on a lead line tied to the back of the carriage. An eighth had replaced the wounded team horse. The party must have been forced to put it down after yesterday's ambush. That probably explained the smell of cooked meat Krenis had noticed last night. It would have been a shame to waste the wounded animal by leaving it all for the scavengers. In a handful of days the journey would end. Krenis would present himself to Lord Yen and then, maybe, he too could get a good meal.

CHAPTER I

Lord Hallis Yen lay on a hastily constructed pallet within the main sitting room of Yen Manor. The pain from his broken body had been deadened with herbs, but the pain was great. Perspiration formed sheens over the lord's pale features. He demonstrated an implacable resistance to both his injuries and the anesthetizing effect of the herbs as he argued with his wife.

"Lady, listen to me!" demanded Lord Yen in a hoarse rasp.

Lady Shara Yen stood next to her husband's pallet with her back to him and her head bent forward. The braid of her long auburn hair hung over her left shoulder and streamed down toward the woven carpet upon the flagstone floor. Her hands gripped the skirt of her gown, the fine brocade wadded within her white-knuckled grasp. Shara's thoughts were in turmoil. She could feel the bedrock of her life crumbling. In her mind's eye the image of her robust barrel-chested husband as he strode across the estate grounds warred with the reality of him grievously injured, unable to rise, almost unable to move at all.

He can't be dying, not Hallis Yen. It's unthinkable. Hallis had been a bulwark that never failed to shelter her and the children. Shara met him after the war when he was at the zenith of his fame, the noonday sun that dazzled a young maiden. Different than other men, he held no buried cruelty or hollow spirit hidden within him. He did not dissemble. Her growing affection for him flowered alongside the realization that he would never last at court. When the king bestowed land and title upon Hallis, Shara saw that it was the most gracious banishment the sovereign could offer. Hallis had known it too and took full advantage of the gift in order to flee Lavembra with his dignity intact. Better for him to be his own master on captured territory at the edge of the kingdom than a pawn in a war of courtly politics. That's what he told her as he struggled for a way to ask for her hand in marriage. He even tried to apologize for having the temerity to ask her. She said yes three times before he'd believed it. She had gone with him most willingly. And he had taken his nowhere and built it into their oasis, the profitable holdings of House Yen. *What anchor will steady House Yen now when the winds of fortune blow cruel?*

"Lord, I hear you," said Shara. Her voice sounded as conflicted as her thoughts. She raised her head. Her own shadow hung across the far corner of the room, wavering and ill-defined in the light of the single lamp behind her. Pushing away the fear, she turned to face her husband. His half shadowed face looked to the ceiling while his fever bright eyes bent toward her.

"At a time like this, when the world is crashing down around your house, you wish to put upon a ten year old boy, a boy who has been in every way our son save name alone, a burden of heritage beyond his years to handle. I believe, Hallis my beloved, that your oath overcomes your reason."

"My oath, dearest Shara, is the reason I must tell him. He was entrusted to us, you as surely as I. But, my sheltering hand will too soon be withdrawn." Hallis could not turn his head. His eyes searched Lady Shara's face for the effect of his words. "Will you stand in my stead? Will Darla? As our ability to protect him wanes, so must his understanding wax if he is to protect himself."

"Husband, Love, how will he take this? If I call him to you he will see the only father he has ever known dying. And when you tell him, it will take from him far more than his father. You will strip him of all family. He is in shock. He holds himself tight against your loss. His mettle is untested. Will your words be one hammer blow too many?"

"How I wish to stay with you sweet Shara. You are right to say it is too soon. Too soon for me to leave you and too soon to reveal the truth of Jalan's family. When I am gone, there will be those who see it as an opportunity. Someone will move against Jalan. If you cannot agree to tell him, then agree to teach him. He must be taught everything."

Lady Shara understood. She had argued against intense training in arms for a child. Now, Jalan would have to master those skills as best and as quickly as he could. He was only ten and his childhood was over, one more thing that passed with her husband.

"I cannot send him to the Society."

"No, that you cannot."

"I... I will teach him what I know. But, it's been a long time."

"It is all we... It's all you can do. It will be enough."

Enough? Is there ever enough? Enough strength? Enough love? Enough time? Shara didn't know.

"I will tell him Hallis. I will tell him when he turns 15. Not before. Let him struggle and learn what he must before he has to know why."

"Very well my love. Do as you deem best. That is the way it must be. I'll not be here. You have made your decision. Let it stand as the decision of House Yen. But, a man needs a reason to work hard. What will you tell him when he asks why his training is so difficult?"

Shara looked deeply into her husband's hazel eyes and said, "I will tell him to put his love for his father into every task. He would never dream of disappointing you."

The choice made, Shara set aside her worry over Jalan's future. Her full attention and anxiety settled once again upon her husband. Hallis's short graying hair and close cropped beard framed the pallor of his pale face. His eyes mirrored the pain of his crushed limbs. She bent low to gently press her lips to his. The thought that this might be their last kiss tore at her heart. She fled from the thought and rose quickly to pursue the next duty that must be performed.

"I will bring in the children. I'm sorry that Guri and Aena are not here. I'm sure they and their husbands will come as soon as word reaches them," said Lady Shara.

Δ

The high collar of Jalan's white linen shirt made his neck itch. He sweltered in the long brown dress jacket that squeezed him like a sausage. His black breeches would have gone well with a good pair of riding boots instead of the low heeled shoes Mistress Cessa insisted he wear with nothing but thin woven hose covering his ankles and shins. He hated being dressed like a little boy. The fact that Tomac was similarly attired or that the girls wore silken and lace dresses made not a crumb of difference.

Darla, his big sister, kept a firm grip on his left hand as they stood waiting in the hallway. She held Tomac's hand too. Vee, barely a step ahead of them, swayed slowly back and forth in front of the closed door as she twisted a brown curl of hair around her finger.

When Jalan tried to raise his free hand toward his neck, Darla looked down at him and said in a loud whisper, "Stop fidgeting."

"It itches," he said.

"Ignore it. It will pass," Darla hissed.

"Why does Vee get to dance in front of the door?"

Darla gave a heavy sigh. "Just keep still."

Darla always told everyone what to do. Jalan contemplated treading on her silk slipper to see how well she ignored that. Before he could do it Mother opened the door and said, "Come along." She beckoned to Vee as the door swung wide. "Father is resting, but he wishes to see all of you now."

When Lady Shara said, "you", she looked right at him. It made him feel singled out.

Vee hesitated and dropped her hand away from her hair before she stiffly entered the parlor. Darla had called it a sickroom, but she had refused to tell Jalan what sickness had struck their father. When Darla followed Vee, Jalan also felt reluctant to pass through the doorway. Before he could decide to proceed or pull away, he found himself being towed along by Darla. She turned sideways and propelled Tomac through the doorway first and then she sidestepped her way in with Jalan bringing up the rear.

The bright flame of an oil lamp drew his eyes to it. The room looked strange. The large comfortable chairs that normally sat before the hearth were gone. In their place a long low pallet lay atop a wooden framework. Jalan's father lay upon the pallet covered by a blanket. The lamp rested on a small table next to the pallet and spilled its light all about him. That single flame did not come close to illuminating the entire room and no fire burned in the hearth to add light or warmth. Gloom enveloped the far edges of the parlor where it added a feeling of heaviness to the still air. The two small windows on either side of the hearth were closed. They shut out the night and yet did nothing to keep the darkness at bay. The door on the opposite wall that led to an adjoining room was closed as well.

Mother shut the hallway door behind Jalan. The sound it made suggested something definite and final. It brought to mind the end of a long day when the whole world seemed tired. He imagined everyone and everything going to sleep. Darla's grip relaxed. He pulled his hand away and quickly looked up to his mother as he held it out to her. Her eyes glistened with reflected lamp light and a small smile made the briefest appearance on her face. She took his offered hand in hers. Jalan moved close to his mother. If all the world fell asleep, he felt better knowing that he would be with her.

Darla went to their father's side first. Their mother kept Jalan and his two older siblings back with her. Jalan asked his mother, "Is Father sick?"

She closed her eyes and took a long deep breath before answering in a soft voice. "Father is dying, Jalan."

"Will he get better?"

"No, dear. He is too badly hurt."

"How did he get hurt?"

His mother glanced toward his father's pallet. "It was an accident at the new windmill. A rope broke and some wood fell."

Jalan remembered playing at the site of the windmill. He and Tomac had climbed the wooden tower and swung from ropes tied to it before the carpenter, Doon, chased them off. What if Tomac and he had broken something? What if he had done something that hurt Father? *What if it was me?* Sadness and guilt spilled over within him and Jalan cried before he even finished his thought. He squeezed his eyes shut to try to stop the tears.

He felt his mother release his hand. He heard the rustle of fabric and an instant later he felt her arms enfold him. Jalan threw his arms around her and buried his face in her shoulder. He shook with silent sobs until the safety and love of his mother's arms pushed away his self-inflicted shame.

"Be at ease now," whispered his mother. "I know this is difficult. So very difficult."

Jalan loosened his embrace and Lady Shara slipped away from him. He watched her hold out her left hand to Tomac who stood nearby. She drew him in until both Jalan and Tomac stood together as she knelt before them.

"My boys," said his mother as she looked at them. "Your lord father and I are very proud of you both. You are brothers and best friends and you have no idea how rare that is. You will grow to be the men of this House. Tomac, take Jalan to your father and show him what fine sons he has. Say your farewell to him with dignity so that he knows he need not fear for the family he leaves behind."

Their mother stood, placed a hand upon Jalan's and his brother's shoulders and delicately turned them to face their father. Together he and Tomac walked the handful of steps to their father's side. Unsure what to say, Jalan reached out and took his father's large hand, much larger than his mother's. His brother did the same. Both of them held their father's hand together.

Father did not look like Father. His skin was waxy like a candle. It made the gray in his beard and hair more noticeable. He looked sick and weak, two things his father had never been. Jalan looked at his and Tomac's hands as his father slowly closed his fingers around them. *The men of House Yen.*

"Remember you are brothers," said Lord Yen. His soft words were simultaneously a command and a request. Jalan wondered which way they were intended to be. "Never fear the future. Never fear change. It always comes, especially when you do not expect it or want it. You are both strong enough to face whatever comes. My pride and my love are always with you."

"Father..." said Jalan and stopped uncertain of how to ask his question.

"Yes?"

"Are you dying?"

"Yes," said Lord Yen.

"But I don't want you too," said Jalan.

"I don't want you to die either," said Tomac.

"I am sorry. I would stop it if I could," came the rough whispered reply.

"But, Father," said Jalan with tears beginning to flow anew. He felt ashamed to cry when Mother expected him to be a man, but he could not help it. He cried more and bent forward laying his head upon his father's arm. No silence this time. Each sob gave voice to his sorrow and fear. His father's grip upon his hand grew stronger.

"It is all right. I love you too. Do not fear for me. The time comes to everyone, the time of death. Everything passes."

Gentle arms slipped around Jalan and helped him lift his head. He heard his mother murmur, "This is too much."

He blinked away tears and saw that Tomac blinked away his own.

"Come away now boys and let your father rest," said his mother. She took her arms from around Jalan and left him to stand on his own. Then she placed her hands upon both Jalan's and Tomac's and lifted them out of his father's loosening grasp.

Jalan looked at his mother. In the lamplight she appeared almost as pale as his father. Her expression confused him until he realized he had never seen her afraid before.

A spasm shook his father. His fingers spread claw like. He relaxed afterward but panted as if he had run a footrace.

"Father needs to rest," his mother repeated. She herded Jalan and the other children toward the door.

"Wait," called out Father, his voice strong for the moment.

Mother stopped. Jalan turned to face his father's pallet. Everyone else did as well.

"Vee, Tomac and Jalan, please do what your hearts tell you is right. Whenever your head is troubled, you have truth in your heart. Listen to it. Do what your mother and what your sister, Lady Darla, ask of you. You must be their support in my stead."

Jalan noticed an unspoken exchange between his mother and Darla. He did not know what it meant, but he had grown up with sisters and seen the way of it many times.

"Yes, Father," said Jalan along with Vee and Tomac.

"Jalan, come," said his father.

Jalan looked at his mother. She frowned. When she saw him watching she said, "Go to your father. Quickly now."

He wiped his nose on the sleeve of his brown jacket as he hurried back to his father's side. At first Jalan worried that his father had called him back to rebuke him for being weak and weeping. Then a chill ran along his spine. Lord Hallis realized Jalan had done something to the windmill which had caused his father's injury. He felt a frozen stone of fear form in the pit of his stomach and a great dread of what his father would say came over him.

"Jalan, I want you to remember something," said his father. Father's voice weakened now and it sounded very rough.

He was too frightened to speak. He could only stand and wait for his father's condemnation. Now everyone would know. He was responsible for his father's death. Jalan began to cry as he imagined his mother's reaction.

"I want you to remember that none of this is your fault," said Lord Hallis. "Your parents love you. Do not judge them until you understand the sacrifices they have made for you. Can you do that?"

What? It's not my fault? Relief flooded through him and it took Jalan a moment to realize his father had asked a question. Could he remember his parents love him? "Yes, Father. Always."

"Good," said his father. The word came out as more of a grunt. His father's face contorted in a look of pain for an instant. Then Lord Hallis continued to speak. "Love will always take you the farthest you can go."

"Yes, Father."

His mother stepped up beside him and said, "Come now. Let your father rest."

His mother took his hand. When she led him toward the door he saw that he was the only child left in the room. His mother silently opened the door and Jalan stepped through the doorway and into the hall where his siblings waited for him. As the door closed he knew without any doubt that he had spoken to his father for the last time and he wanted to say something more.

He stood there with the closed door at his back and started to cry again, unable to stop and unable to tell his father one last time that he loved him. Darla took his and Tomac's hands and along with Vee they made their disconsolate way down the hall

CHAPTER II

The wind gusted at odd intervals as Jalan hurried into the courtyard behind Yen Manor. The sun threw its new-day brilliance across his path and pleasantly warmed the left side of his face. The courtyard was a large open area bordered by many of Yen Manor's workshops and storage buildings. The lancer barracks stood at the far end with a large practice field in front of them. Jalan's training would begin there. He had tossed and turned trying to fall asleep last night as he worried over what training would be like. Tomac usually did everything first, but this time it was his turn and he could hardly wait.

A servant boy carried an armload of firewood as his loose shirt and baggy trousers flapped in the breeze. The wind kicked up dust from the stable yard ahead and forced Jalan to narrow his eyes in order to protect them from the flying grit. The swirl of dust set a lancer to sneezing on his way into the stables. The man stomped a booted foot and shook his shaggy head each time he sneezed. "Huhchoo." Stomp-shake. "Huhchoo." Stomp-shake. "Huchoo!" Stomp-shake.

Jalan skirted the stone wall of the well and felt a light mist across his face. One of Mistress Dahlia's bakers wore a splattered apron and hefted the well bucket in her flour coated arms. As she poured water into a wooden pail, a sudden gust had wafted a remnant of the cascading pour and deposited it on Jalan. The moisture felt almost cold as the wind caressed his skin. It sent a momentary shiver through him.

Far across the expanse of the courtyard he saw Lieutenant Burk waiting for him. Burk wore the regular uniform of a Yen Lancer; blue tunic belted at the waist, tan breeches, knee high leather riding boots. Jalan could just make out the black braid looped over the lieutenant's left shoulder. A saber sheathed in its scabbard hung from the left side of Lieutenant Burk's swordbelt.

Jalan sense of urgency increased, perhaps because of the way the lieutenant stood with feet apart and hands behind his back. Unlike the sneezing lancer, there was nothing shaggy about Burk. He wore his dark hair and beard close cropped. Burk had a thick and muscular frame, built much the same as Jalan's father had been. Jalan started to jog as he imagined the lieutenant as his dead father somehow returned and waiting for him. He knew he only pretended but he broke into a run anyway and finished in a breathless halt before the lancer officer.

Burk cocked an eyebrow.

"Good morning, lieutenant," said Jalan in a rush between breaths.

"Good morning, trainee. You're late. Be here at sunrise tomorrow."

Inwardly Jalan groaned. He had woken with the faintest hint of light coming through his bedroom window, the interior still dark. The rest of the house was a cave. It took much longer to dress than he expected. If he had not stumbled across a servant with a candle, Jalan would still be groping his way toward the winter kitchen and the doorway to the courtyard.

"Here is your saber," said Lieutenant Burk as he produced a long straight stick from behind his back and handed it to Jalan. One end was wrapped tightly with twine. Red pigment covered the length of one side.

Jalan had seen many sabers. He thought of them as elegant weapons. Elegant being a word his mother used to describe gowns, furnishings and various other crafted creations that especially pleased her. The craftsmanship of the well-made sabers of House Yen pleased Jalan. It was the look of them, the slight curve of the blade, the double edged tip. The only one he had ever lifted, his father's, was far too heavy for him to wield. Even when he held the weapon with one hand on the grip and his off hand gripping the blunt portion of the blade just in front of the crossguard, it felt awkward. He had to lean back in order to keep from tipping over forward. Jalan could never hold the weapon with one hand the way the lancers did.

When he took the stick the lieutenant offered, it did not have nearly the weight of a saber, yet its heft felt surprisingly heavy.

"This is a stick," said Jalan.

"Do you think I don't know a saber when I see one, trainee?"

"No."

"No what?"

Jalan hesitated as he tried to guess what the lieutenant wanted. He remembered when his father had prompted him in the same way. "No, sir."

"That's right! I definitely know a saber when I see one and that is a saber." Burk pointed at the twine wrapped end and said, "It has a grip." Next he pointed at the red colored side of the stick and said, "It has an edge. It's a saber. It's your saber and you will practice with it and care for it just as any good lancer would. Understood?"

"Yes, sir."

"Now step over here to the pell."

A large post set upright in the ground a few feet from Burk. Jalan moved toward it and noticed it was the trunk of a small tree with the branches roughly hewn off. It stood about six feet high, well above Jalan's head.

"Watch me and place your feet as I do," said Burk. The lieutenant turned side on toward the pell. He had his left foot back and his right foot forward toward the post.

Jalan peered up the length of the pell as it towered over him.

"Jalan, your stance," said Lieutenant Burk.

Jalan looked away from the pell and saw the lieutenant pointing at his feet.

Jalan looked down. He looked at the lieutenant again and shifted his feet to match his trainer's.

Burk stepped over to Jalan and took hold of his shoulders. The big man twisted him a few inches sideways and said, "Now look down at your feet and think about standing on a straight line that runs directly under both your feet and right through the pell."

Imagining the line, Jalan slid his right foot perhaps an inch to align his feet with his shoulders and place his body, as far as he could tell, in line with the pell. He felt the pressure of Burk's hands leave his shoulders.

"That's a good start," said Burk. "This is your base stance. You will use it when a possible enemy approaches. You will use it for the bow, the sword. It is not the only way you will learn to stand, and even in this position you will learn when to shift your weight between your front and back foot. But, let's not worry about that right now. Now I want you to grip your saber in your right hand."

Jalan held his stick saber in his left hand, letting it hang out and down behind him like a long straight tail. He switched it to his right hand and took a firm grasp of the twine wrapped hilt. Thinking of it as a sword, he raised the tip and held his training weapon up in front of him being careful to extend it out along the straight line between his body and the pell.

"Bend your elbow more. Don't reach out to your adversary. Let them come to you. In most cases you want them to commit or to overreach rather than you doing it."

He wondered how a large post standing fixed in its hole might come to him, but Jalan thought this would be the wrong time to ask. Skipping over his unvoiced question, he bent his right elbow more and that brought his stick saber back toward him.

"Better. Now I want you to relax and stand as you normally would."

Jalan complied. He let his right arm fall to his side and held the wooden sword lightly as it hung down next to his right leg. He stepped forward with his left foot to bring it up next to his right which finished with his shoulders squared to the pell.

"Now, step back into your base stance."

Jalan smoothly slid his left foot back onto the pell line as he returned his right arm and saber to their original position.

Lieutenant Burk walked a circle around Jalan. He wore a slight frown as if in deep concentration. Finally he came to a stop on Jalan's left side and took up his pose of feet spread wide and hands behind his back. "Very good. Now I want you to keep stepping out of your base stance and back into it just as you already did once. Step out and step back in until I tell you to stop."

HIDDEN ABILITY

Jalan brought his saber to his side as he swung his left foot up and squared his shoulders with the pell. Then he slid his left foot back into line as he raised his sword, right elbow bent. He continued the exercise. At first he counted every time his sword tip came up, but at about 20 he lost track as he concentrated on performing each movement in its proper sequence. He breathed harder and his right arm felt much heavier.

Lieutenant Burk called out, "Hold!"

No one had ever yelled "hold" at him before. Burk said it in a way that sounded like Darla, Mother or another adult telling him to stop. He finished his current movement and stopped in base stance.

"I said hold, trainee." The lieutenant's voice had an edge in it that made the words cut. "Hold means stop immediately, not when it is convenient or when you think it is a better time."

"Yes, sir," said Jalan, not sure how he could be in trouble for just doing what he thought the lieutenant wanted.

"I want you to begin the exercise again. Step out of base stance and back in. Continue until I say hold and then stop immediately."

These words did not cut. Jalan said, "Yes, sir", again and began to repeat the same motions he had been doing, ready for the lieutenant to tell him to stop. When the command did not come the first time he stepped back into base stance, he expected it all the more on the second. By the third time, Jalan listened intently for the order to hold, determined that he would not get it wrong. Burk said nothing.

In the middle of a motion, Jalan felt confused, anxious his elbow bent incorrectly or his foot slid out of place. He looked at his feet to check their direction and felt as if his shoulders were out of line. One after another concerns piled up and left him unsure he did anything right.

"Faster!" shouted Lieutenant Burk.

Faster!? Jalan froze for an instant as he tried to comprehend the unexpected command. He rushed to bring the wooden saber down and clipped his right ankle with the tip of the stick. His boot deflected the blow. But, a real sword might have injured him. His face grew hot from the embarrassment. No wonder the captain had only given him a stick. He clenched his jaw. *I will not look foolish! I can do this!*

Jalan swept his left foot back, as he allowed his weight to shift slightly more onto his left leg. The saber point whipped upward in a blurred arc and he ended with his right elbow bent precisely as Lieutenant Burk had instructed. With the wooden saber poised at the ready, a sudden feeling of accomplishment infused Jalan. A new sense of energy and wellbeing supplanted his frustration and fatigue.

In that instant of self-fulfillment something shoved him hard from behind and sent him staggering forward. He took a series of stumbling steps as the wind roared past his ears. He pivoted on his right foot and turned into the wind. He kept his wooden sword raised before him and had only the vague awareness that he had returned to base stance.

Several dark shapes spun through the air toward him. Three he realized before even thinking of counting them. He bent backward at his waist by the smallest degree and the foremost object brushed past his chest as it flipped end over end. With a flick of his wrist, Jalan tapped the next with the tip of his wooden saber and the object deflected and spun past behind his back. The third arced down toward his waist too fast for him to move from its path. He whipped his sword down. Its mock blade edge, driven by all the force Jalan could put behind it, collided with the falling gray rectangular shape. The shock of the contact numbed his right hand and shattered the rectangle. The broken pieces pelted Jalan's lower body and the ground around his feet.

"Hold!" called out Lieutenant Burk.

Jalan breathed hard as he did his best to imitate a tired confused statue. His right hand ached but he still held onto his saber. Its tip rested on the ground where the down stroke terminated. Bits of broken slate lay scattered around him. He knew shards had struck him, but all he felt was exhaustion.

The lieutenant walked around in front of him. He studied Jalan for a moment and then asked, "Are you injured?"

The wind still gusted but nothing like it had when it shoved Jalan forward. However, it nearly carried away Burk's words and Jalan had to strain to hear him. "I'm fine, I think. What happened?"

"You can move. Practice is over for now. We'll start again this afternoon. Go back to the manor and check yourself over. Make sure you are not cut or badly bruised. I'm going to have a few words with the tilers. They'll never be foolish enough to work in a wind like this again."

Jalan dropped his practice sword and sat down heavily among the shattered pieces of slate as he panted hard for breath. The big stone tiles flipping end over end toward him sat vivid in his memory. Now that he had time to think, it terrified him to consider what might have happened. Where had they come from without a nearby roof downwind? Nothing but open courtyard stretched from him all the way back to the manor. Could the wind have been strong enough to carry them that far? "The wind threw roof tiles at me?" he said puzzled.

Burk turned toward Yen Manor and frowned. "Wait a moment longer. I'll walk you to the manor." The lieutenant looked about and called out to a lancer who happened to be passing nearby. "Sedic! Get over here."

The same shaggy lancer Jalan had seen sneezing earlier jogged over to Lieutenant Burk and said, "Quite a breeze we're having, lieutenant. What do you need?"

"Take a couple men and gather up the roof tilers. I have something to discuss with them. Bring them to the Command Room. I'll be there shortly."

"Yes, sir." Sedic made a slight nod of his head to Burk and departed at a trot.

Burk turned to Jalan and extended his hand. "Come with me. I need a word with Lady Darla anyway so I might as well accompany you."

Jalan grasp the lieutenant's offered hand. He did little more to stand than straighten his legs while Burk showed no sign of strain as he practically lifted Jalan off the ground. Jalan shook his hand after Burk let go. It tingled painfully as the numbing shock of his stick's impact with the last tile wore off. Burk's almost crushing grip did not help matters. Lieutenant Burk began to walk. Jalan hurriedly bent and picked up his stick saber and then fell in beside the lieutenant.

"Has anyone else been teaching you how to handle a sword?" Burk asked the question as he casually looked about, his hand rested lightly on his saber's hilt.

"Tomac and I practice."

"Your brother?" said Burk as if there could be another Tomac.

15

"Well, we don't have real swords. Just sticks." Jalan looked up at Burk and added, "Not as nice as this one you gave me. Just plain sticks we find. And Master Hern taught us how to wear a sword and the proper way to draw it and sheath it. He said a gentlemen should know that much at least."

"Hern? The fellow that teaches you children your letters and numbers?"

"The same."

"Hmph. Not someone else then, perhaps one of the lancers?"

"No. Not until today. Mother always said there would be time for it later. She made us learn dancing instead, Tomac and me."

Lieutenant Burk made a sort of strangled noise, but did not say anything further. He just kept looking about as if generally interested in the doings of everyone around him. Jalan followed his example but did not see anything interesting. Just the same people doing the same things they did every day.

Δ

Two weeks later, Jalan walked along the cobbled path between the summer kitchen and the manor. He and Tomac entered together, the doorway being large enough to admit them both, and Jalan pushed the heavy wooden door closed behind them. Within the large dark room sat the empty hearth and cold ovens that were used in winter or when foul weather drove the cooks inside. Various bowls and culinary implements sat upon two worktables, a sign that Mistress Dahlia, the head cook, would soon return. The temptation to search the winter kitchen's larder for a quick bite of anything left unguarded pulled at Jalan.

"Where are you going," said Tomac.

"Nowhere" said Jalan as he glanced about before he retraced the several unconscious steps he had taken toward the larder. "Where are you going?"

"I'm going to talk to Darla about our trip," said Tomac.

"What trip?"

"I'm going with Darla when she inspects the holdings," said Tomac.

"Where?" said Jalan not quite certain what it meant to inspect the holdings.

"All around the estate. Darla said it will take a month and we'll visit each overseer and get to see the crops and livestock each looks after."

As he spoke Tomac led Jalan single file up the narrow servants' stairs that climbed from the winter kitchen into a windowless room on the upper floor. Within the room the servants kept a large cylindrical tallow candle burning atop a squat round pedestal just off to one side of the stairs. Its low flame gave little light. Jalan waited behind Tomac for his brother to get his bearings and start moving again.

"Stop pushing," said Tomac. "I'll go when I can see."

"There's nothing there," protested Jalan. Tomac knew as well as he did that Hint, the household steward, would tar and feather anyone who didn't keep the path clear between the top of the stair and the door to the hallway. He considered pushing past Tomac when his brother finally moved. Jalan breathed a sigh of relief and followed Tomac as closely as he thought Tomac would allow. Once he stepped out of the dark cramped room and had light and air around him, Jalan began to question his brother further. "You get to go riding across the estate?"

"Yes, and we get to look at a lot of different things along the way. That's why it takes so long," said Tomac.

"That's not fair," said Jalan.

"Of course it is. In fact, it is my duty as the eldest son to learn more about our holdings," said Tomac.

The sound of Darla's voice came from directly behind Jalan and caused him to jump in surprise. "Why must you two always argue?" she said.

Intent on the inequity of his situation, Jalan gave no notice to her approach. He wanted to scold her for giving him a fright, but his grievance with Tomac took precedence. He looked at Darla and demanded, "Why does Tomac get a holiday?"

"A holiday? What do you mean?" said Darla.

"You know. The trip he's going on with you." Darla could be a little thick sometimes.

17

"It is not a holiday. Tomac is accompanying Master Chander and me on a tour of inspection. It's long days on the road and endless details to attend to at each stop," said Darla.

"You mean riding out, seeing the countryside and visiting new places. That's what Tomac said. And that's a holiday." Tomac would be free of Master Hern for a month. He would go places and do things while Jalan attended their tutor's lessons and put up with Vee ordering him around. "Why can't I go?"

"Because you're not the older brother," said Tomac with a self-satisfied look Jalan wanted to knock off his face.

"I'm talking to Darla, not you," said Jalan.

"Fine, talk to Darla. But, you better hurry because in a couple of days we will be gone and you can spend a month talking to your bone headed self."

"Tomac! Stop that. Treat your brother with respect," said Darla. "And," she said as she raised her index finger to forestall a comment poised on the edge of Tomac's lips. "Please, do not interrupt me while I'm speaking to Jalan."

"I don't see why he is complaining. He's the one that gets all the training with the lancers. Every time I get something special of my own he wants it. I'm 11 and he's only 10. When do I get to train?" said Tomac.

"That is something our mother decides," said Darla who sounded like her patience had worn thin.

"Why? You're Lady and she always agrees with whatever you do. You could let me train," said Tomac.

"No, that is Mother's decision. But, if you are going to suggest I act as Lady, show me proper loyalty and leave off asking me about training. Go and speak to Mother!"

Jalan forced himself not to laugh at how red Darla's face had become. Instead he watched with satisfaction as Tomac turned away and marched with deliberate angry steps down the hallway.

Darla turned back to him and said, "What are you grinning about?"

"Nothing," said Jalan as he tried to look properly solemn.

"Then go and do your best with what you already have instead of demanding more. You and Tomac, neither one of you understands what you are asking." With a wave of dismissal and the swirl of her

18

skirt, Darla turned away. She drifted off like a tightly contained storm cloud full of fury and lightening that Jalan hoped she expelled prior to his next encounter with her.

What Darla said about doing his best with what he already had reminded him of something Master Hern said. His tutor had commented that people often wished for mastery of abilities they did not possess while never bothering to master those they already had. Jalan shrugged to himself as he trailed along in the direction Tomac had gone. At least Mother allowed him to train with the lancers. He might have felt sorry for Tomac if it were not for the holiday his brother was still going on without him.

CHAPTER III

Jalan felt the extra weight of his jerkin, the vambraces on his arms and the cap on his head. All that leather slowed his movement into basic stance. The padded breeches did not flex well. The entire outfit of practice armor had him feeling hot and tired before the sparring even began. Across several yards of open ground, Tomac mirrored him. Same ill-fitting leathers, bulky breeches and cumbersome cap. Lieutenant Burk had never let them spar before. Jalan tried to forget about his awkward apparel and focus on his chance to prove to Tomac which one of them was the better swordsman.

"You look ridiculous," said Tomac without a hint of irony in his words.

"I'll look better than you when this is over," said Jalan.

Tomac glared at him. Jalan knew it vexed his brother to have had to plead with their mother for permission to train. It had taken nigh on three months for her to agree, time that Jalan had used in preparation for this exact moment. And then Burk made him wait as Tomac learned the basics of the saber. They both had their own stick swords now and Jalan did not want to admit it but his brother showed some signs of skill.

"Black and blue are your colors. Doubtless you will look better with the bruises I give you." said Tomac.

Jalan felt the scowl on his face, the anticipation of welcoming his brother to House Pain. He had overheard Lieutenant Burk stressing defense to Tomac. Being nine months older would do Tomac no good at all on the practice yard.

Lieutenant Burk stepped forward at the point halfway toward Tomac and raised his saber tip into the air between them. "Ready?" he said. He looked at Jalan. Jalan nodded and said, "Ready." The lieutenant looked toward Tomac who nodded and said "Ready," as well. Burk swept the sword down and shouted, "Begin!"

Jalan sprang forward doing his best to look unhindered by his armor. His sword collided with Tomac's. He let the force of Tomac's swing slide along the length of his wooden blade as he sidestepped and pivoted. His brother went by him, the scream he had loosed when he charged Jalan dying in his throat.

Jalan continued his pivot full circle, putting both hands onto his sword as he did so and finished with a strong two-handed swing. He misjudged Tomac's position. The tip of Jalan's stick sword barely grazed the back of Tomac's jerkin as it whipped past his intended target. Tomac responded with his own one-armed counter strike that almost, but not quite, took Jalan in the side.

Lieutenant Burk laughed. "If you two are trying to fan each other to death, you've made a good start! I can feel the breeze from here."

Jalan double stepped backward and pushed his leather cap back in place. Tomac chased him and swung again with a blow aimed at Jalan's sword arm. The block came easy. Jalan felt and heard the solid smack of stick on stick, but the contact denied him position for a counterstroke. Frustrated and vulnerable, he retreated yet another step. Tomac followed up with an offensive onslaught. Jalan slapped his brother's fierce cut with the imagined flat of his own blade, parrying in the fashion drilled into him by long practice.

Wary of what Tomac might try next, Jalan side stepped. The image of two young bulls working themselves up to charge came to him just as he and Tomac threw themselves at each other with a flurry of blows. Jalan deflected the attacks but Tomac did the same with every counter strike. Sweat flowed down his face in earnest. He tried to blink the sting from his eyes. Each step took an extra effort. He labored to breathe and his forearms felt like the vambraces strapped around them were lead instead of leather. His stick sword seemed heavier than a real saber. He feared he might collapse and he had yet to score a hit.

Jalan mustered his remaining strength for a low two-handed swing toward Tomac's right leg and immediately pulled it back in order to cut high at Tomac's shoulder with all the speed he could manage. To Jalan's exhausted delight Tomac fell for the ruse and brought his stick down to parry the initial swing. Jalan's real attack took Tomac in the shoulder and caused him to cry out in pain. Before Tomac had time to recover, he struck him again in the same spot and Tomac let out a howl that turned into a snarl.

Tomac dropped his practice sword and heaved himself at Jalan. He came on like an angry sibling landslide. Hardly able to keep standing, Jalan had no hope of evading him or any desire to try. Tomac slammed into him and bore Jalan to the ground, landing upon Jalan with his full armored bulk. Tomac may have wanted to do more to him, but his brother must have been as bone-weary as Jalan because he merely rolled off and lay on the ground holding his shoulder and panting for breath. Jalan emulated him and looked up at the cloudless blue sky while his heart pounded in his bruised chest and his pulse roared in his ears.

"What... are... you... smiling about?" said Tomac between gulps of air.

"I... hit... you... first," said Jalan.

"I... hit you... best," said Tomac.

Jalan turned his head and saw the smile on Tomac's face.

"Let's call it a draw," said Lieutenant Burk from somewhere outside Jalan's field of vision. "Jalan, you'd better work on your defense. It's not as easy to finish a fight with one blow as you seem to think. Now both of you get up and have another go."

Δ

Time passed in days of training for Jalan. He sparred Tomac regularly and as they progressed Lieutenant Burk would set them against one or another of the House Yen lancers. Jalan anticipated these matches with an intense zeal. He loved the challenge, even the frustration, of facing a superior opponent. He liked nothing more than pondering how to overcome a stronger and more experienced partner.

Tomac and Jalan compared the strengths and shortcomings of various lancers based on their experiences sparring with them. Jalan thought he might be getting better. It seemed the lancers Burk put him against got better too and if they did not, Burk would find someone else for Jalan to face. By the end of the first year of training, Jalan seldom sparred Tomac and occasionally went up against Lieutenant Burk. Those always ended in defeat with Jalan breaking down every encounter in his head as he tried to find anything he could do better.

Riding became a regular part of Jalan and Tomac's training. They were forced to spend greater and greater amounts of time on horseback and tending to the needs of their mounts. They wore real armor for more of their training and actively participated in drills with mounted lancers. By the end of the second year, they both felt like lancers even though everyone stilled called them trainees. They knew the mounted formations and basic tactics. They had been allowed to ride along on road patrols.

Jalan found the patrols to be far more boring and tedious than many of Master Hern's lessons. Nothing ever happened. They rode out for a day, camped overnight and rode back the next. Some of the lancers talked of bandits, wolves or troublesome villagers and farmers, but Jalan and Tomac never saw any of these. He and Tomac became convinced Captain Erida assigned them to the dullest, and probably in the captain's mind, safest patrols. Clearly, thought Jalan, the captain did not understand the lethal power of boredom. The current assignment was no exception.

On the second day of the patrol, the cold early spring night had given way to the warmth of early morning. But a stiff breeze kept the five lancers wrapped in their cloaks. Jalan and Tomac plodded along side-by-side on their mounts as the gathering clouds finally blocked all sight of the sun. Sergeant Jonas rode in front. Two lancers followed, riding next to each other. Jalan and Tomac rode last. The weather had been wet which did away with dust but occasionally left the road a muddy track that slowed the riders' progress. They had just negotiated yet another muddy patch when the sergeant signaled a halt.

Jonas turned to one of the men behind him and said, "Do you smell smoke?"

The man nodded and said in a quiet voice Jalan only just heard, "Yes, sergeant."

Jonas frowned and in an equally subdued tone said, "I didn't think anyone was supposed to be in this section of our lady's woods. We'll have to go look." The sergeant began to dismount and said, "Patrol, dismount." Once on the ground he said, "You two," indicating Jalan and Tomac with the point of his finger, "stay here and watch the horses."

"Why not take them?" said Tomac.

"These woods are overgrown. The undergrowth is heavy in places. Horses have a hard time. We'd have to lead them and watch for whoever made the fire we smell. Better to keep them safe here with you while the rest of us investigate."

With that the three lancers handed their reins to Tomac and the sergeant said, "Stand watch. I'm sure we'll be back before midday."

Thoughts of a good fire and a warm drink receded in Jalan's mind with every step the three lancers took into the woods. He smelled the smoke too and knew the searchers would retrace the path of the wind to find its source. That might become more difficult once they were surrounded by trees and brush. He and Tomac had nothing to do but watch the horses and wait. A few minutes after the three lancers disappeared into the woods, the clouds opened and a steady cold blowing rain began.

"I hate patrol," said Jalan.

"What? I thought you loved playing the lancer," said Tomac, he looked out from beneath his hood while the rain pelted him, having almost shouted in order to be heard over the sudden storm.

"I don't love standing on the road in a storm and we wouldn't be here if we were not on patrol." He put a grumble into the word patrol to emphasize his displeasure and his point.

Tomac looked around and said, "Let's get under the edge of the trees. That's barely off the road at all and should be no problem for the horses."

They stopped after they led the horses several yards in under the trees. The undergrowth did not seem that bad to Jalan. It must get worse further in he decided. The sound of the storm still surrounded them. Very large raindrops fell frequently from the treetops above them, but the wind no longer lashed them with the downpour.

25

"I'm going to mount," said Tomac after a few minutes.

"Why?"

"It'll be warmer sitting on a horse."

Jalan followed Tomac's example and climbed into the saddle. He draped his cloak over his thighs and soon felt warmer just from the body heat of his mount.

"Now I guess we wait here until midday," said Jalan.

"Any idea when that will be?"

Jalan looked up and got hit in the eye with an especially large raindrop, having seen nothing but tree branches and early spring foliage for his trouble. They had no view of the sky and even if they did, the complete overcast prevented them from ever ascertaining the sun's position. Jalan rubbed the water from his eye, ready to declare it hopeless, when he thought he saw something on the road.

He crouched low in the saddle for a better view. The rain fell even harder now and tree trunks partially obscured the road, but it looked like several people moved along it. He counted five figures and turned to tell Tomac.

"I see them," said Tomac before Jalan had opened his mouth.

"Who are they?"

"Don't know."

"I think they are looking for something," said Jalan.

"Us maybe? But, how could they know we are here?"

Concern for the sergeant and the two lancers with him sprang up in Jalan. "What if they captured the others? Maybe they've come looking for the horses?"

"It's dark under the trees and I don't think they can see us," said Tomac.

"Let's lead the horses in the direction the others went searching. Maybe we'll find them. With all the noise from this weather I doubt they could ever hear us no matter how much brush we have to break through."

Without further discussion, Jalan and Tomac slipped out of their saddles. In short order they had each horse's reins tied to the saddle of another horse and formed a train of all five. Jalan, the lead horse's reins in his hand, followed Tomac deeper into the woods in the direction they supposed Sergeant Jonas had taken.

They traveled in silence. Jalan strained to hear any sound of pursuit but between the storm and the procession of horses the only thing he heard clearly was his own labored breathing. Tomac raised his hand several times to indicate a halt as he scouted the path ahead. Jalan felt his nerves settle and his fear of pursuit lessen. He concentrated on keeping the horses moving. At the point where he seriously pondered telling Tomac they should turn back and aim for the road to keep from being lost in the woods, he smelled it. And a moment later he saw the firelight through the trees.

Jalan got his brother's attention with a wave and then tied the lead reins to a tree. Together, Jalan and Tomac crept closer to the light to see what they could discover. The storm's fury began to die down and it became easier to hear the large drops of rain that collected and then fell from above with a splat, splat, splat all about them. Someone near the fire spoke and Jalan could just make out a few words as he inched closer.

"... are they?"

"Maybe the rain slowed them down," said a familiar voice in response.

Tomac put his hand on Jalan's shoulder. When Jalan looked at him, Tomac mouthed, "Jonas."

The recognition shocked him. Jalan pushed closer to where he could see Garvin, one of the two lancers that had accompanied the sergeant, standing on the far side of a campfire. The fire burned in the center of a small clearing overhung by tree branches. Sergeant Jonas sat on the near side of the fire with his back to Jalan and Tomac.

Garvin said, "It's never taken this long before. You don't think they wondered off do you?"

"I told them to stay there and keep watch. It's not that complicated," said Sergeant Jonas. "Besides, they've had a couple of years training. They know how to obey an order. Winst will scoop them up and bring them here shaking in their boots."

A second shock jolted Jalan. Those figures on the road were men sent to capture Tomac and him. Jonas plotted with bandits to kidnap them. He knew stories of nobles held for ransom, but Jalan never thought he would be one. Jalan swore silently that he would never let that happen and from the look on Tomac's face, his brother felt exactly the same. Jalan signaled Tomac that he saw two opponents. Tomac nodded and signaled the same back.

Jalan swallowed. What if they had to fight? What if they couldn't take them by surprise and subdue them? Something else bothered him about the situation. He placed a restraining hand on Tomac's arm and jerked his head back to indicate they should move away. Tomac looked like he wanted to say something. His hand grasped the hilt of his saber as if he might draw it. Instead Tomac released the saber and followed Jalan's lead as he crept back toward the horses.

No matter how carefully Jalan stepped, he could not help snapping a twig or scraping against brush or low branches. The retreat from the clearing seemed much noisier than their approach. The wind had dropped to a whisper. Fewer over-large raindrops fell. Every sound grew louder in the ebb of the storm. That included the words spoken by the two lancers back at the fire.

"Did you hear something?" said Sergeant Jonas.

"Vidrus? Is that you?" said Garvin.

"You try tromping through the trees with an armload of firewood and see how much noise you make," said a third voice a short distance to Jalan's left.

Jalan froze, almost not daring to breathe, afraid that even his pounding heart might give him away. Jalan now heard Vidrus moving very nearby. The furtive sounds Tomac and he made while retracing their steps must have been enough to disguise the rustle of Vidrus's passage. With luck Vidrus had not heard them over the disturbance he created.

"Bring it then. We could use fresh fuel for the fire. I don't know what's keeping the others, but they're bound to be wet and cold," said Jonas.

Vidrus quickened his pace. Jalan let out the breath he'd been holding and took a tentative step. They were going to make it. The horses were close. All this time the horses had been quiet and amenable. Then, one of them whinnied, not as a gentle greeting but a full protest, most likely a complaint against being left wet, cold and tethered. The whinny made a deafening uproar. No one had to guess its source or the direction from whence it came.

"Run," Jalan urged Tomac in a tense whisper as he sprang forward. Tomac ran only a step behind. If they could quickly free the horses they could escape. What Jonas said about the undergrowth being too thick must have been a lie. Nothing Jalan had seen supported that statement.

The horses were just ahead, five shapes beneath the trees.

"Hurry, get a horse and scatter the others," said Jalan.

Even as he spoke, his mind signaled a warning. Two of the shapes leapt forward, not four legged horses, but two legged men with strong arms and grasping hands. He fought them. They wore armor too and had the advantage of size and surprise. He delivered two ineffectual blows that did nothing. They wrestled him to the ground. In the next instant he lay face down on tree roots, ferns and bracken, his hands tied behind his back. Tomac lay next to him, similarly immobilized. The bandits had them.

Δ

"Stand up," said the bandit that grabbed Jalan's left arm. Another took his right and together they lifted as he got his feet under him. Two more did the same with Tomac. The four cloaked and hooded men kept hold of their arms and marched them back to the campfire which now burned higher with new wood. The fifth bandit walked behind them.

He said, "The two of you led us on a nice hunt. I have to say you surprised us by coming here. But, things have a way of working out, don't they boys?"

The men holding Tomac and Jalan laughed.

"It would have been easier for us to have captured you on the road where you were ordered to stay. Not sure the sergeant's going to like that. We could have ridden back on the horses and this would have all been over by now. Instead, you two got burrs in your saddles and took off into the woods. I've got to say you didn't put up much of a fight either. Did anyone tell you what those knives are for? Good for close quarters. I guess I shouldn't complain that we didn't have to ruff you up taking them away. I'd say you were smart not to draw your sabers in among all these trees. Since you didn't have your knives out, I'm wondering if maybe you don't know how to use the sabers either."

Jalan strained against the cord lashed around his wrists and twisted against the hands that held his arms. "Untie me and I'll show you I can use a saber, you varlet," he said.

"Easy boy. You're outnumbered and you're a prisoner. Not a good time for big talk," said the bandit holding his left arm.

All his twisting and pulling did no good. The knot and his captors' grips held firm. He looked over at Tomac who struggled against the two scoundrels that held him. He made out no better than Jalan.

Sergeant Jonas stood on the other side of the campfire now. "I'll admit that Winst has a way of irritating his prisoners. But, he brings up one good question. Why," said the sergeant as he looked between Jalan and Tomac, "did you leave the road?"

"What difference does it make to you? Why should the orders of a traitor matter?" said Tomac with real heat behind his words.

"The orders of a superior always matter. What does not matter is your opinion of the man giving the orders. You boys have been training as lancers. You should realize by now that why you are given an order is not important to you. Did you abandon your post because you assumed you could just do as you pleased? Did you fail to learn even the most basic lessons of your training?"

"We didn't abandon our post. If anyone abandoned anything it's you and the two with you that have abandoned your honor," said Tomac.

"Really boy, how so?" said Sergeant Jonas with a crooked smile.

"You're in league with these brigands. You left us on the road to be taken. What did they promise you that made you forsake your oath to House Yen, a share in the ransom?"

"Oh, so they are brigands are they? And we," said the sergeant with a sweep of his hand to include himself, Garvin and Vidrus, "are oath breakers. Well, if that's the case exactly how much ransom do you think we could get for the two of you?"

"What?" said Jalan.

"I'm curious. Tomac seems to have this all figured out. Do you agree with him? If so, if you are both so clever, then surely your wisdom extends to how much wealth we can extract from House Yen for your safe return. Please, tell us how highly you value yourselves."

"This is ludicrous," said Tomac. "You've kidnapped us and now you want us to set our own ransom?"

"A man should know his own worth," said the fifth bandit, Winst, who still stood behind Jalan and Tomac.

"True, friend Winst," said the sergeant. "Which begs the question, what are we worth? What are you and I and our men worth, Winst? What are eight lives dedicated to serving as steel in the mighty hand of House Yen worth? What is a Yen Lancer worth?"

Jalan tried to follow the twists of the conversation. Were they attempting to set a ransom based on what they saw as the value of a lancer's service to House Yen? Why would anyone kidnap two sons of a noble house and not have already decided the ransom they would demand?

"What is going on here?" said Jalan. "What kind of kidnappers are you?"

"The very best kind," said Jonas. "We are the kidnappers that allow you to ransom yourselves and all you must do is answer the question."

"What question, how much a Yen lancer is worth?" said Jalan.

"Yes. As two boys who may one day command lancers to obey orders that may seem to make little sense or expect men who dislike you to obey you, what are those men worth? When you hold a lancer's life in your hand and choose how it is spent, how high a payment will you demand for that life? What is it worth to you?"

"This is some kind of trial, a test for us?" said Tomac.

"It is," said Jalan before anyone else spoke. He thought he understood. He could be wrong. "Winst berates us because Tomac and I didn't make you pay dearly enough for our capture. We set too low a price on ourselves. And you, sergeant, want us to think about what a lancer is, what he means to House Yen, what it means for him to spend his life, either in years or in a moment, in service to House Yen and what that sacrifice is worth."

"And," said Sergeant Jonas, clearly expecting something more.

"And," said Tomac, "what House Yen owes to that lancer, what his officers owe him and what anyone who commands him owes him."

Jalan felt a knife slip between his wrists as it slashed through the cord the bound his hands. The two men who held him let go and stepped away. He glanced at Tomac and saw his brother freed as well.

"But we didn't answer your question," said Jalan.

"How you answer that question will be important. However, only a fool would expect two unseasoned boys to have an answer," said Jonas.

"It is enough that you know the question," said Winst who stepped around the man at Jalan's left side and walked over to stand beside Sergeant Jonas. "You will likely spend the rest of your lives discovering your answer. Although, I trust you will raise the value of your own freedom after today."

"So you're not bandits?" said Jalan.

Winst and the others laughed again. "I think you've guessed we are Yen Lancers. I'm Fist Leader Winst, Southway Outpost. Your unwelcome escorts are my men."

"What happens now?" said Tomac.

"First, we drink." said Sergeant Jonas. Several of the men cheered and pulled flasks from beneath their cloaks. "Then, you tell me why you left the road, and it better be good. After that, we convince you to not report us to Captain Erida for putting you through this."

"He doesn't know about this?" said Jalan.

"Don't look at me like that. He knows. He just doesn't want to."

"You see, this is our informal indoctrination for new lancers and it's not exactly sanctioned by the officers," said Winst as he accepted a flask from one of his men.

"You kidnap everyone?" said Jalan.

Jonas shook his head. "No. We have a couple other things we do too. It happened that our patrol and Winst's patrol would meet today. I took advantage of the schedule and sent a message with the last currier so that our brothers from Southway would be prepared to assist us."

"It's better when the victim doesn't recognize any of his captors," said Winst with a wink. "All the patrols from Yen Manor and the outposts help each other whenever we can."

Jalan took the flask Winst passed to him. He raised it to his mouth to take a drink and stopped when his nose caught an unfamiliar sent.

"What's in here?" he said.

"It's not watered wine. Go ahead. It won't kill you," said Winst.

The way the swallow set fire to his throat said differently. Even Tomac laughed as Jalan sputtered while warmth spread outward from his belly. He did not think it funny until he saw the round eyed look of shock on Tomac's face when his brother swallowed his first mouthful.

Jalan and Tomac tried to explain to Sergeant Jonas why they left the road. Despite the stern expression he wore as he listened it soon became apparent their story satisfied him. Everyone relaxed as they talked and shared flasks. The Yen Manor horses were added to the picket line the Southway lancers had already set up for their mounts. The picket line, located just inside the trees beyond the clearing seemed hard to miss.

"How did I not notice this?" wondered Jalan as he secured his mount to the line.

One of the Southway lancers said, "You were distracted. You didn't even notice us sneaking up on you."

Jalan admitted the truth of that. Startled by the presence of Sergeant Jonas at the campfire, he had not given much thought to anything else.

"Say, um..." It seemed a little difficult to concentrate. He had a question, but forgot it as he spoke. Then it came to him. "Why were you on foot? Why not ride your horses?"

"Lancer's ride. A gang of skulking highwaymen who steal horses can't possibly be lancers can they?"

"So that's another distraction?"

"Or one less maybe. You can throw a cloak over armor and house colors. It's harder to hide a well-tended and trained warhorse."

The image of a lancer trying to sneak about with a warhorse tucked under his cloak leapt into Jalan's mind and he began to laugh. The lancer laughed too and that seemed even funnier.

The man threw an arm around Jalan's shoulders and said, "We better find you a place to sit down."

Jalan remembered laying out his bedroll and laughing at various stories told by some of the lancers. Tomac seemed to enjoy himself as well. At some point, Jalan must have crawled into his bedroll because he woke up there in the morning.

ALDUS BAKER

His head hurt and he wanted to sleep longer when the sergeant ordered everyone up. Warm bright sunshine replaced the gray overcast of yesterday. A few minutes after leaving the woods, Jalan yearned for clouds to dim the daylight that pierced his eyes and stabbed into his head. Winst told him the contents of the flask would not kill him. He rather wished it had.

Tomac said nothing all morning. When Jalan forced himself to turn his head and look, Tomac's eyes were nearly squinted shut and his mouth formed a sullen frown. Sergeant Jonas rode at the head of their file. His voice boomed whenever he gave an order or asked a question. Jalan thought he might learn to hate the man by the time they reached Yen Manor.

CHAPTER IV

Jalan and his brother stood before Lieutenant Burk as the sun rose above the rooftops of the eastern buildings that lined the courtyard.

"You two now have sufficient stamina and strength to learn the longbow," said the lieutenant with just the hint of what Jalan thought was pride in his voice. He directed them to take one of the unstrung bows from the wooden weapons rack and then spent the next couple of minutes teaching them to step through the bow in order to string it. Burk performed the action with his bow almost without looking at it.

Jalan's bow stood taller than he did. When he fumbled the string's loop while trying to slip it into place on the noch the strain of holding the bow bent rapidly overwhelmed his arm and he had to stop, rest a moment and start again. A quick look at Tomac showed his brother had fared better and strung his longbow on the first try.

"These are not like the little hunting bows you are used to," said Lieutenant Burk. "A heavy longbow requires strong shoulders and back muscles to bend it." He demonstrated by raising his bow, right hand holding back the string while his left pushed the bow forward. The lieutenant leaned into the weapon until it fully bent and his right hand held the string even with the side of his right cheek. The lieutenant counted to five in a measured pace then slowly eased the taunt bowstring forward and lowered the bow.

"Your bows have a light bend weight. A lancer would have no trouble holding one for a five count. And even though you are both stronger and hardier than when your training began, you do not have the strength of a grown man. You should find bending these longbows challenging enough," said Burk. "You shall bend with me. We will count together as I have just done and then you will allow the string to slowly ease. You will not loose the string. If you find holding the bend to be too difficult, let the string move forward slowly to ease the tension. Questions?"

Burk paused. Jalan waited. Tomac remained silent.

"Good. Imitate my stance and we will begin on my order."

Jalan satisfied himself that his stance closely resembled that of Lieutenant Burk.

"Trainees, bend!" said Burk.

Jalan immediately raised his longbow with a simultaneous pull back on the string and push forward against the bow in the way he had seen the lieutenant do. His right hand came back to rest against his cheek with the string digging into the three fingers that held it. The tension within the string seemed familiar and the wood of the longbow responded to it. Together the strain of the string against his right fingers and the pressure of the wood against his left hand played off the sinew and muscle of his arms, shoulders and back in a harmony of exertion that felt more natural to Jalan than anything he had ever experienced. He recalled back before his training began, the last time he had drawn a bow. He and Tomac hunted rabbits. Drawing that bow should have been easier according to the lieutenant. He remembered it as more difficult.

"Five," said Lieutenant Burk. "Now slowly ease the string forward."

What happened to one through four? He had barely drawn the bow. The full count could not have been complete. He saw both Burk and Tomac easing their bowstrings forward in his peripheral vision and decided he should do the same. He would figure out what happened later. Burk had said he was stronger. Probably that explained it. Maybe the bend of his bow was even lighter than Burk thought.

"Remember to breathe when you hold the bend," said Lieutenant Burk.

Jalan took a deep breath. He could not remember if he breathed while holding the bow taut.

"Trainees, ready. Bend!" said Burk.

His right fingers protested as the string dug into them again while his shoulders, back and left arm exerted to push the longbow out and bend the yew wood. Again his body held in check the bow's desire to release the power he had put into it. Jalan felt the effort it took to a greater degree. Holding the bend was not as easy this time. He told himself to breathe and eased the string forward as quickly as he could after the lieutenant finished the count.

He shook and flexed the first three fingers of his right hand to relieve the pain from the string. Warmth rose in his back and shoulders, not a burning and not an ache, almost a pleasure of tense muscles relieved by use. With a heavier heartbeat and increased need to breathe, his body became a little more alive, awakening to the demands of the longbow. He could think of no other way to express this unexpected enlivening.

Burk took them through bending their bows again and again, having both Jalan and Tomac call out the count with him. By the end, Jalan's tunic clung to him and he could feel a weariness overtaking his mysterious vitality. Even the lieutenant's face glistened with sweat. Except for his sore fingers, Jalan would have welcomed more repetitions if only to keep experiencing the odd sensation of it.

He watched Tomac tug at his own damp tunic. Tomac looked as though he needed to work out a strain. He swung his right arm in a circle and used his left hand to massage his right shoulder. Because of their months of sparring, Jalan knew his brother was exhausted. He could read it in Tomac's face. Tomac and he had learned to hide fatigue. They both knew the fresh energy and determination they got when their opponent appeared to be on the brink of defeat. Tomac would stand tall no matter how much he wanted to bend over with his hands on his knees and let his head hang down while sucking in all the air he could and allowing his spent muscles to rest. Jalan admired Tomac's fortitude, the way his brother projected a readiness to continue forever even as he teetered on the edge of collapse.

It seemed Tomac's bluff did not fool Lieutenant Burk either because he said, "Unstring your bows, drink some water and rest for a few minutes."

Jalan placed his unstrung bow back in the wooden weapons rack and walked over to sit beneath one of the few mature trees in the courtyard. The morning sun had not climbed far toward zenith, but its warmth left little doubt about how hot the day would become. The water bucket sat on the ground among the roots. He lifted the ladle from the bucket and drank water as Tomac lowered himself to the ground.

Jalan passed the ladle to Tomac. He drank and leaned back against the tree trunk as he closed his eyes. Jalan reached over and took the ladle back. Tomac gave no sign of caring. Jalan dipped the ladle in the bucket and raised it in a salute to his brother. He drank and dropped it back into the bucket.

Jalan surveyed the practice yard. Lieutenant Burk examined the bow Jalan had used. The lieutenant strung it and bent it as Jalan had done during practice. Burk eased the string forward and bent the bow a second time. Then he unstrung it and repeated the same actions with Tomac's bow.

Burk walked to the tree and Jalan stood, ready to continue with training. Tomac appeared to have fallen asleep and remained where he was.

Burk glanced at Tomac and then placed his full attention on Jalan. "How do you feel?"

"Fine. Tired, but fine," said Jalan, not at all sure why Burk asked.

Jalan heard Tomac start to stir, perhaps begin to rise. Burk looked toward Tomac and said, "Stand easy." In a somewhat sleepy voice Tomac said, "Sir." Jalan glanced over and saw him sink all the way back to the ground.

"This afternoon you practice archery with the regular lancers. Sedic holds a practice each day just after midday bell."

"What about Tomac?" said Jalan.

"A good lancer doesn't ask questions, he follows orders," said Lieutenant Burk.

"Yes, sir."

"I'll see you tomorrow morning. Be ready to spar."

"Yes, sir."

"Take your bow, find Sedic and let him know I've ordered you to attend his archery practices."

"Yes, sir."

"Dismissed."

Although Jalan's head filled with questions he knew Burk expected him to be a good lancer and not ask. He would have to wait and see what Sedic might say and what he could learn from Tomac later. He turned toward the lancer barracks and jogged away to look for Sedic. He only had to ask any lancers he came across. One of them would know where Sedic was. He definitely would not be asking Lieutenant Burk.

Δ

Jalan asked after Sedic several places until finally running down his new archery master at the fletcher's shop.

Sedic creased his brow and gave Jalan a slight tight-lipped frown as he listened to him relay Lieutenant Burk's order to begin training that afternoon. The shaggy headed lancer made no comment except to direct Jalan to set down his bow. Sedic then slipped a quiver strap over Jalan's head where it ran diagonally across his chest and back to an oiled canvas quiver that hung low at his left hip. Sedic slung a second strap over Jalan's head to hang another quiver at his right hip. The lancer did the same with two more, positioning the quivers just to the rear of those Jalan already wore.

"What are you doing?" said Jalan. The quivers were not very heavy individually, but four of them with 24 arrows in each put a discernible pressure on his neck and shoulders.

"What are you doing... lancer," said Sedic in response.

Jalan suppressed a sigh and repeated the question with the correct form of address, "What are you doing, lancer?"

"We, you and I, are picking up an order of flight arrows and I am arranging them for you to carry. Hold out your arms."

He listened to Sedic's response, held out his arms and began a mental calculation of the distance from the fletcher's to the archery field.

Sedic grabbed up two more quivers by their straps and dropped them, one, two, across Jalan's outstretched arms. "That's done then," said Sedic. He turned directly for the shop's door and walked out.

"My bow," said Jalan as he stood loaded down with a gross of arrows.

"You'd better bring it," came Sedic's voice from outside as if he were making a helpful suggestion.

Jalan wanted to drop all the quivers, pick up his bow and tell Sedic to carry his own arrows over to the cursed archery field when Sedic popped back into the shop, grabbed Jalan's bow off the floor and laid it across Jalan's armload of quivers.

"There you go. Hurry now or we'll be late," said Sedic as he again left Jalan standing there and exited the shop.

With a six foot longbow laid across his outstretched arms there was no way for Jalan to walk straight through the shop's door. He almost dropped his entire load in frustrated disgust. It occurred to him that he would still have to report to Sedic for archery training. If he did not do what Sedic demanded of him now, things would go badly for him later. Lieutenant Burk had ordered him to train with Sedic. Not doing as Sedic directed might be consider disobeying the lieutenant. What if the lieutenant stopped Jalan's training? What would his mother say? Jalan had promised to do his best and give honor to the memory of his father.

"Have a care," said the shopkeeper as Jalan turned in order to walk sideways through the door. The end of his bow nearly knocked a rack of freshly fletched arrows to the floor. "You'll ruin a morning's work."

"Sorry," said Jalan in more of a growl than an apology. He sidestepped his way to the door where he struggled to squeeze through. His upturned forearms scraped on the door frame as he fought to hold the two quivers and his longbow. The quivers at his back tried to wedge him in place. To his relief, no such thing happened. Having forced his way out, he inhaled deeply to convince himself that he could still breathe.

He expected to see Sedic waiting for him. Instead he had to make due with giving his angry scowl to the back of the lancer's head as he quickened his pace to catch the man. Sedic had a long stride. The four bouncing quivers hanging off Jalan buffeted his hips and posterior. He could do nothing about it with his arms full. At least when he sparred he could hit back. Jalan imagined taking a particularly wicked swing. He made Sedic the recipient of his vicious strike. Sedic did not seem to notice, but that did not stop Jalan from mentally pummeling him all the way to the archery field.

HIDDEN ABILITY

It only took a few minutes to place all the quivers inside a hut used specifically to keep arrows, bows and other equipment out of the weather and secure.

"You will keep your bow here. It is a weapon and until you have shown the skill and responsibility required, I cannot entrust you with it," said Sedic.

Lieutenant Burk had given him the longbow this morning and let him take it when he left to find Sedic. Jalan had not loosed arrows randomly into the air or behaved in any fashion he considered to be irresponsible. What did the lancer think he would do with the longbow, hunt rabbits at 150 yards? "I can be careful with it," said Jalan.

"But can you keep it safe?" said Sedic. "That longbow is the most dangerous weapon you will ever use. Because of that, it is also the most coveted. This is foreign yew, long grained and strong. We have to trade for it. The wood alone is valuable. Once it is shaped, bent and tested by a bow master it becomes one of the rarest weapons we have, more valuable than most swords and strong enough to pierce armor. There are thieves who would slit your throat for it. I cannot leave it in the hands of an untrained boy."

"I'm trained..."

Sedic kicked Jalan's feet out from beneath him. In the blink of an eye Jalan lay on the ground with a knee pushing into his chest and a knife pressed against his throat.

"I'll be the one to decide that," said Sedic as he eased his knee off Jalan and let him take a breath.

"That wasn't fair," said Jalan.

"Thieves aren't fair and brigands don't care." Sedic took the knife from Jalan's throat and slipped it back into the sheath at his hip. "You'd best remember that." The lancer rose and frowned while Jalan picked himself up. "Get something to eat and be here on the first bell of the afternoon."

Δ

Sedic passed out longbows to the dozen lancers milling about near the equipment hut at the archery field. He pointed at each of them, one by one, as Jalan waited his turn. With each bow, Sedic

41

handed out a quiver of arrows. There were a dozen lancers and they were all equipped before Sedic pointed a finger at Jalan.

Without a word between them, Jalan took the bow offered to him and his own quiver of arrows. He could not be certain, but the bow seemed to be the same one he had given over to Sedic earlier. Jalan walked to his place at the near end of the archery line where all the others already stood shoulder to shoulder. A few of the lancers watched him openly. He caught a couple of others looking away before he could meet their eyes. None of them smiled and even those he knew gave no sign of recognizing him. Jalan had never seen a more somber gathering of lancers. The shortest and youngest, he felt the years that separated him from the rest most keenly.

Sedic stepped out before the line and let his gaze move freely across them as he said, "At Lieutenant Burk's order we are joined by our new little brother." There were a few snickers and a whispered comment Jalan could not quite hear followed by a low chuckle. Sedic paused only a moment to let the response to his words die before he said, "Some of you know Jalan. All of you probably know he is the youngest child of House Yen. Whatever claim to title or fealty he has means nothing to us here. Here he is another archer in training and must prove himself just as any man must." Sedic placed extra emphasis on the word man. "You need not show him deference or quarter." Sedic said the last after catching and holding Jalan's eye. He had his left hand resting on his belt knife.

Jalan knew all the lancers had stopped looking at him as Sedic spoke, but he felt as if he were being scrutinized by each of them and that none of them considered him to be a man, a lancer or an archer. Sedic had driven a wedge between him and the others. Jalan wished to blend in or at least be overlooked. Now they thought of him as some form of little brother interloper. It angered him that Sedic, who could have eased his way, seemed intent on making it an uphill struggle.

"Lancers, spread apart, set your arrows and string your bows. Begin!" ordered Sedic.

The men shuffled a little further away from each other. Jalan stayed in place on the end of the line as the lancer beside him moved a sidestep away. He immediately felt a little more at ease with more space between himself and the next person. Gratitude for having no one to his right lifted his spirits as well.

The lancers pulled back the cloth flaps that covered the tops of their quivers and remove the arrows. As they took an arrow out they jammed it point first into the ground next to them until they had porcupined a small plot of earth. Jalan followed suit and soon had his own little forest of feathered shafts sprouting from the ground to his right. He strung his longbow the way Lieutenant Burk had showed him. Once he finished he noticed that Sedic watched him with a neutral expression. Jalan could not tell if that was good or bad.

"If it takes this long to make ready tomorrow we will have to start skipping the midday meal in order to have enough time for practice," said Sedic.

Jalan knew what Sedic meant. He had been the last one to string a bow. If he failed to perform any task well enough to satisfy his new archery master, Sedic would punish everyone and make certain they blamed Jalan. He could feel his teeth grinding together in frustration.

"Everyone look out across the archery field. For the benefit of our newest trainee, I will explain once again the range markers. At the farthest extreme is 300 yards. Only the strongest of you with the best technique will ever have a hope of sending an arrow that far." Sedic swept his open hand palm up toward what appeared to be a short length of fence or several wooden posts set close together. Given the distance it might have been either or something else entirely. "Moving closer is a marker at 250 yards, a range that certainly requires strength and skill to achieve. Closer still is the 200 yards marker, the distance that you must all reach with reasonable accuracy to be of any value in battle. Stepping in we have the 150 yards, the 100 yards and the 50 yards markers."

Jalan easily discerned the construction of the 50 yards marker, several wooden posts set side by side with planks lashed horizontally across them. The other markers seemed to be of the same sort. Sedic began to speak and Jalan returned his attention to his instructor.

"We will begin at the 100 yards mark." Sedic walked up to the line of men and passed through to stand behind them. "Lancers. Noch arrows. Begin!"

Jalan reached over, grasped the noch of an arrow and pulled it free of the ground. He tilted his bow slightly to the left, placed the shaft of the arrow against the arrow rest and slid the arrow along the rest to maneuver the noch into position on the string. It took very little time and relieved some of his tension when he noticed others finishing after him.

"Lancers. Bend bows and take aim. Begin!" called out Sedic.

He leaned into his bow as he had done at Lieutenant Burk's direction that morning. The initial resistance made him worry that he would fail to duplicate his earlier success. His body did not disappoint him however. Again the muscles of his shoulders and back took over and a warmth of exertion spread through him. He felt strain and pleasure as if he vibrated with the power of the longbow. Instead of becoming lost in the sensation he raised the arrow tip up to what he thought was the same angle the lancer to his left had chosen. Then he blew out his breath and listen for Sedic's next order.

"Lancers, loose!"

Jalan moved the first three fingers of his right hand and let the bowstring have its way. The tension and power in his muscles and longbow were given to the arrow and propelled it up and out in a blur of motion. An awareness deep within Jalan reached out and went with it, arcing to the summit of flight and plummeting to earth. *Short.* The word appeared in Jalan's mind with certainty. He did not even think to question the thought. He knew it beyond all doubt. He even knew how short. The arrow protruded from the field 25 yards short of the target.

From behind him he heard, "Are you sure you're up for this? Is that the farthest you can send an arrow?" Jalan flinched, surprised by the unexpected words that were so close as to almost be in his ear. "I don't know what Burk is aiming for by sending you to me, but there is no shame in admitting you can't do this. You're a boy. In a few years, when you have grown, I am certain you would make a fine archer. There is no reason for you and me to continue to be the brunt of the lieutenant's bad joke. Say the word and I will send you back to him. Your humiliation will be over," said Sedic.

Heat rose in Jalan, not the heat of shame, the fire of anger. "Say the word and I will put one dead center in the marker."

"Just so. I see that spirit I've watched burn in you today has come forth." Sedic walked forward from behind Jalan to stand once more in front of the archery line. "Our newest trainee wishes a trial," said

Sedic in a strong voice that everyone present could hear. "He will, in his own words, 'put one dead center in the marker'. Should he fail, he will stop playing at being a longbowman and wait until his proper time."

All the lancers on the line looked at Jalan. Some stared. A couple laughed. One or two looked as if they might be embarrassed for him. None looked like they believed Jalan could do it. They saw some boy who stood on the archery line with them, a momentary aberration soon to be ended. His own confidence began to falter in the face of so much doubt until he heard Sedic speak again.

"Trainee. Noch arrow. Begin!"

Jalan pulled an arrow from out of the midst of his little forest and smoothly noched it.

"Trainee. Bend bow and take aim. Begin!"

He had no one else with which to compare his angle. Nor did he feel the need. His bow bent and took on the aspect of another part of himself. With his right eye he sighted along the arrow and brought its tip up into a square patch of sky that seemed to brighten when the arrow point settled within it. That patch gave him the angle and direction he needed. It compensated for the breeze and banished his creeping worries. He knew it as he knew his own name.

"Trainee, loose!"

He did not know what the men who watched did as the arrow lofted into the sky. Jalan felt only the flight of it and the bite of the point into the wood were it struck home. A slow smile spread across his lips.

Sedic sent a lancer to survey the 100 yards marker and report back. When the man returned Sedic asked, "How many arrows were lodged in the marker?"

"Four."

"Could you tell for certain if any of them were put there by our trainee?"

"No, master. But only one was centered."

"Unfortunately, that could have been done by any one of you," said Sedic to everyone present. He faced Jalan and said, "We will need more from you than laying claim to an arrow that could have been loosed by any man here."

Until now Jalan would have sworn that only Tomac, or possibly their sister Vee, was capable of displaying such a stubborn wrong-headed ill-natured attitude. His fingers started to ache from the stranglehold he had on his longbow and his shoulders felt tighter than while he held the bow bent. He shook himself and threw off the stress and anger like a horse bucks a rider, caring only to be free of the unwanted burden. He stepped off the archery line and over to Sedic where he held out his bow.

For Sedic's part, the lancer did not look happy but rather disappointed. "Giving up?" he said as he reached out and took the longbow Jalan offered him.

"No, master," said Jalan as he turned and started walking.

"Then where are you going, trainee?"

"To get another bow," said Jalan. He walked into the open storage hut and in moments put his hand to a bow that had the right feel. If he had not been so driven to act, to prove himself to that ox brained archery master, he might have let the doubting part of himself question what he did. Instead the inner fury fanned by the injustice of his situation burned away all hesitation and uncertainty.

He returned to the line. He put all he had into stringing the bow because he knew that if he failed then everything would collapse. He would not give Sedic the satisfaction. As his body shook from the strain, the loop slipped into place. Jalan closed his eyes for an instant. His muscles relaxed, his breathing slowed and relief filled him.

"Congratulations, you've strung a heavy longbow. I'm surprised you had the strength to do it. Do you propose now to bend it because I would not want you to look foolish in front of all these lancers? There is no way a boy possesses the might to use that bow."

Sedic spoke the truth. A boy would never be able to do it. So why did he think he could? He did not have words to explain it. The bow spoke a language that his body understood and his mind lacked a way to express. The touch of the wood told him he could do it. This bow, this wood, with it he could.

Jalan plucked another arrow out of the ground and noched it. He leaned into the bow while drawing the string back in unison with the song the bow sang, a song of earth and sun, of strength and strain, a melody that rang within him. String to his cheek and arrow to the sky, he stood poised at the farthest edge of his ability. His heart beat once and the world shook. He exhaled and the wind died. He loosed his arrow and it pierced the sky, destined to strike its distant target, the mark he had chosen, the mark only the strongest and the best could ever hope to reach.

This time Sedic said nothing. He nodded once to Jalan and started walking out into the archery field. Jalan laid the longbow down. He had no strength left to unstring or carry it, but nothing would stop him from following Sedic. The absolute certainty he possessed the moment he released the arrow dwindled little by little. His arms hung at his sides like two slack ropes. His legs, heavy as stones, made each step a challenge. He had done the impossible and now he bore the physical cost.

Sedic stood before the 300 yards marker when Jalan slogged up beside him. There, with its feathered end raked steeply upward and as close to dead center as to leave no argument, stuck an arrow. Its head had splintered the wooden plank and lodged deep enough to hold. Sedic turned toward Jalan. Jalan met his gaze. Sedic did not speak, but Jalan felt the lancer's careful study of him, almost as if Sedic had never really looked at him before.

Sedic called out, "Do you see this?"

Jalan wondered what was wrong with the man that he had to ask. Several voices surprised Jalan as they responded, "Yes, master."

The others were all there, standing in a rough semicircle behind him. The ringing in his ears must have prevented him from hearing them.

"By your honor as Yen Lancers, do any of you claim to have loosed this arrow?" said Sedic.

Responses of "No," and "No, master," came from all the lancers.

"Then by your honor you are bound to tell the truth of this when any question it. And, they will question it." Sedic looked directly at Jalan and said, "You deserve something for such an achievement, but I think you will find the fame from it to be no reward at all. However, you have more than earned my apology. I thought you were a child fallen into deep water. Who knew you could swim so well?"

"Not I," said Jalan as he sank to the ground to sit upon the very comfortable looking grass.

Sedic chuckled and several men laughed. Someone said, "Boy, you are spent."

The warm sun and soft grass seemed like the perfect place for a nap. Jalan almost lay down when strong hands lifted him to his feet and got him walking. The trip back to the archery line was a stumbling blur. At some point he stopped moving and lay down, the last memory before sleep took him.

When he woke, Sedic stood over him giving light kicks to the sole of Jalan's booted foot.

"Wake up, trainee. What kind of example are you setting by only loosing three arrows and then taking a nap? I'll expect better of you tomorrow," said Sedic.

Jalan pushed himself up, uncertain about where he was or how he got there. The sun outside the storage hut hung only a little above the horizon. *Why was I sleeping?* It only required that he think the question for all the events of the day to come flooding back to him. For an instant, Sedic's words angered him. Sedic's face showed no rancor or disdain. In fact, the man smiled, a thing Jalan had not seen today.

Sedic offered his hand to help Jalan up. "You were joking weren't you?" said Jalan once he'd gained his feet.

"Just then? Aye, I was," said Sedic.

"It's hard to tell," said Jalan.

"So I've been told," said Sedic. "We could all see you were done in. I let you sleep in here. We needed to get on with practice and you'd more than earned a rest. I still don't believe it." Sedic shook his head. "Think you could do it again?"

"Maybe, yes, if the bow lets me," said Jalan.

Sedic's eyebrows rose in puzzlement, but he did not ask any more questions. "You'd better find your evening meal," he said.

Jalan's stomach growled loud enough for both of them to hear and the thought of food drove all other considerations out of his head. He bid Sedic good evening and promised to return the next afternoon. He even looked forward to it now that Sedic appeared to want him there. He glanced at the longbows in their racks and wished them a silent good evening as well.

CHAPTER V

Jalan held the lieutenant off all morning as his leathers grew hotter, his movements slower and every muscle in his body protested his abuse of them. As it approached midday, the hot sun boiled him in his own sweat and his lungs burned with every new breath.

"Keep your guard up!" shouted Lieutenant Burk.

He raised his practice blade higher and nearly groaned from the effort needed to do even that.

The lieutenant moved in with a low slash toward his thigh. He stepped back and swept the tip of his blade in a circle to intercept the attack. Burk surprised him by curving his slash upward. In a panic, Jalan twisted away as Burk's blade came toward his head. He jerked his sword hilt up, desperate to raise his weapon fast enough to block Burk's blade.

Burk's strike battered Jalan's sword, almost knocking it from his hand. The big lancer followed immediately with a kick that took Jalan in the side. Already out of position and hopelessly off balance, Jalan toppled over like an uprooted tree in a windstorm. He barely had time to consider which hurt worse, the kick or landing sprawled across the practice yard, before Burk expressed his displeasure with Jalan's performance.

"What kind of stance was that? My grandmother could have taken you boy," said the lieutenant as he stood over Jalan scowling.

Jalan raised his arm and reached for the lieutenant's offered hand. After Jalan stood, Burk continued.

"If you are going to step back, step all the way back and plant that heel. Where does your strength come from boy?"

"My heel", said Jalan for what he was certain must be the thousandth time.

"And!" called out the lieutenant.

"My hips", responded Jalan.

"And don't forget it. Ready to try again?"

Jalan learned early that the lieutenant did not ask for another round if he believed Jalan was too exhausted to hold the practice blade. At first, that only took a few rounds of sparring. Now, Jalan could go 10 rounds of the sand glass. Lieutenant Burk claimed the sand ran for three minutes, but it seemed closer to six. There were occasional breaks in the routine whenever Jalan had to pick himself up off the ground. He tried taking his time getting up, but Burk only went at it harder when he judged Jalan to be idling. Jalan preferred more sparring over nursing all the extra bruises.

A real enemy would never care how Jalan felt or let him prepare. An enemy would like him rattled, pummeled and weakened, the way he felt right now. He shook the sweat out of his eyes, forced himself into a neutral defensive stance and ignored his anatomy's objections. He waited for Burk to make the first move. When not beaten down, he could quickly close with the lieutenant and strike a blow. In his current state, the big lancer's greater reach would never allow it.

"Trying to wait me out, eh?" said Burk. "You know I'll just get close and batter your guard until you can't hold me off."

Jalan stifled a groan. He did his best to look unconcerned. He tried to keep his face still and his posture relaxed. *Burk is taunting me.*

"Perhaps you'd prefer to spar someone less skilled? You might stand a chance against your sister Vee. Although we both know she is the better dancer."

Not the dancing again. One time he said something about dancing lessons and Burk never let him forget it. He felt his jaw tighten and knew he had made a mistake.

Burk charged with a two handed stroke that would split Jalan from top to bottom. Jalan's parry collided hard and a tingling numbing jolt ran through his right hand and forearm. The next attack was one handed and slower. Jalan tapped Burk's blade with his own and deflected it past him. He lunged, pressing the tip of his practice sword into Burk's underarm. The weak hit, made in desperation, seemed destined to have little effect. The lieutenant bellowed in pain and dropped his sword arm against his side.

Shock kept Jalan from following up on his unexpected advantage. Burk seemed to have lost control of his arm and Jalan worried he might have done the lieutenant real harm. The lieutenant, on the other hand, wasted no time as he switched his sword to his off hand even while he still grimaced in pain. Burk began to circle Jalan, looking for an opening with murder in his eyes. He hoped Burk remembered they were only sparring.

A thought grabbed hold of him and Jalan reversed his stance. He too traded hands and held his sword in his left.

Burk faltered and snarled, "This is a bad time for honor, boy."

It sounded like a rebuke and a warning. Jalan heard a hint of admiration too. He decided to heed the warning and save the admiration for later, assuming he'd be in any condition to appreciate it. "Let's dance," he said.

Burk gave him an evil grin. The big man came at him with three quick strikes. Jalan managed to parry each one. Burk feigned a slash. Jalan moved to counter and met an unexpected trust that scrapped across the front of his jerkin as he twisted sideways to avoid it. He wanted to scream as he watched Burk's leg sweep his feet from beneath him. His back slammed into the ground. His cry of frustration suffocated when the wind was knocked out of him.

Burk's booted foot weighted on his chest. The lieutenant's sword point pressed against his throat. Jalan forgot everything except his desire for air, but his lungs refused to fill.

"Yield!" said Burk.

A wheezing sigh escaped Jalan's throat.

"I accept your yield," said Burk as he lifted his boot and removed the sword point. "Well fought."

"...thank you...," Jalan managed between gasping breaths. He did not see the hand Burk offered him until the black dots swarming before his eyes cleared a bit. As he staggered upright, he relied mainly on the strength of the lieutenant's left arm to lift him.

"Next time, wait until after you've won to display your finer qualities. It will not serve if all that can be said about you is, 'he died with honor'".

"Yes, sir," said Jalan, speaking to the ground as he bent double to catch his breath and wait for his head to stop spinning. "How is your arm, sir?"

"Whatever you did sent fire through my arm and left it useless for a moment."

Jalan saw Burk move his arm about and flexed his hand.

"It seems fine now. I've seen a man taken in battle that way, but that was with the thrust of sharp steel. I had no idea a blunted sword could cause such an effect. Why didn't you press me when you had the chance?"

Jalan rose slowly to his full height and shrugged. "I worried I hurt you. I mean really hurt you, not just a bruise."

"Takes more than a poke to stop a lancer, boy."

"Yes, sir."

"Sedic tells me your knife throwing is coming along and your slinging needs more practice. That's a difficult weapon to master, but that's no excuse for not doing your best."

Jalan thought about his practice with the sling. A bow made sense. He could feel it. That affinity did not translate to the sling. "Yes, sir," was all he said.

"Captain Erida said you've been drilling well with the lancers. Running them through formations and maneuvers almost like a real officer."

"He told me I ride like a plowboy."

Lieutenant Burk barked a laugh. "From him that's a complement."

Jalan rubbed his head, trying to massage away his sudden headache.

Lieutenant Burk straightened even more than his normal honed lancer posture and said, "Captain."

Jalan turned and his head barely spun. The tall broad-shouldered captain approached as if conjured by the mention of his name. The midday sun lightened the officers brown hair to blond. The silvering at his temples and the streaks in his short beard looked white. He wore the same uniform as all the lancers, blue belted tunic, tan breeches, tall riding boots. A saber hung against his left hip. His captain's braid stood out bright white on his left shoulder. "Captain," said Jalan as he looked up at him.

"Lieutenant. Trainee," said Captain Erida addressing both of them in turn. Jalan's unofficial induction into the lancers had been almost five months ago. Since then many lancers started calling him by name instead of saying trainee or boy. The officers, especially Captain Erida, were not among them.

Unexpected interruptions in his training caused Jalan to worry. He never admitted it to the captain and especially not to Burk, but he enjoyed training. He still recalled his childhood before the intense instruction and practices began, how he waited for something to happen. Once his training began, it seemed to be exactly the thing required to fill the hollowness within him. He could imagine nothing worse than having it taken away. Nothing except the death of his father which required no imagination at all.

"...with me," said Captain Erida.

Jalan shook himself to clear his head and rein in his wandering thoughts. "Yes, sir," said Jalan in the hope he had made an appropriate response to whatever the captain just said.

"Lieutenant, what have you done to the boy? Has he been climbing ropes with that weighted pack again?" said Erida.

"Sparring, sir," said Burk as he held up his wooden practice sword. "He's had the wind knocked out of him, but will soon be himself."

"Good. Assuming you've finished, it's time for another lesson. Jalan, we were discussing some of the battles from The Chalmar Wars. Find a good stick for scratching out representations of the key engagements."

Another history lesson. Maybe not for Erida because he fought with Jalan's father in the last of the three wars, but it happened before Jalan was even born. Captain Erida favored the practice yard for his history lessons. He claimed sketching battle scenes in the dirt made them easier to understand. The captain taught strategy, tactics, military formations, troop units, their use in battle, how to support them, how to advance, and how to fall back. The where and why of it all, and more, explained by the scrape of a stick across the ground.

53

It seemed a lot to learn. Perhaps they expected him to be an officer one day. Jalan, despite the mental and physical struggle of it all, could conceive of nothing better. Early on he asked his mother why he must work so hard. She said his father had wanted him to be well trained. He honored his father's memory by doing his best.

The captain sketched several terrain features and filled in various spaces around them with military units that had been present at the Battle of the Three Ridges, the initial encounter credited with starting The Second Chalmar War. Jalan crouched down a few feet in front of Captain Erida. He watched and listened to his explanation of why the House Martris Lancers were improperly deployed.

As he spoke, Captain Erida glanced at something behind Jalan. Erida dropped the stick on the dusty ground and sprang from his crouch. He drew his sword in a single fluid motion. Jalan thought it was graceful, impressive and frightening. Almost without thinking, Jalan launched himself into a forward roll that brought him to his feet behind Erida where he spun to face whatever danger made the captain draw steel.

A man of average height with lean solid features and shaggy white hair walked toward them. He had a long nose and his square face held an expression of mild interest. Jalan though he looked very relaxed especially with Captain Erida's saber threatening him. The stranger wore a dusty weather stained travel jacket. It may have been green at one time. The jacket moved slightly about his torso as the listless breeze chanced to catch its open front. The legs of his equally worn breeches hung around the outside of his boots rather than tucked within and they too flapped and swayed with each step. Jalan thought they looked brown but could originally have been gray or even black.

"Lieutenant!" shouted Erida over his shoulder without taking his eyes off the white haired stranger. Jalan's heart pounded as he watched the man continue to walk toward him and the captain as though taking a pleasant stroll.

"Captain, I had hoped we'd gotten past this," said the stranger.

"They were good men, Enmar. I don't forget my men."

Lieutenants Burk and Goss along with two other men stormed around the corner of the stables at a full run. They drew weapons as they sprinted toward the confrontation between Erida and the stranger.

"Captain", said the dusty man in a soft voice that carried a strong undercurrent of disapproval despite his mild tone. The man stopped walking and stood looking relaxed and unconcerned with the end of Erida's sword no more than a long stride away.

Erida did not remove his eyes from the fellow as he threw up his left hand palm out toward the reinforcements and yelled, "Hold!"

Jalan felt himself stiffen even though the command had not been for him. All four soldiers stopped immediately and waited with weapons at the ready, eyes on the new arrival. The stranger, Enmar, gave them all a brief polite smile.

"Why are you here, Enmar", said Captain Erida as he returned his left hand to his sword hilt." Jalan noticed the captain had taken a strong defensive stance. That seemed odd because the stranger appeared to be unarmed.

"I'm here on the kings' business to speak to the head of House Yen," said Enmar.

Jalan saw some of the tension slip away from Captain Erida's shoulders and back. He did not lower his sword. Burk, Goss and the two men with them still stood ready as well, but they exchanged glances with each other, eyes no longer locked upon the stranger. Beyond the earlier smile, Enmar paid no attention to them. Jalan did not understand how wanting to talk to Darla made the man less dangerous.

"You have a copy of your orders?" asked Erida.

"I do. May I present them to you, captain?"

"We are servants of the king," said Erida as he lowered his weapon and eased the blade back into the scabbard strapped to his left hip.

"And the king is the servant of the people," said white haired Enmar as he slowly reached into an interior pocket of his travel jacket and withdrew a small leather messenger's tube.

The words each man spoke seemed like part of some ritual. Judging by the orders Lieutenant Goss started issuing and Burks cajoling of the gathering crowd to move off and be about their business, things were, if not normal, then at least no longer on the verge of bloodshed. Jalan decided to remember those words.

Captain Erida looked up from the parchment he read. He held the open leather tube. Its cap, covered in the remnants of a green wax seal, dangled by a string. Given the look on Erida's face, Jalan expected to be ordered to labor in the stables. The captain rolled up the parchment and slid it back into the open tube. He held the tube out to Enmar and said to Jalan, "Take Messenger Enmar to Lady Darla immediately."

When Jalan hesitated as he tried to sort out this bewildering turn of events, Erida barked out, "Today!"

"You can hardly blame the boy for being confused," said Enmar as he took back his document. "A moment ago you wanted to split me down the middle."

"I still do," said Erida.

Enmar laughed deeply as though enjoying a great jest. He turned toward the manor house and started walking without waiting for Jalan to lead him. Jalan pushed his sore body into motion while trying to puzzle out how the man had gone from extreme threat to someone Jalan could safely deliver to Darla.

Δ

Krenis Enmar strode toward the manor, certain the front door remained were he had left it years earlier. No one could say he had not been patient. But the boy was so old now. He could wait no longer to begin real training.

The boy arrived after jogging to catch up. He appeared to be lean and fit. Grime covered from whatever Erida had him doing, sparring by the look of his leather jerkin and the wooden sword he carried. Dirt and sweat matted his sun bleached hair. The perspiration carved rivulets through the filth on his face.

As the boy was about to speak, Krenis raised one finger. "Jalan is it?"

"Yes," he replied.

"Yes, what?" said Krenis in a firm voice.

Jalan appeared to consider a moment before answering, "Yes, sir."

Krenis nodded approval and asked, "You're not going into the house like that are you?"

The boy looked truly puzzled and said, "Like what?" Belatedly he added, "Sir."

He's quick. "Are you going to wash up first?"

"Well, err..." stammered Jalan.

"Go get a bucket of water. Wash your hands and douse your head. One does not enter the presence of the head of a landed house while wearing most of that land upon his person."

"It's just Darla. She's seen me before."

Krenis smiled and said, "I'm sure she has. Now go on." When Jalan still hesitated he added, "I'll wait here."

The boy shrugged and left with the air of a child complying with one more pointless adult demand, completely unaware that his life had just changed. It might have happened sooner if Hallis Yen had not died. No wall stood around the manor. No guards challenged Krenis's approach. Lady Darla Yen seemed competent, but she was definitely not her father. Lord Yen's presence had kept away some searchers. It had taken time to deal with the repercussions of his death. After so long, Krenis looked forward to ending his vagabond existence and eagerly anticipated the challenge of training young Jalan.

A wetter and cleaner Jalan returned to interrupt Krenis Enmar's thoughts. The boy had stripped of his leather armor. His damp tunic clung to him. Krenis thought it likely the moister did not come from the bucket he used to wash.

"I'll take you to Darla now," Jalan said.

Krenis raised his left eyebrow in a querulous fashion but spoke with no hint of criticism. "Lady Yen, or if you please, Lady Darla."

Jalan sighed and said, "I'll take you to Lady Darla now."

"Most kind of you. Lead on, please."

Jalan opened the front door of the manor house and stepped inside. Krenis followed and closed the door. A short portly man in a Blue and Tan shirt hurried toward them.

"Jalan, who is your, ah, guest?" said the man.

"This is Messenger Enar..."

"Enmar," corrected Krenis, "Krenis Enmar".

"Enmar," Jalan repeated with exaggerated precision. "He is here to see D... Lady Darla." Jalan looked toward Krenis and said, "Messenger, this is Steward Hint."

"Does Lady Darla expect you, sir?" said the steward in a polite but neutral tone.

"Unlikely, unless Captain Erida sent word of my arrival. I am here on king's business and found it expedient to present myself to him first, as he made a point of greeting me personally."

"The Captain told me to bring him to her right away," said Jalan.

Hint looked at Jalan and back to Krenis. He said, "Please take a seat in the parlor while I announce you," and excused himself with a slight bow.

"The parlor is this way," said Jalan with a halfhearted sweep of his hand.

"Is something wrong?" said Krenis

"I don't like the parlor."

"Why not?"

Jalan shrugged and looked down. "I just don't." Then he walked away.

Krenis followed him in silence.

Δ

Lady Darla rose from her seat behind her worktable and moved to a mirror hung on the wall. She was not fussy about her appearance, but others judged her by it. Taking a moment, she felt for the bow of the blue ribbon that tied back her brown hair. It seemed to be in place. No ink smudged her face as sometimes happened. Her undyed cotton and flax dress had no intricate design or lace accents. The worn cuffs and ink stains told of her days pouring over ledgers and reports. She had expected no one and dressed accordingly. *I am once again undone by circumstance and station.*

Darla pick up a bell from beneath a small table covered with reports and rang it vigorously. Within the minute a servant knocked and inquired after her needs.

"I wish to continue my work here as long as possible. Please ask my maid to bring the blue gown and the tan sash so that I might change without returning to my chamber."

When the maid and gown arrived, it seemed as if no time had passed and Darla set aside the report she annotated, frustrated with how little she had accomplished. She allowed the maid to assist her as she changed into the more appropriate gown for receiving the royal messenger. She turned once more to her mirror and watched as the maid placed a necklace about her throat. Having judged herself prepared, she wondered about what type of man the messenger might be.

How had he so discomfited Captain Erida? Should she worry for her own safety? The man claimed to be a messenger from King Tamaron and Erida confirmed it. Darla had no choice but to receive him.

There came a tapping at the door and Lady Shara stepped in. Her mother smiled with a hint of anxiety in her blue topaz eyes. "I wish to be present when the messenger speaks to you."

"Of course," Darla said as she returned her mother's smile.

Lady Shara, as usual, had no need to change. She wore a gown of emerald green silk brocade that lay across her form in the most flattering way.

Darla envied her mother's easy grace. "I was going to ask Steward Hint to find you before bringing the man to my study. But, now you have saved me the trouble. And, as I think on it, I believe the parlor is a better place to greet this visitor."

Almost as if need alone could summon him, Steward Hint appeared at the door behind Lady Shara. "My lady, I have requested the cook bring refreshments as you directed," said the steward.

"Thank you, Hint. I am afraid I will have to ask you to redirect Mistress Dahlia and have the refreshments taken to the parlor instead of here. It just seems the more suitable place to greet a messenger from the king."

"Very well, my lady. Will there be anything else you require my ladies?"

"If you would ask Mistress Dahlia to put some of Jalan's favorite cheese on the tray, I would be most grateful," said Lady Shara. "I know he is with the messenger and I am certain he has not eaten since breakfast."

"As you wish, my lady," said the steward. He bowed slightly at the waist and departed.

Shara closed the door and slowly turned toward her daughter. She began to speak, paused, and turned slightly away. "There are things I should have told you," she confessed.

Darla moved closer to her mother and asked gently, "What things?"

Looking away Shara said, "Things about Jalan, about our fostering him. About whose son..." Lady Shara drew herself up and faced her daughter, "About whose son he really is. Now, when you need to know, we are out of time."

"Mother," said Darla softly. "There are many things I did not know when Jalan came to us. For instance, I did not know Black and Green are the colors of House Mar. Now I do. I know that Jalan is my brother and your son, no matter what other claims the world makes of him. Even the words of a king cannot change what is in our hearts. Jalan loves you. It is all right."

The women embraced; each gained strength from the presence of the other. Then hand in hand they left Lady Darla's study.

Δ

Jalan sat in one of the four chairs arranged around the fireplace. There was no fire. It was too hot for that. The windows on either side of the fireplace were open. Little gusts of wind pushed the curtains aside. He did not look around the room. He looked at the curtains. And sneaked glances at the messenger.

The man's eyes were closed. He wondered if the stranger slept. Because the messenger's eyes were shut, Jalan felt free to take a longer look. The man sat up straight. His head did not hang down chin-to-chest. Perhaps he only rested his eyes.

His white shaggy hair made him look old, like Captain Erida. His square face sported a long nose. His neck and arms looked solid. Not as big as Lieutenant Burk, but thicker than most men Jalan knew. Jalan wondered why Erida disliked him and why he wanted to talk to Darla.

Jalan sighed and let his eyes wander about the parlor. There was nothing to see other than the fireplace, chairs and the closed door to the adjoining room Darla called the Business Room. *Where was she?* Darla always took a long time. She could be fast if she was talking to him. But, he had to wait and wait if she was seeing someone else first, or reading some report, or working on a ledger. She made a list of things to do each day. Jalan was certain he and the messenger were not on it.

He remembered his father was like that to. *Except father would just let me walk in and stop whatever he was doing to talk to me.* It made him feel good and bad to remember.

The messenger looked at ease. Maybe he was used to waiting. Maybe being a messenger meant that you were always interrupting people that had lists which did not include you. He wondered if the messenger liked waiting. Jalan definitely did not.

Maybe the messenger only pretended to like waiting. People always said to be patient. Is that what patience was? Pretending to like waiting? *I could ask him.*

Jalan's study of the messenger was cut short when the white haired man breathed deeply and opened his eyes. Jalan kept watching him to see what he did next.

The messenger smiled and said, "You can stop fidgeting now. The lady is here." The man stood and the hallway door began to open. He looked at Jalan and waved his fingers to signal that Jalan should stand as well.

As Lady Shara and Lady Darla entered, Jalan slipped out of his chair and turned toward them. Lady Darla looked at the messenger and then at Jalan. He took her look as an indication that he should introduce Enmar.

"Darla. I mean Lady Darla," said Jalan with a sideways look at the messenger and a slight emphasis on the word lady. "This is Messenger Enmar. Captain Erida ordered me to bring him to you."

Darla nodded and said, "Thank you, Jalan." She turned her attention back to the messenger and said, "Welcome Messenger Enmar. What is the nature of your business with House Yen?"

While Darla addressed Messenger Enmar, Jalan watched his mother. Lady Shara stood a step behind and to the left of Darla and pretended to listen, but Jalan could tell she worried about something.

Lady Shara noticed his attention and flashed him a brief smile before looking as if she might cry. Her behavior confused Jalan. This was the room where Father died. He did not want anything to happen to her here. Jalan moved to a position between her and the stranger.

Darla asked something about wanting to listen to the messenger. Focused on his mother, he missed what she said. He nodded, hoping that response would do.

"Very well," said Darla.

The parlor door opened after a quick tap on the exterior. Mistress Dahlia and Juna, a girl that sometimes helped her, entered. They carried a pitcher of wine and a tray of cheese with bread and dried fruit. Steward Hint followed them with a small serving table that he placed in an open space near the center of the room. Jalan paid particular attention to the tray of food. His stomach growled and he realized it had been a long time since breakfast. He decided to pretend he liked waiting and tried not to fidget.

Lady Shara caught his eye after the tray was set on the table and wine had been offered and poured. "Go ahead, dear," she said. "You must be hungry after your practice this morning."

Jalan needed no more encouragement. He filled a small plate with little cheese wedges, some dried figs and a large slice of crusty bread. He picked up his cup of watered wine. He preferred it to the sharp overpowering flavor of undiluted wine and considered himself fortunate that his mother and sister tended not to offer him any. Jalan carried his plate and cup to a small end table and carefully placed them on it. He looked quickly around to be sure no one would tell him to wait and then started eating.

The servants had been dismissed and the parlor door closed. The Ladies politely nibbled at offerings carefully selected from the food tray. Messenger Enmar had taken a number of items as he conversed with Lady Darla and Lady Shara about the weather, the condition of the roads in the district, the expected crop yields and other boring things.

Jalan had time to get some dried apple, another fig and one more cheese wedge before the three of them finished their plates.

"Now that we have had a chance to refresh ourselves, let us allow Messenger Enmar to deliver his missive," said Lady Darla.

The messenger had taken a chair on one end of the semi-circle. Darla and his mother were seated with an empty chair between them. Jalan moved from where he had eaten and took his place there.

The remaining cheese still occupied his mind as Messenger Enmar said, "Here, Lady Darla, are my credentials and the orders I was issued by King Tamaron." Enmar handed Darla two pieces of parchment he extracted from his leather messenger's tube.

Darla examined both papers and then passed them to Lady Shara. Once his mother finished reading she returned the parchments to Darla.

"How long ago did you follow the band of travelers from Lavembra?" said Darla.

"Twelve years ago, lady," said Messenger Enmar.

The number caught Jalan's attention because it matched his age.

"Your orders were to present yourself to Lord Yen. My father never mentioned you."

"I did present myself as ordered. Your father was not pleased to see me and neither was Captain Erida. Fortunately, I was already speaking to Lord Yen before Erida knew of it and I was able to keep the king's words private."

"Captain Erida does take issue with you; however he did not explain the cause. Perhaps you would?"

With a steady look Enmar replied, "I cannot speak for the captain. He will have to explain himself. It would be inappropriate for me to speculate on his motivations."

Darla's hazel eyes flashed as she gave the messenger a thin lipped look of dissatisfaction. She seemed to consider her words further before she said, "Perhaps you would speculate on why my father was unhappy to see you. As you know, I cannot ask him and therefore I must seek your opinion."

"He thought I was the king's royal assassin," said Enmar as if he still casually commented on the weather.

Jalan stopped thinking about cheese entirely. He tried not to look too interested or they might change the subject.

"Before you feel the need to find a polite way to ask, the answer is no. I am not the royal assassin. I suppose the distinction between what I was and an assassin could be lost on the less well informed. To put it plainly, the king would send me into difficult situations where diplomacy had failed. Violence was certain to ensue in one form or another. I did my best to minimize the violence so that it impacted only those most in need of the experience."

"Who needs violence?" Jalan wondered. He felt embarrassment for having spoken his thought aloud. But, no one else seemed bothered by it.

"That is a keen question," said the messenger as he turned in his chair to look at Jalan. "Those who wish to subvert the will of the king or harm his subjects often choose violence as a way to accomplish it. Those that would use violence need violence."

Enmar returned his gaze to Lady Darla as she asked, "So you were sent with the travelers from Lavembra to bring violence to those who needed it?"

"I was ordered to protect them," said Enmar.

Jalan's sister looked puzzled. He turned to look at his mother. Her face showed a calm mask, but she sat back in her chair with her arms crossed and looked as if she doubted the messenger's word.

Before Darla could respond, Lady Shara said, "There were six lancers escorting that carriage. And Lern, that huge fellow with the broadsword, was the bodyguard for... for them. If the company could not protect itself, what was one man supposed to do?"

"I asked myself the same question, Lady Shara," said Enmar. "In the end, I found a way to be useful. You can ask Captain Erida about an ambush that occurred in the Sand Hills and the fate of three archers. Although, I doubt he'll be pleased to credit me for my anonymous assistance."

Jalan's mother had just said there were six lancers with a carriage. She said nothing about archers. Those three must have been attacking the people traveling from Lavembra. But, what does that have to do with Captain Erida?

Lady Darla leaned forward and said, "You followed the travelers. You protected them. And, you made contact with my father. Your orders state that you were to enter his service. Why didn't you? Did my father not accept you?"

The messenger looked from Darla to Shara and back again before he said, "I did enter your father's service. The king not only sent me as a protector, but as a teacher as well. I am charged with teaching Mer Tung to the king's heir." Now Enmar looked only at Lady Shara and said, "Lord Yen directed me to wait. He expressed Lady Shara's concerns with it. That she and he both felt the intense training was not advisable until the boy grew older or until his own survival required it."

Turning to look at Shara, Lady Darla said in a slightly elevated voice, "Mother, you knew about this?"

Jalan saw his mother frown and then nod once. She said, "Yes. I knew. Your father's last wish was that..." Lady Shara stopped speaking. She looked at Jalan and seemed uncertain. Then she turned back to Darla and said, "His last wish was that Jalan receive the training. And, I said I would do it. But, Mer Tung, or what I know of it, seemed too demanding. Jalan was only eight, a little boy. But I promised Hallis. I had Captain Erida expand Jalan's training. And he has worked him so very hard." Shara looked between Darla and Enmar both as she added, "I hoped it would be enough."

Jalan could hardly follow what they said. He was supposed to be trained? Why would he need training to survive? Certainly he trained. He practiced with knives and swords and bow. He worked with a lance too. But, everybody did that. Well, maybe his brother Tomac did not do everything he did. And, outside of the lancers nobody trained with as many weapons. Even most of the lancers only worked with sabers, lances and bows. Staves, he'd forgotten about staves.

With the thought of one more weapon the entire swirling mass of practice sessions and multiple weapons crashed together to form a single image, his image. Jalan. The only thing all the practice, exercise and chores had in common was Jalan. He was the only person doing them all. "Why?" he asked in a puzzled expression of his bafflement.

Lady Shara looked distressed and said to him, "Because I love you."

Jalan never thought of that. He never knew that someone could make things difficult because they love you and also make things easier at the same time. He knew his mother told him why she hoped all the training was enough even though he had asked why he did more than anyone else. Love answered both questions.

"I love you too, mother," said Jalan as he looked directly at Lady Shara. "But, do I do more than anyone else has to?"

Lady Shara's lower lip quivered for a moment and her eyes looked moist. "Every one of my children is special. Each has different abilities and needs. You, you need your training."

"Why?"

"There is something you need to know, something..." Shara hugs herself and blinks rapidly several times before she continues. "Something I promised Hallis I would tell you. I intended to wait longer, but Messenger Enmar's arrival forces me to tell you now. You are my foster son, Jalan. Mine and father's."

"Foster son?" said Jalan. "What does that mean?"

Her voice sounded tender and reluctant as Shara said, "That means that we, Lord Hallis and I, are... That we are not your real parents. But your father and I have always loved you as our own. We never treated you differently except as our oath to your birth parents decreed we must."

Jalan stood and took several steps before he spun around. "But you are my parents, you and father," said Jalan. He almost shouted it. In the back of his head a part of himself watched in confusion, frightened by the way he spoke to her.

"Oh my son, of course we are. In every way any parents could be we have been parents to you and all our other children. It is merely that you were not born of father and me. We have loved you no less for it."

"Wait," said Jalan as he held his hands palms out to push back Lady Shara's words. "Not born of you? I am not a Yen?"

His mother's brows pressed together in a look of pain, "Please Jalan, don't think of it that way. You are, in the hearts of all of us, one of us."

"But, I am not a Yen?"

Lady Shara bowed her head and spoke without looking at him. "Your birth parents still live and have never relinquished their claim. You are their son in name." She lifted her head and looked at him. "I will never think of you as other than my own. You are Yen among us, but the world knows you by another name."

"What name?" Now that the question escaped his lips, Jalan wanted to unsay it. "No! Wait. I am Jalan Yen. I don't want another name."

"You don't want to know who your birth parents are?" said Lady Shara, her voice almost hopeful. She uncrossed her arms and leaned forward with her hands on the arms of her chair.

What difference does it make? Whoever they were they had nothing to do with him. They sent him away. They did not care about him.

66

Why should it matter what their name was? Jalan crossed his arms, ready to deny any interest in the strangers that claimed him.

"Jalan, look at me," said Enmar.

When he did, Jalan felt relieved at being able to do something other than answer his mother's question. Seeing the fear on her face and the sadness in her eyes caused him anguish. He wanted to reject these unknown parents he never had. Except that down deep in him, a small curiosity had taken root. If he was not a Yen, then who was he?

"I am a messenger. I tell people things. That's what a messenger does."

That made sense to Jalan. A messenger gave you a message. He could see that. Jalan nodded.

"I would like to tell you something. Would that be all right?"

"I don't know," said Jalan.

"I wish to tell you who your parents are, your real parents." said the messenger.

"My mother is right here. She is the only real parent I need."

Enmar gave Jalan an understanding smile and said, "I do not mean to say that Lady Shara is not your mother. However, as she already told you, she is not your birth mother, not the mother to whom you were born. Are you not a little curious?"

"No."

"You see how your mother cares for you, how it distresses her to speak of this?"

He looked at Lady Shara and back to Messenger Enmar. "Yes."

"Imagine if you had been taken from her and raised by someone else. Consider how distraught she would be. Even now I judge her disquiet is due to the thought that she might lose you to another. Would her heartache not be great? Don't you think she would miss you, pine for you and worry over your fate?"

"Yes."

"Then consider further that there is a woman whose heartache is great. A woman who does miss you and longs to see you again. I ask you once more, are you not the least bit curious to know her name? I assure you she knows yours."

"No." Jalan refused to hear of such a person in the presence of his mother.

"Very well," said the messenger with a sigh. "I will not force it upon you. You asked why your life is different. It is different because your parents are different. Knowing who they are will take you a long way toward understanding your life."

"Mother, I wish to be excused," said Jalan to Lady Shara.

Lady Shara looked between Jalan and Messenger Enmar. Jalan watched emotions flow across her face too quickly to follow.

"You may go, dear," said Lady Shara. She sat back in her chair and clasped her hands together.

Jalan could not tell if he had pleased or displeased her. Tired and still hungry, he ached in ways that had nothing to do with his muscles. Driven by needs he did not understand and could not fulfill one thing he could satisfy remained. He walked to the table with the platter of leftover food. He filled his plate with favorites and left. No one spoke or questioned him. Once he stood in the hallway with the parlor door closed, he felt like crying. He had been bruised many times, but never before had it been his heart.

He meant to walk away and assuage his discontent as best he could. But, he heard Darla speak and listened at the door in spite of himself.

"Make it clear for me, please. My mother and you know what I am almost certain is true. But, tell me plainly. As Lady I require no doubt in this matter. Who are Jalan's parents?" said Darla.

A voice in his head screamed at him to run. Curiosity held him fast. His mother could not see him and he had not allowed the messenger to tell him what he feared would hurt her. The messenger spoke to Darla now, not him. It was by chance and not choice that he would learn the answer.

"Jalan's parents are King Tamaron and Queen Urala," said the messenger.

The names meant almost nothing to Jalan. It was as if the messenger said his parents were the sun and the moon.

CHAPTER VI

Jalan walked down the hallway with his freshly loaded plate of cheese wedges and dried fruit. He wandered without thinking about it, compelled by conflicted emotions to move. Tomac and Vee hurried toward him. Tomac still reminded Jalan of a smaller copy of their father. Vee, taller and thinner, had a countenance more like Mother's or maybe Darla's. Vee and Mother shared the same blue eyes, but Lady Shara and Lady Darla had rich brown hair that fell straight while Vee had long dark curls that framed her delicate face. The pair of them made an imprecise imitation of his father and mother. It struck him suddenly why he looked so little like either.

"What did the messenger say?" asked Tomac in a voice rich with curiosity. And with barely a breath in between he added, "Can I have a fig?"

"Me too, please," said Vee.

Jalan held out plate he had almost forgotten he carried. Tomac took two figs and a cheese wedge. Vee took the last pieces of dried apple.

"Thanks," said Tomac as he popped a dried fig in his mouth.

Vee just smiled and ate a piece of apple. Jalan finished what remained while he still had something to call his own. He turned toward the back of the house to return the empty plate to the kitchen.

"Well?" said Vee as she stepped beside him. Her eyes shone with interest.

"The messenger wanted to tell me who my parents are," said Jalan without slowing.

"What do you mean?" said Tomac from behind.

Vee rolled her eyes and said, "He means his birth parents."

"His what?"

Vee stopped walking to look directly at Tomac. Jalan stopped walking, surprised that Vee knew about his parents.

"His birth parents are the people he was born to. Our birth parents are mother and father. Jalan was born to someone else. He is our foster brother," Vee explained with exaggerated patience as though she thought her words might really be too complex for Tomac to understand.

"But, Jalan's our little brother," said Tomac with a hint of uncertainty.

"Yes, our foster brother. He is also mother and father's foster son, which means he has real parents and father agreed to foster him, to raise him as one of our own family."

"What?" said Tomac as if Vee spoke another language.

"Darla said a carriage brought Jalan." said Vee. "His real parents sent him here to grow up with us."

Mother said something about a carriage to the messenger recalled Jalan. "What carriage?" he said, hoping the answer would help him remember Lady Shara's words.

"I just said," replied Vee. Exasperation filled her response. "Not that you would remember as you were a tiny infant. You came in a carriage. I heard Darla and Guri talking about it once. Guri said Captain Erida led the escort. Lieutenant Burk came with him and some other lancers too."

Guri, their eldest sister, had married and moved away. Jalan subtracted twelve years from her age and arrived at 13. Guri would have been 13 when the carriage arrived. And that was what his mother had said, a carriage with six lancers. The messenger said Lady Shara could ask Captain Erida about an ambush. None of it had made sense. Now Vee claimed Captain Erida escorted the carriage that brought Jalan to House Yen. Captain Erida knew where he came from. He might even know Jalan's real parents. It had not occurred to him that anyone he knew might know his parents.

If the captain came with the carriage, then he must have been at the capital and Lieutenant Burk had been there too. *What about the messenger?* The messenger worked for the king. The king was far away in Lavembra. But Jalan began to think that the king's influence was much closer.

"Who are his real parents?" said Tomac.

"I don't know that," responded Vee with a look that called Tomac foolish for asking.

Appearing unfazed by their sister's dismissive tone, Tomac turned to Jalan and asked, "Who are your real parents?"

"He didn't tell me. He told Darla," said Jalan.

"What did he tell her?" said Tomac still undeterred.

"Yes, what?" said Vee.

Jalan looked at their expectant faces. Mother knew. Darla knew. Lieutenant Burk knew. Captain Erida knew. Why not tell them and get it over with he thought. "The messenger said my parents are the king and queen," Jalan said. He shrugged and added, "But, I don't know. That's just what he said."

"You are making that up!" said Vee. "If you are not going to tell us what he really said then say so, but don't make up stories."

Vee's disbelief angered Jalan. She knew more about him than he did and the one thing she did not, the only thing he knew before she did, Vee refused to believe. How could he help it if his parents where King Tamaron and Queen Urala? The only parents he wanted were mother and father and he would trade the king and queen to get Lord Hallis back if he could.

A deep undercurrent of outrage welled up in Jalan. It took control and he did not know what to do. His fury pushed at him and he pushed back harder. It crystallized and he put this new thing completely into the words he yelled at Vee. "I am not a liar!"

The color drained from Vee's face and she staggered back while reaching out to the hallway wall. Tomac dropped to one knee and shook of his head.

"Jalan!" shouted someone.

Feeling very tired, it took Jalan a moment to focus on the person who called him. Lady Shara, with her skirt caught up in her hands, ran toward him. *How odd. Mother never runs.* Jalan half lowered himself and half collapsed to a seated position on the floor.

Even though she shouted his name, his mother moved past Jalan and wrapped her arms around Vee who still had trouble standing. Shara assisted Vee as the girl lowered herself down to sit on the hallway floor. Lady Shara put her hands on both sides of Vee's head and examined her. An expression of relief formed on his mother's face.

Lady Shara left Vee sitting on the floor with her back and head propped against the wainscoting and went to Tomac. Tomac struggled to stand, but Lady Shara instructed him to sit down for a moment until his head cleared.

Finally, Jalan's mother came to him. She looked frightened, perhaps more than when she examined Vee. She took one of his hands in both of hers and looked at Jalan closely as if watching for something dangerous. Again she looked relieved, but wary too and let go of his hand.

"Stand up," she said. His mother hesitated a moment before reaching out to help him rise to his feet.

He felt less tired, more like right after sparring instead of the exhaustion that forced him to the floor.

"Go to your bed and sleep for a bit. I'm sure you'll feel better afterward," said his mother as if coaxing a sleepy child to take a nap.

Jalan's head felt stuffed with wool. He did not know what had happened. His mother's fear registered in his clouded mind, not fear in general, but fear of him. She had feared for Vee and Tomac, her real children. But her gaze held fear when she looked at Jalan. *Is this what it means to be a foster son?*

Worried and dejected Jalan looked down. Still foggy and fatigued he said the first thing that came to him, "The plate."

Lady Shara followed his gaze and frowned. "I'll take care of it."

Δ

Jalan woke. Sunlight streamed through his window and his mother sat on a chair next to his bed. Her smile brightened his morning even more.

"Good morning, Jalan," she said. "How did you sleep?"

Too long judging by the sun. "Too well," he said.

"Don't worry. I sent word to Captain Erida not to expect you first thing this morning."

Relieved and curious, Jalan sat up in bed and asked, "Why?"

"I knew you would need rest," said Lady Shara. "All of you," she continued. "It was to be expected after you, Vee and Tomac ate that bad cheese yesterday."

Something about the hallway and his brother and sister almost became clear in Jalan's memory before it slipped away. "Bad cheese?" he said.

"Yes, you had taken some cheese with you from the parlor and shared it with them. Apparently, the cheese had gone bad. It made all of you ill very quickly."

"But, Vee didn't eat any cheese," Jalan said.

"Jalan, my son, please listen to me. If it was not the cheese then it was the fruit. There is no other explanation for it." The last sentence sounded as if his mother meant there was no other explanation allowed.

"We didn't all eat the same thing. If all the items were bad, why didn't you, Darla and the messenger fall ill too?"

His mother's expression looked strained. He thought she hid something. She said, "We were very fortunate and you three were not."

"But mother, I..."

"Just accept it," snapped his mother. Then she seemed to think better of the outburst and added, "Please, Jalan, you don't know everything. Sometimes things happen and the explanations are unsatisfactory. What else could it have been?"

Jalan had to admit he had no other explanation and he said as much. This seemed to calm his mother a little and she gave him a smile.

"There you are, dear. There simply is no other explanation," said Lady Shara.

"Yes, mother," said Jalan.

His mother looked even more pleased. She reached out and patted him on the arm. Then she leaned forward. When she spoke, he had to listen closely to hear her. "Now, just between us, let's play a game."

Jalan's wanted to avoid further upsetting his mother. "All right," he said quietly in return.

"It is an imagination game. We will pretend that there might be some other reason for what happened in the hallway. But, this is just our game, our secret. Yes?" Her voice sounded light and happy, but she looked serious and a little desperate.

Uncertain, Jalan said, "Yes, mother."

Shara gave him a tight smile that barely touched her eyes. "If what happened was not tainted food, then it must have been caused by something else in the hallway."

"But Tomac, Vee and I were the only ones there." That much he remembered for certain.

"Are you saying that Tomac or Vee did something to cause it?"

Jalan pictured the hallway with his siblings and himself in it. Beyond the food there was only Tomac and Vee's curiosity about his parents. He remembered telling them what he overheard the messenger say...

A feeling of being overwhelmed and alienated swept through him. It brought the realization that the mysterious occurrence in the hallway came from him. When he shouted at Vee, something more than words came out. He hurt her. He hurt Tomac. He frightened his mother. And now he felt fear because he did not know how he had done it, how to stop it from ever happening again.

"Please, Jalan, try to breathe slower."

His breathing came in rapid gasps. He shook as though he had a sudden chill.

His mother threw a blanket around his shoulders. With tears in her voice she whispered, "I'm so sorry. I did not mean to frighten you."

Jalan forced himself to take deep breaths of air. He wanted to tell her that she had not frightened him. He frightened himself. As his breathing became regular and even, the shaking subsided. Lady Shara sat on his bed with her arms around the blanket, holding it against him.

"What is wrong with me?" said Jalan.

"You are cursed."

"What?"

"You have the magic, The Ability."

"Master Hern taught us only those in The Society have it," said Jalan bewildered by his mother's explanation.

"Only those who submit to the authority of The Society are allowed to live. Anyone else with The Ability is hunted down like a rogue animal and killed."

"Then I have to join The Society?" said Jalan.

"No! Never do that. If anything happened to you..." Lady Shara drew back and placed her hands on his shoulders. She looked into his eyes and said, "Promise me you will never do that. Promise that you will keep it hidden and never use it. Promise me."

His mother did not look frightened now. She looked terrified.

"I promise. I will never use it. I will keep the magic hidden." He would have said anything to remove that look from her face. He could not explain how he had used magic or how he would stop himself from ever using it again.

He almost asked, but Lady Shara stood abruptly, terror replaced with relief, and said, "There is much of the day left and you have much to do. Go to Mistress Dahlia and tell her I wish her to give you a light breakfast now that you are feeling better. I'm sure Captain Erida will have something for you to do after that."

CHAPTER VII

The messenger, Krenis Enmar, approached Jalan as he walked across the courtyard on his way to one of the lancer barracks.

"You're with me," said Enmar.

"What do you mean, ah, sir?" said Jalan

"I spoke with Lady Darla and Captain Erida yesterday. It was agreed that I am training you from now on."

The messenger's dusty faded clothing of the day before had been replaced by a tan tight-fitting tunic and loose pants. Instead of boots, the man wore shoes. His large nose hung above a broad smile.

Jalan was of two minds about Enmar. He upset Captain Erida and Jalan's mother. His arrival caused turmoil, most of which seemed to fall squarely on Jalan. For those reasons, Jalan found him unsettling. Enmar also seemed unperturbed by danger and the chaos he caused. That and his welcoming attitude intrigued Jalan. He thought he might almost like the messenger. Not much new happened on Yen Estate.

He had trained with several people because each one was best at teaching specific things. "Are you going to teach me to be a messenger?"

Enmar roared with laughter. When he finally stopped he wiped an eye and said, "I just might. I just might." Then the man sighed deeply. "But we'll leave that for another day. Right now I want to see you run."

"Run? You want me to run? All right." Jalan took a step. Before his next footfall, Enmar snatched Jalan's shirt collar and plucked him off the ground with one hand.

"I meant with me, boy," said Enmar. "You run with me and we'll see how you do."

His new trainer sat him back on the ground. Jalan waited for Enmar to start running and then he matched the man's pace.

Enmar followed the paved way out of the courtyard and continued on toward the gates of the Manor grounds. The two iron gates sat open. An armsman stood watch and ignored the runners as they passed by. Enmar turned right onto the road and Jalan stayed with him.

"I can run faster than this," said Jalan.

"It's not about speed. It's about distance," said Enmar.

Δ

When they finally crossed back through the gates and jogged to the manor, Jalan wished he could have sparred with Lieutenant Burk instead. He thought Enmar slowed down about half way. Not that he had any idea where half way really was. He had long since stopped thinking about how far he ran and only concentrated on keeping pace with Enmar. Lost in his exhausted haze, Jalan did not even notice where they were when Enmar stopped running. He was too relieved to care. Even when Enmar poured a full bucket of well water over Jalan's head, the boy stood there dripping into the puddle at his feet.

Enmar stripped off his tunic and sat it aside before pouring water from a fresh bucket over his own head and briefly scrubbing his face and arms with his hands. He then rinsed with the remaining water and sat the empty bucket back on the edge of the low stone wall that surrounded the courtyard well.

Enmar grabbed up his tunic and started to walk. Jalan followed almost out of habit now. They walked toward the workshops. His trainer moved with an easy stroll and Jalan hobbled and squelched in his wet boots. When they reach the leather shop, Enmar discussed something to do with shoes. Jalan concentrated on standing and let the conversation drift past him.

Ritka, the leather crafter, had Jalan sit on a stool and take off his boots. Then Ritka had Jalan put his feet on a couple of pieces of leather and inscribed marks in the leather that seemed to roughly correspond to the size of Jalan's feet. Too tired to care, he did not ask why Ritka would make him new boots when the ones he had were still in good shape.

"Come along. Let's get something to eat," said Enmar. He looked at Jalan. "Ritka is going to want that stool back."

Jalan accepted the hand Enmar offered and let the man pull him to his feet.

Carrying his wet boots and soaked woolen hose, Jalan trudged toward the manor's kitchen entrance. His bare feet felt sore and swollen and he winced when he stepped on a sharp stone.

"Don't worry. Your feet will get a rest tomorrow," said Enmar.

Δ

The next evening Jalan sat at the family dining table and wondered if he could eat the soup in front of him without using his arms.

"He made you walk on your hands?" said Tomac as if it was the most outlandish thing he had ever heard.

Jalan had to admit that it might be.

Lady Shara said, "That is what your brother said, dear. Now please stop badgering Jalan about his training, unconventional as it may be."

"Yes, mother," said Tomac.

Across the table Vee smirked and tried to hide it by eating another spoonful of soup.

A silence ensued and Jalan noticed his mother never seemed to meet his eye. Usually she questioned the children about details of their day, but tonight she had not asked a single thing.

Besides prodding Jalan about what happened to his arms, Tomac said little. And Vee, often the most talkative, said nothing so far. Jalan worried that his accident with The Ability changed things. Mother had not said if the others suspected what had really happened. Perhaps he only imagined it, but something seemed different.

Darla broke the silence by sharing details of the new book she was reading. Vee told everyone what she had heard about a traveling singer rumored to be performing in the district. Lady Shara spoke then and asked questions about the children's various lessons with Master Hern.

With what he considered to be a heroic effort, Jalan managed to feed himself. He asked to be excused at the meal's end. As he walked the candle lit hallway to his room, he wondered if the stone of Krenis Enmar's arrival struck the quiet pond of Yen Manor so hard that it made waves instead of ripples.

Δ

Later, after Jalan settled himself for the night, there was a tap at his door and his mother spoke from outside, "May I come in?"

Lying on his bed, his mind wandered on the edge of sleep. Her voice roused him. He sat up and said, "Yes, mother."

Lady Shara entered the room holding a short wooden dowel with a small candle lantern hanging from its notched end. Outside the window, dusk's muted glow had not yet given over to full night. The last bird song of the day drifted in along with sporadic sounds of workers in the courtyard that finished today's tasks or prepared for tomorrow's. Inside Jalan's dark room the candle sent wavering suffused light dancing across the walls and over his mother's form.

She softly closed the door behind her and gave a wavering shadowed smile. She took the few short steps to his bed and sat on the edge of it. "How are you feeling?" Lady Shara asked.

He wanted to say confused, lost or maybe alone. "Tired," replied Jalan.

"If you like I can speak to Master Enmar about..."

"Mother, no!" blurted Jalan. He felt his face color with embarrassment. He hoped it was not visible in the candlelight. "I mean, please don't. Everything is fine, really." Jalan heard the edge of pleading in his voice.

"If you are certain," she said. The words held grudging acceptance of the outcome to a battle she knew she could not win.

"Master Enmar said the beginning is the most difficult time. It will get better. But, I have to do this. Father wanted me to do this."

Again, he heard himself pleading with her. The thought crossed his mind that it was the wish of his foster father. He could only guess at what his real father wanted. The same, he supposed. Perhaps Lady Shara knew. He dared not ask. What if his questions only pushed her further away? His curse had done enough harm already.

Lady Shara reached out and sat the little candle lamp on the night stand near the bed. She moved closer to Jalan. He leaned into her arms. Jalan knew his foster mother only objected to his training because she loved him and wished to spare him. And, he knew she only allowed him to continue for the same reason. He fell asleep while thinking again of the two sides of love and how he and Lady Shara tried to make each other's suffering easier.

CHAPTER VIII

The next day Jalan found Krenis Enmar running flax string between stakes positioned in a big rectangle. As Enmar finished his last knot, two of the estate's craftsmen arrived.

"Good day, Krenis. This where you want it?" asked Master Anton the stone mason.

"I've staked it out for you," said Enmar. "Now I'll be off and let you good men get to work. I know Master Doon has the plans well in hand."

"What are they doing?" said Jalan as he followed Master Enmar and hoped that today's training was less torturous than yesterday's.

"Building a Training Hall!" said Enmar with exuberance.

Jalan had done a lot of training, but never suspected there were buildings dedicated to it. "Why?" he said, feeling puzzled.

Master Enmar stopped to face him. "Because, you are not being trained for a month or a season; you are being trained for a lifetime. That takes more than running around a dusty practice yard can do."

Enmar moved off again and led Jalan to what looked like a plank leaning against a tree at a shallow angle. When he looked closer, Jalan saw a stout dowel mounted horizontally on a wooden block. The block connected the center of the dowel to the surface of the plank. With the dowel attached in that fashion it looked like a crossbar handle to Jalan. The purpose for mounting a handle three quarters of the way up on the top side of the plank eluded him.

"Lie down on the plank with you head here," said Enmar as he pointed to the lower end of the plank, "and your ankles here," added Master Enmar as he pointed at the gaps between the dowel and the plank on either side of the block that held the dowel in place. "Hook them under the dowel at the high end to keep yourself from sliding down the plank."

Jalan creased his brow as he examined the plank more closely. When he thought he knew what to do, he straddled the plank. He reached up to grab hold of one side of the dowel. Then he remembered he could not hold himself in place that way and still manage to raise his ankle and slide it under the dowel at the same time.

He reached behind his back with both hands and leaned backward to grasp both sides of the plank. He wanted to get his hands in place and then sit on the plank using his own hands and arms as a backstop to hold him as he raised his legs. It was more of a stretch than he realized. By the time he managed to touch the wooden plank with both hands he was overbalanced and flipped feet over head backwards to land seat first on the hard knobby roots of the tree.

Finally he gave up on holding anything with his hands. He straddled the board and swung his right leg up, aiming to slip his ankle beneath the dowel in one smooth motion. It worked but left him in the very awkward position of having his right foot and ankle in place on the plank and his left still on the ground as he struggle to maintain his balance. He grabbed both sides of the plank in front of him. But, his left hand and arm blocked his left leg from swinging into place.

He reached behind himself again. With his right ankle already in place, he did not topple over backwards. After three attempts he managed to swing his left foot up and hook his ankle under the left side of dowel.

All this time, Master Enmar stood and watched. He offered no advice and gave no assistance. Jalan perspired as he lay on the plank with his feet up and head down. He was a little winded from his struggle to get into position and his head felt like it was growing from the inside. He suspected the entire point of this exercise was expending all the effort required to get on the plank. It would have been easier if he had not exhausted his arms yesterday when Master Enmar insisted he use them as legs.

"Ah good, you're finally ready to get started," said Master Enmar.

Started!? What devious torment could his trainer have in mind now?

"First I want you to sit up." As Jalan reached for the sides of the plank, Enmar said, "Without using your hands."

Jalan could feel the frown on his damp face. He took a deep breath and tried to relax. Then he tried to sit up. It was more difficult than sitting up while lying on the ground, but it was not a struggle. Jalan raised his upper body until his head and back were straight up.

"Well done. Now reach out and touch your toes."

When Jalan completed that to Master Enmar's satisfaction, Enmar instructed him to lie back down. Then Enmar said to do it again over and over.

At first the repeated laying back and sitting up was almost pleasant. The strain inside Jalan's head diminished whenever he sat up and laying back gave him a nice stretch. He kept a silent count, but lost track around 50 or 60 when he needed to concentrate on maintaining a good rhythm. An even pace made repetition easier and he had no idea how brutal Master Enmar intended to be.

Eventually there was nothing remotely pleasant about the exercise. Jalan toiled as sweat dripped and soaked into his clothing. He breathed more and more like the bellows at Master Brunt's forge and his muscles threatened to give out entirely. When the time came that he could no longer force himself to rise up, he lay with his head down as it pounded in time to his heartbeat and pondered how he would ever free himself from the accursed plank. Having no better idea and once again getting no aid from Master Enmar, Jalan put his hands down onto the ground and strained until he was able to force his body to slide upward sufficiently that he could work both ankles free.

His arms gave out the instant his ankles came loose. He slid down the plank on his back. His head and neck scrapped across the root covered ground at the end of the plank as Jalan forced himself to roll off the side. He tumbled into a fatigued heap and struggled to sit up. When he tried to stand, his legs would not support him.

"You did well enough. Sit and rest. I'll get you some water," said Master Enmar.

Jalan, too weary to protest, thought he'd done better than well enough. He would gladly trade places with Master Enmar and let him collapse from exhaustion as Jalan watched. Instead he sat on the ground with his head hanging down and waited for the water Master Enmar had promised.

Enmar returned with a waterskin and Jalan drained it. Before his trainer could direct him to do something more, Jalan asked a question. It might have happened because the consequences of asking eluded his tired mind or that his curiosity overcame him. "Do you know my parents?" he said.

"Yes," said Enmar from where he stood in the shade of the tree. "Although I have not seen them in years."

"I haven't seen them at all." Jalan spoke with more bitterness than he intended.

"You have, but you don't remember. You were two months old when you left."

"You mean when they sent me away," said Jalan.

"True enough. It wasn't that you had a choice," said Enmar. "But why the sudden interest. You said you did not wish to know."

Jalan looked away from Master Enmar and confessed he had listened at the parlor door. He could not meet Enmar's gaze.

"All right. Now you know. That is more important than how you learned it."

Jalan expected a lecture or at least a rebuke for having listened to another's private conversation. The easy acceptance encouraged him to ask more. "Why? Why did they send me here?"

"I don't know, but I can make a guess. By the time the carriage spirited you from Lavembra there had been at least two attempts on your life. It is likely they did it for your own safety."

"But, they are my parents. Didn't they care enough to protect me?"

"You should think more and talk less. You look rested. Time for the next exercise."

Master Enmar set Jalan to doing push-ups. He explained that those would be easier because Jalan did not need to stand up to do them.

After pushing while on his fingertips, then knuckles and finally palms, Jalan had to walk on his hands again. Several times he managed to stay upright, or maybe it was downright, a little longer than yesterday before he fell over. It annoyed him when his sweat ran toward his head. Perspiration got in his eyes and ran up his nose while he was helpless to prevent it. Once his arms became too weak to support him, Master Enmar allowed him to take another rest and drink more water. He used both hands to lift the waterskin and had a difficult time holding it to his mouth.

Master Enmar directed Jalan to stand on one leg with his other leg held out in front of him and then to squat down and stand back up. He repeated this in a series of ten repetitions for each leg until he could no longer push himself back up from his squat.

This time Master Enmar helped Jalan rise to a standing position. Then he said, "Time for your run. Run around the courtyard until you don't feel tired anymore."

Jalan did not even bother to groan. Every muscle felt like wet sand. He swayed where he stood. It seemed his body had forgotten how to hold still. He started to jog and his mind drifted back to his questions. Master Enmar had only been training him a few days. Jalan could not decide if he was being punished for asking questions or if he could expect a physical pummeling as a matter of course. Today was terrible, but yesterday had been as well. The same was true for their run together.

The master had answered some questions. He knew Jalan's parents. Maybe asking Enmar questions made his training worse. It did not matter. He did not think he could stop as long as there was a chance to learn something. His real parents might be awful people, cold and heartless. He still needed to know because something about them might hold the key to an even darker secret. He could deal with physical pain and cruel parents. He felt helpless when it came to his magic.

Jalan stumbled on, running the same questions through his head in time to his footfalls against the hard ground. At some point, Master Enmar waved him over and sent him to eat his midday meal. The mindless exercise ceased, but the questions continued to occupy his mind.

Δ

After his meal and a short rest, Jalan stretched as he stood and found he felt much better. That feeling dwindled quickly as he and Master Enmar practice longswords and sabers. He practiced with both arms equally and Enmar called a halt when Jalan's swings were no better than feeble flailing as his arm muscles burned.

Jalan sat waiting for his arms to recover. Master Enmar showed him a long hollow tube he called a blowpipe. A large needle with down or a bit of feather affixed to one end, called a dart, was placed in one open end of the blowpipe. When Enmar blew into that end, the dart flew out the other end and stuck in the bark of the tree they sat beneath.

Jalan could not keep form laughing. It was the oddest weapon he had ever seen and the only one that required a man to blow into it. The image of a lancer who rode into battle blowing little darts at the enemy was too funny for words.

"You think this is a joke?" said Master Enmar.

"I just can't imagine how anyone would use it in battle," said Jalan. "It could never stop an attacker like a bow or a sling could."

"That is true. The use of a blowpipe is more subtle. It can be a good weapon for hunting small birds and animals. In a tight spot you might be able to spook an enemy's mount with it." Holding up the dart he retrieved from the tree trunk Enmar said, "Imagine how that would feel in a horse's thigh."

Jalan was unconvinced. "What if the horse is armored?"

Enmar waved his hand in a sweeping gesture to indicate the estate grounds. "How many armored horses do you see? For that matter, how many armored men?"

"Us," was Jalan's flippant reply.

"Besides us and anyone else sparring? Perhaps a handful of lancers on watch? Maybe ten people on the grounds of Yen Manor. Many more go without."

"All right. I see your point. There are fewer than a dozen men in any type of armor and no horses."

"Why is that?"

"Because no one wears armor unless they think they need it."

Enmar nodded. "And if all you have is a blowpipe, how will you use it?"

"Attack when the enemy is not ready and retreat when they are," said Jalan.

"Very good. When there is no advantage in victory, it is better to deny your enemy the battle. Even if you win, the cost of victory is likely to destroy you anyway."

Master Enmar had not only burdened Jalan with physical challenges the last few days. He had also hammered him with ideas. Denying the battle was the first of them. The second was that if battle cannot be avoided then be the one to choose the battleground. Third, if you cannot choose the battleground then control the conditions of the battle. And, forth, if you cannot control the conditions of the battle, change the conditions.

Jalan had never been in a battle and did not know if Master Enmar meant these ideas to apply to more than fighting, but he noticed one corollary to attacking when the enemy was not ready. When the kitchen ran smoothly, Mistress Dahlia denied his requests for extra morsels or only allowed him a small sample. But, if several things happened at once and her attention became scattered, Jalan often got a larger portion.

He noticed a pattern in his training as well. Captain Erida, Master Hern and the other teachers all taught him things in stages. It was not obvious at the start. Only as the training progressed did it become possible to look back over the pattern. Jalan expected that once Master Enmar's new training hall was completed all the physical destruction he endured would become the beginning of something greater. That or he would be dead soon.

Δ

Jalan thought Lieutenant Burk and Sedic knew how to run him ragged. They could both take lessons from Master Enmar. After the first week of Enmar's training, Master Hern petitioned Lady Dara to order Master Enmar to allow Jalan time for his studies. Jalan did not know what Master Enmar said to Darla, but afterward, Master Hern excused Jalan from lessons for three months. Although, Jalan was given a stack of books to read during his spare time. Spare time turned out to be after nightfall when it was too dark to continue training.

One night as Jalan drug himself toward his sleeping room he happened upon Tomac in the upper hallway of Yen Manor.

"How's your holiday from Master Hern," said Tomac.

"Terrible. I never thought I would miss Master Hern's lectures," said Jalan. "Did you know that there are people that fight with sticks? And, I don't mean staves or wooden swords but two hardwood sticks? I expect Master Enmar will one day hand me a feather and expect me to fight with it. Oh, wait! That already happened? Did I tell you about the blowpipe?"

"Only a few times," said Tomac.

Jalan continued, oblivious to his brother's sarcasm. "Do you know what he did today? He threw rocks at me and expected me to dodge them. He didn't even allow me a sword to deflect them or shield to block them. I swear he is eager for the day he can use a sling."

"Then why don't you quit?" said Tomac.

"I can't do that," said Jalan almost stunned that Tomac would suggest it.

"Then stop complaining."

"You'd complain too if you had to put up with Master Enmar's devious tortures."

"No I wouldn't. And neither should you. At least you're getting the training. Look at me. I'm still practicing under the eye of Lieutenant Burk while you whine about learning things I never get to try. You're Sedic's golden boy. I heard about what you can do with a longbow. Everyone's heard about what you can do. You want something to complain about try living in your shadow."

"What?" said Jalan.

"That's the most vexing part. You don't even know. I'm your older brother but I'm constantly compared to you. And all you do is complain."

"Then why did you ask me about it?"

"I don't know!" shouted Tomac as he turned red faced and stalked away.

CHAPTER IX

The large rectangular Training Hall had taken shape with the framework of the walls. A series of wooden trusses with interlocking posts supported the roof. Waddle and daub panels filled some of the gaps in the walls. Workmen busied themselves completing more. From inside the building the wooden skeleton was exposed. No interior wall paneling had yet been placed. Looking up showed an open ceiling all the way through the trusses to the bottom of the roof planks.

Six men could easily have stood side-by-side across the width of the hall and with their arms outstretched not touch each other or the walls. The length must have been ten men at least. From the floor to the bottom of the roof trusses was nearly the height of two men. Jalan could not understand why the room needed to be so tall. When he mentioned it to Master Enmar his teacher gave him another one of his knowing smiles and leapt up to touch a roof truss. Jalan thought he had imagined it. Surely no one could jump that high.

Master Enmar simply turned to him and said, "That's why."

Jalan, Master Enmar and others smoothed the plank floor. After two days of rubbing abrasive glass paper over the rough wood the soreness wore off as his shoulders and arms became accustomed to the work. Today even his knees seemed to have toughened enough to take another day of crawling across the plank floor.

Master Enmar surprised him when he said, "That's enough. We'll leave the rest to Cress and Carpenter Doon's other apprentices."

Jalan pushed himself up off the floor and followed Enmar out the large opening where the double doors where to be installed. Master Enmar insisted they use the doorway rather than any random opening that still remained in the unfinished walls.

He followed Enmar to almost the exact spot where his first day of training with Lieutenant Burk had taken place two years earlier. The place was quite near the Training Hall. Jalan forced himself to stop watching the workmen and listen as Master Enmar spoke.

"You've learned to run well. You move side to side quickly. Your rolling and tumbling are good, but now we need to work on your jumping," said Master Enmar.

"But I can already jump higher than Tomac," said Jalan. He realized belatedly that Tomac had a point about the two of them being compared. He worried that his desire to prove himself better than his older brother drove a wedge between them.

"Just because you are better at something than another person does not mean you cannot become even better than you already are. Now watch me and imitate what I do."

His master squatted down and waited until Jalan did the same. Then Enmar sprang straight up into a jump that took his several feet above the ground. He landed and then squatted down again. "You're turn," said Master Enmar.

Jalan pushed down with his legs as hard as he could. His body sprang up, although not as high as his teacher. He crouched back down, knees bent as far as they could go. His fingertips lightly touched the ground near his feet.

Master Enmar jumped up again and Jalan did the same. Together they continued. Although Master Enmar had just cautioned Jalan about comparing himself to others, he could not help but try to push off harder and jump as high as Enmar did. It was frustrating not to be able to do it, and humorous to watch as his master performed the exercise.

Some passersby stopped to watch and Jalan overheard one of them say, "My, those are some large frogs." A general chuckle rose from the impromptu audience. In his imagination, Jalan pictured what it must look like to see the two of them and he started to laugh despite the strain of leaping and landing over and over.

Master Enmar paused his jumping and said, "Any of you with no duties to which you must attend, step over here and join us."

The handful of onlookers dispersed after appearing to recall various tasks they needed to complete.

Jalan continued to spring up, squat down and spring up again as Enmar gave his ultimatum to the onlookers. When Enmar turned his attention back to Jalan, he gave a wry smile and said, "And you wondered why we need a training hall."

The frog hop, as Jalan could not help but think of it now, had quickly become more difficult and his jumps were lower and lower as his legs weakened. He could not imagine jumping up and touching a beam in the training hall any time soon, if ever.

"You may stop now," said Master Enmar.

Jalan turned his final squat into a cross legged seat on the ground. He felt his heart pound and his breath bellowed as it would after a challenging run. He remembered to keep his back straight and elbows slightly out to aid his breathing. It was more work than bending forward and resting his head in his hands, but that made it harder to breathe. Proper breathing, as Master Enmar always told him, was necessary to recover quickly from exertion.

As Jalan rested, Master Enmar said, "That exercise is the secret to jumping high. There are more elaborate movements that I will teach you once the training hall is finished. You have most of the physical conditioning required for Mer Tung. But, I cannot teach the secrets of the art in the open. The right to learn it is earned and attempting to copy a part without knowledge of the whole could do great harm. What you learn in the training hall is not to be shared."

The set of Master Enmar's mouth and the fire in his eyes showed that what he said mattered as much as anything he had ever told Jalan before. "Yes, sir," said Jalan with a feeling that his words had committed him to a lifelong oath.

Δ

"What are you doing?" Tomac's voice pulled Jalan back from the edge of his soft downy somnolence.

"Training," said Jalan.

"But you're just standing there," observed Tomac.

"How long have I been here?"

"I don't know. Maybe an hour."

"Must be time to switch legs," said Jalan.

"What? Are you going to just stand here on your other leg for another hour? I could do that!" said Tomac.

"Try it then. But, stand over there." Jalan pointed to a patch of ground well away from him.

"Why over there? Why not right here?"

Jalan tried to think of a nice way to say Tomac would fall over and Jalan didn't want Tomac to bump into him. "We need room. If one of us starts to fall, we might bump into each other and then we'd both have to start over," said Jalan.

"Oh. All right," said Tomac as he moved to the spot Jalan had indicated. "Which leg should I stand on?"

"You're right handed. Start with your right leg."

"What difference does being right handed make?"

"Maybe none. But, maybe, your right leg is stronger just like your right arm."

Tomac frowned in concentration and raised his left foot off the ground. He attempted to emulate Jalan's stance. After three tries, Tomac was able to rest his booted left foot in the crook of his right leg.

"Why are we doing this?" asked Tomac.

"Endurance and balance," said Jalan.

"This doesn't seem like much exercise," said Tomac.

"You've only just started. It gets harder."

Tomac did not say anything more. With a slight frown upon his face he moved his arms around several times in halting jerks of motion until he seemed to have settled into a somewhat poor imitation of a resting crane. Jalan wondered if he looked that way as well.

After a few minutes of silence and the occasional arm flap, Tomac said, "Is your leg starting to burn?"

"No," said Jalan.

A moment later Tomac asked, "Are you sure?"

"It's just your leg getting tired. You can try to bend or straighten your knee a little so the muscles can move around."

Jalan watched Tomac gently bob up and down in very small increments.

"That feels a little better," he said.

Jalan closed his eyes and listened to the sounds of the workman performing their tasks at the Training Hall. He felt the light breeze across his exposed skin. He heard Tomac breathing hard and the rustle of cloth. He opened his eyes in time to see Tomac windmill his arms for balance as his booted left foot touched the ground. Even with both feet back on the ground, Tomac stumbled sideways for a few steps. "You can switch legs if you want," said Jalan.

"I think you're cheating," said Tomac.

"How?"

"Well, you don't have boots on. That makes it easier."

"Take your boots off then," said Jalan.

Tomac sat on the ground and pulled off his boots. He gave Jalan a defiant look and stood. With only one attempt, Tomac mimicked Jalan's stance, his right foot tucked in behind his left knee.

Jalan closed his eyes again.

"Why do you close your eyes?" said Tomac.

"I'm relaxing."

"Resting?" asked Tomac.

"In a way. I am relaxing all the muscles I don't use for standing. You probably have your shoulders and neck tense, and your stomach is tight. All your muscles are working harder than they need to. It makes you tired faster."

Tomac said nothing. Perhaps he thought about what Jalan just said.

"Whaw!" said Tomac.

Jalan heard him fall to the ground.

"I know. I know. Don't relax so much."

"That and your leg started to shake," said Jalan.

"How do you know? Your eyes are closed!"

Jalan did his best to smile like Master Enmar. *Is that how the master does it? He makes a good guess?*

"Humph. Fine, don't tell me." Tomac sounded angry.

"If you'd like I will ask Master Enmar if you could train with me sometimes."

Jalan only heard Tomac breathing and then Tomac said, "Well, um, that might be all right."

Tomac did not sound enthusiastic, but at least he didn't still sound angry. "I'll ask him. I'll see what he says."

"He says keep your eyes open."

Master Enmar's voice was right next to Jalan's left ear. At the same time he heard his master's words he felt a push on his left shoulder that tipped him off balance along with pressure against his right foot and the back of his left knee. His left knee bent forward. He could not get his right foot to the ground and ended up landing hard in the grass on his right side.

"Or," added Master Enmar, "sharpen your hearing. I suggest you try both. Turning to Tomac he said, "That is your first lesson. Did you like it?"

"Very much, Master Enmar," said Tomac with a huge grin on his face.

"If you are serious about training, you will have to get your mother's permission. When you have it we will set up a training schedule."

"Yes, sir," said Tomac.

"Get up, Jalan. You already have your mother's permission," said Enmar. "Apparently, standing on one leg is not enough of a challenge for you. Let's see how well this frog hops!"

Δ

Within the open cavernous interior of the Training Hall, Jalan stood barefoot in his loose fitting tunic and trousers made of heavy flax. Master Enmar and Tomac wore the same. The long row of windows high up on each side wall had their shutters pushed open to allow whatever breeze might enter. The shadowed inside of the hall was almost as cool as standing in heavy shade. On this summer day, it was far preferable to toiling in the bright hot sunshine.

Master Enmar taught Jalan and Tomac Mer Tung, the complex and secretive fighting style native to the Turngow Islands. Shortly after his arrival Enmar revealed a few little things from The Art, but the real training started once the Training Hall was completed. In the two years since then, Jalan and Tomac trained for several hours each day.

"Jalan, show me the targets," said Master Enmar.

Tomac held still. Jalan stepped up to him and threw a stream of punches, elbows and kicks as he called out the name of each blow's intended target. He concentrated on technique as Master Enmar watched and evaluated every move. None of the strikes were allowed to land. They had to be fast and accurate, but truly hitting Tomac would be a failure.

Jalan felt winded after his intense minute of concentration. Even that short period of fast hard movement caused perspiration to spring up all over him. When it was Tomac's turn he showed his brother the same respect and stood still as fists, elbows, knees and feet flew at him from what seemed like every direction. It was easier when Tomac moved behind him because Jalan did not have to watch what Tomac did. He only had to feel the movement of air or hear the light brush of a strike against his uniform. That sound came more frequently in the last couple months as his brother's speed and accuracy increased.

"Good. Now, to me," said Master Enmar.

Jalan's breathing was normal as he sprinted to Master Enmar. He heard Tomac's more labored breathing as he recovered from his target practice.

"Backs to the wall and prepare for the crossing," said Enmar.

Jalan placed his back against the wall and faced the far end of the hall. Tomac did the same on the other side of Master Enmar.

"There and back in no more than..." Master Enmar paused as if considering and then said, "Five steps."

Flips front or back, cartwheels, diving rolls and walking on hands were not considered steps. The trick was to reach the far wall and return as fast as possible without walking or running. Jalan started with a diving roll, followed by a cartwheel and then a shoulder roll. Tomac thought him crazy, but Jalan always challenged himself to not immediately repeat the same move during the crossing. He pushed on with a leap that ended in a handstand. It gave him an upside down view of Tomac not far behind. Jalan walked on his hands as quickly as he could then tucked his head and rolled back up onto his feet where he took his first step to turn himself and perform a back flip.

Tomac tumbled even with Jalan who tried harder to spin, twist and vault like a crazed acrobat during the performance of a lifetime. The staggered pounding thumps echoed in the huge hall each time Jalan landed and forced his burning muscles to propel him into the next maneuver. The sounds from Tomac's passage ensured the din never died out entirely.

Jalan reached out and touched the wall next to Master Enmar. Several heartbeats later, Tomac did the same. Jalan leaned on the wall and marshaled his body for further exertions. A pounding began at the closed double doors to the hall. The sound of someone shouting accompanied it. Master Enmar rolled his eyes and Tomac gave a tired laugh.

Master Enmar walked over to the two large doors, undid the bolt and swung the right door open. On the porch of the hall stood a young lancer, a look of worried concern on his face.

"Is everyone all right?" said the lancer.

"Of course, but you had better come in and see for yourself," said Enmar as he pulled the door open wider and stepped aside to let the young man enter.

"Dark in here," said the lancer while he blinked a few times and peered around the big empty room. He looked from Master Enmar to Jalan and Tomac "Just the three of you? It sounded like a regiment."

"As you see, it is only the three of us and we are fine. The hall is fine. No trouble here."

The lancer blinked once more and shrugged. "It sounded like chaos and ashes," he said.

"Just our regular practice. Tell your fist leader hello for us," said Master Enmar as he closed the door and threw the bolt.

Jalan could not hold his laughter any longer. Tomac guffawed and even Master Enmar chuckled.

This was the third time a young lancer recruit ran to their aid because of the noise they made during training. As usual, it was the crossing exercise that drew him. Jalan suspected the other lancers were having fun with the recruits. The bewildered look on the lancer's face made the pummeling he gave himself beating Tomac across the floor even more worthwhile.

Δ

Jalan left the Training Hall and walked to the new bath house near the lancer barracks. People had grown accustomed to his Mer Tung uniform and either ignored him or greeted him exactly as they would when he wore his lancer uniform.

Sedic approached with a wave and asked, "Is it true?"

"Is what true?" said Jalan.

"The proposal. Everyone is talking about it, but I thought if anyone knew the real story it would be you."

"I have no idea what you're talking about."

"That's what I thought. Just another rumor," said Sedic with a look of mingled disgust and disappointment.

Curiosity prompted Jalan to ask, "What proposal?"

"It's nothing. Some story about Lord Shrift proposing to Lady Darla. An idler's fantasy it seems."

"But Guri is married to Lord Shrift. That doesn't even make sense."

"There it is then, a rumor and nothing more," said Sedic as he walked away.

Jalan entered the bath house with a shake of his head and wondered how such a story ever got started.

After he cleaned up and changed into his lancer uniform, Jalan hurried to the mess hall for a midday meal. Several other lancers sat scattered around the long trestle tables eating the stew the cooks had prepared. Jalan took a bowl along with bread and cheese. As he ate he heard others talking. One conversation caught his attention.

"Lord Shrift. That's what I heard," said a lancer.

"But, Lord Shrift's already married to Lady Darla's sister," said the man next to him.

"No, no, no. Not Juin Shrift. Don't you know there is more than one Lord Shrift?"

"Why would I know or care?"

"Because one of them is marrying Lady Darla."

"So you said. But what I'd like to know is when will you pay me those coppers you owe me?"

"You know we don't get paid till the end of the month."

Jalan stopped listening to the two lancers. The possibility of a second Lord Shrift consumed his attention as he hastily consumed his meal. It seemed possible that both Guri and Darla could marry a Lord Shrift after all. He pushed away his half empty bowl uncertain if the stew or the conversation sat less well with him. Lieutenant Burk expected him. He would wait until the evening meal to speak to Darla.

As he rose to leave, Tomac entered. When he saw Jalan he waved him over.

"Have you heard the news?" said Tomac.

"The proposal?" said Jalan.

"Yes. What do you think is going on?"

Jalan glanced about and then beckoned Tomac to follow him outside. Once they reached a place of relative privacy, Jalan said, "I heard Darla received a proposal of marriage from Lord Shrift."

"That is what I heard as well. Why would Darla tell everyone before talking to us?"

"I don't know and I don't have time to ask her. I have to report to Lieutenant Burk."

"Well I've got time. I'll tell you what I learn," said Tomac as they parted.

It bothered Jalan that he did not feel excited for Darla, perhaps if she had told him herself before he heard it from others. She headed House Yen. What would happen to the family and to Yen Estate if she married? Would she renounce her role as Lady? Would it pass to Vee or Tomac? And, how would it affect him, the foster son. He knew he had parents, but they never showed any indication they wanted him with them. He was 14. How much longer could he live in Yen Manor?

He tried to ignore his questions about an uncertain future as he jogged to the practice field in search of Lieutenant Burk.

CHAPTER X

Jalan had missed any number of evening meals, but nothing kept him away tonight. Tomac had no luck speaking with Lady Darla and neither of them knew anything. The rumors of the afternoon still burned in his thoughts. Not one had yet been confirmed by his sister.

He stood beside his chair. Tomac and Vee stood next to theirs. They awaited the arrival of the Lady. Once Darla took her place the meal could begin, except Darla was late. The three of them nodded occasionally to each other in awkward silence, too preoccupied with their own thoughts to even make small talk. Jalan reminded himself for the hundredth time that wars are won through patience. He felt quite near losing his war when his mother, Lady Shara, entered the room.

"I bring your sister's apologies. She was overwrought by a very taxing day and has retired early," said Lady Shara.

"But...," said Vee.

"Do not worry. She will be fine after a night's rest," said Lady Shara. "Let us be seated so that our meal may be served."

Even before he lowered himself into his chair Jalan said, "What about..."

And at the same time Tomac said, "How are we..."

Jalan attempted to defer to Tomac by allowing him to speak first. Tomac raised his eyebrows and looked at Jalan.

When neither spoke for a moment Vee stepped in and said, "What about the proposal?"

His mother's mouth fell open for an instant and then she gathered herself together and said, "How could you possibly know about that?"

"Mother, it's the gossip of the entire estate," said Vee. "How could we not know?"

The color rose in Lady Shara's cheeks. She said, "How could that possibly be? I only received the proposal this morning and other than me only Darla knew of it. She can't have told anyone."

"Someone found out. The talk of Lord Shrift's proposal is everywhere," said Jalan.

"Lord Shrift? What are... Oh," said Lady Shara. "Oh dear, this has become terribly muddled. You're talking about a proposal for Darla's hand?"

"Of course, who else could it be," said Vee. And then her eyes widened and she said, "Oh no. It's not me is it? It can't be me."

"Vee, it's all right. No one has asked for your hand. Although, it would not surprise me if it were to happen in the next year or so. But, not yet and I certainly would not tell you of it at table."

The conversation halted as servants arrived with the start of the meal. Once the first course had been laid Tomac said to Lady Shara, "You spoke of a muddle. Is there a proposal or isn't there?"

"There is no proposal for Darla. There is, however, a proposal for," Shara paused and again her cheeks colored as she said, "me."

"Mother!" said Vee.

"Oh please, don't act so shocked daughter. After all I am quite enough amazed and dismayed for both of us."

"Who is it?" said Tomac.

"You recall Lord Brace?" said Lady Shara.

The image of a short older man with a bit of belly and a kind smile popped into Jalan's head. "Of course," he said. "The gentlemen that has called upon you several times."

"But Mother, he is so old," said Vee.

"Not much older than I," said Lady Shara. "And the pleasure of his company counts for a great deal to my mind."

"So you will accept?" said Tomac.

"Don't be hasty," said Lady Shara as she waved a finger at Tomac. "It is never as simple as accepting the first proposal. But, I am considering how to respond," she said with a little smile.

"If the proposal is yours, then why is there talk on everyone's lips about a Lord Shrift and Darla?" said Vee.

"That would be the muddle. Although Darla has received no proposal, a letter from Guri did mention the possible intent of Lord Merk Shrift, one of her husband Juin's cousins, to offer a proposal of marriage."

"That is still potentially earthshaking," said Jalan.

"In what way?" said Vee.

"If Darla marries will she still be Lady? Will her husband become head of House Yen? Will there even be a House Yen?"

"Jalan, be calm. Nothing has happened yet. Every question would have to be answered to the satisfaction of us all before it ever did," said Lady Shara. "It is not as if anyone could force your sister into a marriage."

Jalan did not worry about Darla being forced to do anything. He worried about the aftermath of her choice and what it would mean to all of them. And especially, if he allowed himself to admit it, what it would do to him.

Δ

Lord Merk Shrift watched the gardeners as they tended the meticulously sculpted greenery below his office window. He sighed as he considered the constant vigilance required to impose an esthetically pleasing symmetry on the world around him. But, the landscape was the least of his concerns today. He turned back to his desk and his final reading of the marriage proposal that would be delivered to Lady Darla Yen. He tried to think of anything else that might strengthen his offer. The document spelled out several advantages to a union, the increased holdings, the family contacts, the business relationships, the generations of fine men and women that have borne the Shrift name and the final temptation, Shrift armsmen ready to fight alongside House Yen. The lord nodded to himself in acceptance of the properly crafted proposal.

He sat the pages aside and took a fresh sheet of parchment, newborn goatskin, the finest he had. He pickup up a quill with a nib newly cut that morning by is secretary. Lord Shrift delicately dipped the quill into the ink and began to compose the final part of his proposal, a personal note to Lady Yen. Upon the finely scraped and chalked surface of the parchment he carefully outlined his intent to be an exemplary husband. He made certain to let the lady know that he was attracted to her because of her fine mind, the keenness of which was evidenced in the skill with which she had led House Yen after Lord Hallis Yen's untimely and tragic death. He mentioned the memory of her beauty accented by the emerald gown she wore and the lovely green of her hazel eyes from when they first met. He implied his longing to once again be blessed by Lady Yen's charming tone of voice and turn of phrase.

Shrift assumed that Lady Darla would realize on her own that his holdings and the Yen holdings had become competitors. The merging of the two houses would make a strong financial union. She would see the sense of it, how the sum of the parts created a greater whole. Rather than competing they would control the majority of grain and flax in western Ojmara. The financial advantages aside, his offer of military aid was not something House Yen could afford to ignore.

After completing his personal note, Lord Shrift rang a tiny high-pitched hand bell. His personal secretary, Yartin, entered the room through the double doors that faced the lord's large and ornately carved desk.

"My lord?" inquired Yartin with a slight bow.

"This final draft is good. Please prepare the copies and send one to my cousin."

"Yes, my lord. And, by some coincidence, a letter from Lord Juin has just arrived. Would you like me to bring the correspondence now or at the customary time?"

Merk Shrift considered a moment. With so much going on he preferred to keep to his daily schedule. "Just the letter. I will take the remainder at its proper time."

Yartin accepted the draft proposal from Lord Shrift and left only to return an instant later with a sealed envelope. He offered it to the lord on a silver tray.

"Thank you, Yartin," said Lord Shrift as he took the envelope. "Has the special report arrived yet?"

"No, lord," said Yartin with a hint of apology.

Shrift sighed. "Things have gone well enough. I suppose no news is not bad news," he said quietly. "See to those copies and bring me today's reports. I'll look them over after reading Lord Juin's letter.

"My lord," said the secretary before he made another slight bow and left again.

Lord Shrift examined the envelope. Anticipation was often the best part of any experience, the moment before the first sip of wine, the pause just prior to the musicians beginning to play, or the instant before opening a letter. At these moments, he could still imagine that the best was yet to come. Before it begins, any event was still a mystery that held a great and terrible potential. It could be sublime or second-rate. He hoped for the sublime. But as a realist, he had learned to deal with inferior outcomes.

Shrift cut open the envelope without disturbing the wax seal. He removed the letter and plunged into reading it. Passing quickly over the customary familial platitudes, he searched for the meat of the missive. "... anticipated arrival..., ... accompanied by...," muttered the lord as he scanned the document.

The lord looked up from reading as Yartin entered with a loosely bundled sheath of papers. "Yartin, I have one more thing for you before the reports. Please, tell Cartlyle to prepare the guest suite for the arrival of my lord cousin and his wife. They anticipate their arrival in two days, but you know how my cousin likes to surprise people. He'll likely arrive early so let's have everything, including those copies, ready by tomorrow."

"Yes, my lord," said Yartin.

The secretary began his slight bow when Shrift thought of one more detail. "Oh yes, please be sure that any of Kressel's men are tucked away somewhere out of sight during my cousin's visit."

"Of course, lord."

Lord Merk stood and turned back toward the window. He heard Yartin close the door upon leaving the room. The lord contemplated the order of his garden. It was as it should be, as he had set his mind to make it. A frown pulled down the corners of his lips as he considered something, or rather someone that was not as he should be. Kressel's report should have arrived. The mercenary had been reliable but he kept his own schedule which vexed Shrift.

Δ

Lancer Zahn watched the caravan move sedately toward him along River Road. From his marginally higher vantage point, he counted two large wagons and four mounted riders. Four horses drew each heavy wagon and canvas tarps covered their beds. The lancer tried to imagine what the wagons contained. He suspected cloth, seeds and perhaps lamp oil. Oil had some value. Experience told him there would be more guards for rare goods or if the merchant had made a nice profit in Nakra. Besides, they looked like oil wagons. He had an eye for that sort of thing.

Zahn turned toward the gatehouse to write down the description of the caravan before it arrived. Beyond the gatehouse stood the rest of Southway Outpost. A handful of people moved between the barracks and mess hall. A few horses stood in the corral outside the stables. It all looked as plain boring as the caravan. And neither outpost nor caravan would be here if River Road had not turned onto Yen land to climb east until it changed course southward and plunged into the Sand Hills.

Travelers that passed that way were usually bound for Lavembra. But, they had to stop at Zhan's gate first. A long bar across the road blocked the way until the tariff was paid. Then Zahn would swing the bar aside and let the travelers pass. First, he had to inspect the loads and tally the tariff. *Most likely lamp oil.*

A short distance up the road sat the other gatehouse where travelers in the other direction stopped. When Lancer Zhan glanced that direction he noted that Lancer Mikel stood waiting for a second caravan. Three wagons and several riders slowly made their way down the hill toward Mikel. Probably loaded with goods from Lavembra, or even the Turngow Islands and bound for Nakra. Mikel would brag later about all that exotic cargo. Zahn already pictured Mikel as he asked what Zhan had seen today. Zahn would have to return the favor. Then Mikel would go on and on about spices, and artwork and such. Zahn turned his head and spat to clear the bitter taste of the anticipated conversation from his mouth.

HIDDEN ABILITY

Something hit Lancer Zahn hard in the back and sent him stumbling forward.

"What the...," was all he could say before it happens again and he fell to his knees. He felt something on his back. He tried to reach around and touch whatever it was but his arm failed to move right. Pain sliced through his awareness. He tried to call out to Mikel, but could not make the words come out. He looked toward Mikel's gatehouse. Things were darker than he remembered and people were running past him. He tried to see. He was trying. Somehow he had fallen on the ground. He wondered how he got there and why everything had gone black.

CHAPTER XI

Captain Erida's presence dominated the opposite side of Darla's new desk as he stood in her private study and waited for her to acknowledge him. She had risen early hoping to make up for lost time. Yesterday could not have been more chaotic. Two proposals in one day. The future of House Yen flapped like a flag in the changing winds of matrimony. Darla wanted to talk with Lady Shara, but she barely settled into her chair when Captain Erida appeared with an uncharacteristically dour look upon his face.

"Captain," said Darla.

"My lady, I have news of great concern to House Yen. Our outposts have been attacked," said Captain Erida. "We only have initial reports, but it appears the damage and loss of men may be extensive."

"Attacked?" said Darla trying to make mental room for this new crisis. "By whom?"

"The survivors arrived early this morning. They report that the attackers did not wear uniforms or carry banners. They came disguised as merchant caravans and attacked each road gate. A few said that foreign lancers and archers entered the fight once the initial attacks began."

"You said, 'Attacks'. How many outposts were attacked?"

"All three of them, my lady. That has added to the confusion of determining exactly what occurred. We believe it may have been a coordinated assault on Southway, Midland and Pass all at the same time. Southway may be the most severely damaged, but it is the attack we know the least about. Midland's commander, Lieutenant Caser, reports that the fires set by the attackers have been put out. The only large structure not damaged is the mess hall. Most of their horses were driven off or killed, and 15 lancers died with another 10 wounded. He has secured what is left of the outpost. The report from Lieutenant Niksus at Pass Outpost is the most detailed. It is from his report that we have the best description of the supposed merchants. Pass is the least damaged. Something about the merchant trains made them suspicious and they immediately formed up their available lancers and met the attackers head on. They still took heavy casualties, but Pass Outpost appears to be the least damaged of the three."

"How many men were stationed at each outpost?" Darla remembered something about this, but it was years ago when her father discussed it with her.

Captain Erida's frown appeared to deepen as he said, "There are approximately 30 lancers at each outpost if you include farriers, smiths, supply personnel and the like. There would be about 15 civilians working at each post as well.

Darla was surprised that the number of civilians was so high. She tried to imagine what they would all be doing there. "Why so many civilians?" she asked.

"My lady, there is a cook and maid for each officer. A cook and his helpers to prepare food for the lancers. Laundresses. Stablemen. Assistants to any of the tradesmen as needed. It is no small task to keep an outpost running, even such as these."

"Such as these?" Darla was puzzled as to what Captain Erida meant by his comment.

"I only meant that even when undermanned it is still necessary for each outpost to have a sufficient number of support staff."

"The outposts are undermanned?"

Captain Erida blinked several times before he answered. "Yes, my lady. The outposts were constructed for upwards of 300 lancers each. We barely had a tenth that number at each one."

Now Darla felt even more confused, "In that case, why weren't there more lancers at each outpost."

Darla watched as Erida seemed to be at a loss for words. He started to speak but then said nothing. The Captain looked about as if he might find the words hanging in the air around him and at last settled on a response. "I had assumed you would know that answer, my lady. The cost of the lancers is paid by House Yen, and you, not meaning to be too direct, are House Yen."

"Oh," was all Darla could think to say. The outposts were paid for by the road tariffs. The amount collected was relatively steady over the years. Therefore, it maintained the same size force at each outpost year after year. Darla had not considered that the tariffs were perhaps only meant to supplement outpost expenditures and that she should be developing ways to pay for more lancers. Possibilities for funding begin to come to mind and Darla started to mentally evaluate them before she realized that Captain Erida was still standing there. *No time like the present.* "How long does it take to recruit and train new lancers?"

"A call can be put out for young men of standing. Most would have some equipment and at least their own horse. These men could be ready with a week of daily training after their mounts and equipment pass inspection and they have proper weapons. Given time for the call to go out and a response, plus equipping and training it could be as soon as a month when we could have new lancers in the field. If my lady is considering this, might I also make additional suggestions?"

"Of course, captain. I welcome anything you can offer."

"We do not know our adversary or his mind. I have dispatched scouts to learn what they can. But, we must assume the worst and prepare as if a new Chalmar war is upon us."

Even though Darla half expected the captain to say it, she still found it difficult to believe. "But, my father put that to rest. He led our forces to victory and ended the war."

"My lady, that was almost 30 years ago. Ankena has had decades to nurse its wounds and rebuild its army. They still claim grievances against us. It is conceivable that they would start another war with Ojmara. They would be ready for it, but we are not. In order to survive until the king can marshal his army, there are things we must do immediately."

"What things?" asked Darla.

"We need to recruit lancers, archers, mounted archers and foot soldiers. Yen Estate needs to be fortified. Various strong points need to be established to form a network of defensive positions and sally points. Supplies must be acquired and stored. The estate's workshops need to be expanded. The three outposts should be rebuilt and manned with double the usual number."

"What you are asking for is a fortress, an army and renewed and revitalized outposts? Is that it?"

"That is correct, my lady."

"And what will happen to House Yen if we are beggared by it?"

"Less, I believe, than what will happen if we are overrun by an enemy that hates the name Yen and all for which it stands," said Captain Erida.

Darla sat back in her chair as thoughts raced through her head. Her father had been a brilliant military commander. No matter how well she fulfilled the role of Lady Yen, she could never be General Yen. Darla looked at Captain Erida. "Be seated Captain. Let us work together on a list of all that must be done and order it by greatest need. And then a second time by what may be accomplished most quickly. It may be that some needful things are quickly done and that several goals might be achieved together if we carefully consider who leads the effort and what resources are required."

Δ

Today was Jalan's Name Day. He wondered if it would have any special significance. At 15, would he see a difference in his life? Having been 14 yesterday, what did one day matter? It seemed unlikely that today would be special or exceptional when compared to any other day. Life on the Yen estate moved as it always had. He would spend his day training, being made ready to either save his own life or for a glorious future that no one could describe or promise to him. Today would be like yesterday and tomorrow. It was a special day for him, but an ordinary day for everyone else.

Jalan had slipped his foot into a boot when the knocking began. Seated on the edge of his bed, he grabbed his other boot and said, "Yes?"

"Your sister, Lady Darla, summons you. She sent me to relay her request that you proceed to her study with all haste," said Steward Hint from the hallway side of Jalan's closed door.

He pulled on his other boot before he rose and stepped to the door to open it. Steward Hint was gone. Jalan saw him almost running down the hallway toward the main staircase. "What...," said Jalan before he decided there was no point in asking what his sister wanted. He would have to go and find out for himself.

When he reached Darla's study he would have knocked, but the door stood wide open and several people were already in the room. Darla and a woman Jalan did not know were sorting papers and placing them in boxes. Maid Ranie dusted a set of empty shelves and the cook's helper, Juna, swept the floor. It almost shocked Jalan to see so much activity in this normally sedate quiet space.

"Lady Darla," Jalan called into the room.

His sister turned to him. "Jalan? Oh, yes, yes. You need to go see Captain, er, Major Erida. He's been promoted and you'll need to remember to call him major now. He was just here, but left to see to several things. You will most likely find him at the lancer barracks." Darla went back to looking through the papers she held.

Assuming he had been dismissed, Jalan proceeded down the hall. As he reached the stairway to the first floor he heard Darla call to him.

"Good fortune on your Name Day!"

Jalan could not help but smile as he bounded down the stairs two at a time in search of Major Erida. He had no idea what was going on, but Darla remembered his Name Day.

Jalan dodged past two servants who scurried along so intent upon their own tasks that they nearly collided with each other. He bolted out the front door of the manor house as one of them called out, "Your pardon, young master."

The manor grounds looked abnormally empty and the half dozen lancers he saw jogged or ran instead of walked. None of them looked in his direction. They all seemed intent on going somewhere in a hurry. He decided to emulate them and ran toward the barracks. The barracks were actually three large, two story wood frame structures on the far side of the corral and stables. The corral was all but empty with only one horse in it, a fine heavy warhorse. The strong shoulders and quarters were obvious even from a distance. The stablemen seemed to be working on the barn they had talked about ever since learning of Master Enmar's Training Hall.

Outside Lancer Barracks One, or just One as it was usually called, men busied themselves with polishing pieces of plate armor, oiling leather and repairing their Blue and Tan uniforms. These chores were easier to perform outside where the light was better. Jalan wondered if there was an important ceremony coming up that he had forgotten. "Major Erida?" asked Jalan of the lancer nearest the main barracks doorway.

The man cocked his thumb at the open door and said, "Inside."

Jalan knew all the lancers on sight after his years of training. He said, "Thanks Yustel," and sprinted inside.

The main doors of the long barracks building opened into a wide hallway which ran straight through to another set of double doors on the other side. Immediately to Jalan's left and right were stairways that ran up to the second floor. He walked past those to the center of the hallway and turned left to pass through a wide single door. As he hurried between the two rows of pallets stuffed with straw that jutted end out from the walls he thought about how little used the barracks were. Most of the deep closets that set next to the pallets were empty. The rest held a combination of armor, weapons and personal belongings. Unmarried lancers were the primary residents. A portion of their pay was set aside as rent for their pallet and to cover meals at the Mess Hall.

Jalan reached the door at the end of the double row of pallets and went through it into the Command Room. Within the Command Room were two tables and several chairs. Shelves and chests for storage lined the walls to Jalan's left and right. A large fireplace sat centered in the wall across from the doorway. This provided the only source of heat in the barracks during cold weather. A small widow on either side of the fireplace allowed natural light to enter the room.

The newly made Major Erida stood in the room along with Lieutenants Burk, Martus, Rinlan and Sert. They surrounded one of the two large wooden tables and studied a map that had been spread out upon it. Major Erida looked up as Jalan entered.

"Good," said Major Erida, "Now that we are all here we can discuss assignments." Jalan and the four others focused their attention on Erida and listened carefully as he continued. The Major addresses each of them in turn. "Captain Burk, you will lead a company of lancers to secure the area around Southway Outpost. The reports state that there is very little left of the outpost. You will need to take the appropriate supplies and support for one month in the field. Report daily on your status. Reestablish what you can of the outpost. You will be the provisional commander there."

Major Erida turned to the next man. "Captain Martus, you will lead a similar company provisioned and supported for a month to Midland Outpost. Work directly with the outpost commander, Lieutenant Caser. Secure the area around the outpost and assist in rebuilding and repair. Report daily on your status and have Lieutenant Caser do so as well."

Now Erida addressed Lieutenant Sert, but Jalan discovered quickly that Sert was now a captain as well. "Captain Sert, you will lead a third company of lancers to Pass Outpost. You will secure the general area and reinforce the outpost. Congratulate Lieutenant Niksus on his promotion to captain and relieve him. Captain Niksus is to return here for further orders. You will report daily on your status."

Next the major spoke to Jalan. "Captain Yen, you will lead a company of mounted archers. Find your old archery instructor, Sedic. Inform him of his promotion to sergeant. After Captains Burk, Martus and Sert have formed their companies and moved out, you and Sergeant Sedic will choose the best mounted archers you can from the remaining lancers. You will need to select at least 10 men as the core of your company. As new recruits are trained or skilled riders join us, you will need to add men until you have at least 20 under your command."

Finally, Erida directed his attention to Lieutenant Rinlan who also must have been promoted. "Captain Rinlan, you will begin a sweep through all settlements within the Yen holdings and recruit as many able men as possible. Take a fist of lancers with you. Before you leave, stop at Yen Manor. A sheath of public notices is being prepared for posting wherever you think appropriate. Lady Yen is also being quite generous. Any man that joins will be given a horse if he does not own one, or if he does, the new man will receive the equivalent value of his horse as a bonus. The value will be determined by the Yen stable master. Hopefully, that will induce men to bring a good mount with them."

Jalan tried his best to keep a neutral expression on his face as his curiosity climbed almost beyond enduring. The lieutenants were all captains. Captain Erida was now Major Erida. He was now Captain Yen. Not Mar, his true last name. His identity was still a secret it seemed. But, captain? *What is going on? I'm 15. Is this a joke?*

"Captain Yen, do you have a question?" asked Major Erida.

Apparently his confusion was obvious. "Yes, major. What has happened?"

All the men in the room stared at him. Major Erida said, "The attacks on the outposts? Didn't Lady Darla tell you? Didn't anyone tell you?"

"No, sir. They didn't."

"Welcome to the military," said Erida with a wry smile. The other men chuckled politely. "Our outposts were attacked yesterday. Southway may have been destroyed. The others are damaged. Pass faired the best. You just heard the orders I gave each officer here." Erida swept his glance across everyone else in the room as he asked, "Are there any further questions?" The response was silence and after a brief moment the Major said, "Captain Yen, I'd like you to stay for a minute. Everyone else dismissed."

The other four captains filed out of the room. Burk was the last to leave and he closed the door behind him.

Major Erida's manner relaxed a little and he said, "Your sister really said nothing to you about any of this?"

"No, sir. She only told me to see you."

"Let's sit down and talk for a minute." Major Erida pulled two wooden chairs close together and sat in one. Jalan sat down in the other.

"I could tell by the look on your face that something was wrong. You did well not to balk when I gave you your orders. You've been made a captain because of who you are and because you have demonstrated the ability to do the job. You've had extensive training in weapons and lancer tactics. If you were a little older, no one would question your appointment. We, your sister and I, discussed it and Lady Darla agreed that because of the attacks and the lancers that

116

have been killed we need everyone who can serve. Do you understand?"

"I think so, sir."

"I'll be honest. We're doing our best to give you a command with the least chance of getting you injured or killed. You are a prince and serving in the lancers is a normal part of learning to command. But you are also, just today, the minimum age for a lancer recruit. No matter how extraordinary your skills are, I am not putting you in the van. You are part of our reserve force, once we actually have enough men to create a reserve. If things go as I am afraid they will, you will see battle and have your trial. There will be no need for you to seek out the fight. It will come to you. Is that understood?"

"Yes, sir."

"Good. And, there is one last thing. I'm not going to be able to take you aside like this in the future. When I give you orders you have to carry them out no matter what your misgivings. You have to appear confident in front of your men and the other captains. If anyone questions your authority, you have to find a way to deal with it without running to me. That's the only way the men will respect you."

"Yes, sir."

"I'm not telling you what to do. But, if I were you, I'd find Sedic. Then I would let him know he's a sergeant and that he reports to me. I imagine he has an opinion on which lancers you might want in your new company."

Δ

Jalan needed a way to hang on to a handful of good archers. Once the other captains gathered their companies he would be left with the least desirable lancers. He thought he knew how to do it. First, Jalan followed Major Erida's advice and sought out Sedic. In short order they compiled a list of good archers and Jalan went to see Lady Darla.

The earlier bustle of reorganizing and cleaning appeared to be complete when he returned to Darla's study. She sat behind a desk that lacked all appearance of ever having been cleared of papers.

Without looking up, Darla raised one finger in a sign that she needed a moment before she could turn her attention to Jalan.

When Darla did look at him, all she said was, "Yes?"

"I need to beg a favor," said Jalan.

"What is it?"

"When you send riders to the other houses, I would like you to send men from this list." He handed her the list of lancers he and Sedic had compiled.

"Have you been talking to Major Erida?" said Darla.

"Only to get my orders. Why do you ask?"

"Did he say something about riders?"

"No. I just assumed you'd send them," said Jalan.

"So you thought of it yourself?"

"It only makes sense. We have to consolidate our position and contact allies."

"That is almost word for word what the major said. And, yes, I am sending messengers to the other houses." Darla scanned the list and said, "Very well. I'll request the first five men on your list to act as messengers." She handed the list back to Jalan.

"Don't you need to write them down?"

Darla looked skeptical. "Do you think I can't remember five names?"

Jalan had never known her to forget anything, especially not any childhood infraction of his, but this was important. "All right, if you're sure," said Jalan.

"I am," said Darla

Next Jalan visited Mistress Treana, the Yen family seamstress. He did not recall any time in his life that he actually sought the woman out. Past visits had all been made under silent protest and lasted only as long as it took the seamstress to measure him. His sister Vee, on the other hand, had to be told to stop requesting new garments. She was now limited to one new dress every season and could not approach Mistress Treana without mother in tow.

The seamstress was the only practitioner of a trade that worked exclusively for the family. Jalan did not know how it came to be, but Mistress Treana had her own quarters and salon tucked away in one wing of Yen Manor. He suspected that between mother and his four sisters, there had always been enough work in progress to justify the close proximity. Even after marriage and moving away, both Guri and Aena had visited Yen Manor in order to have Treana create gowns for them.

At the door to Mistress Treana's salon, Jalan knocked and waited. Before he drew two breaths the door was opened by Mistress Treana's personal maid, Brianne.

"Young mister Jalan! What a nice surprise," said Brianne in a lilting singsong as she gave Jalan a wide-eyed smile. She reached out and took gentle hold of his left arm, drawing him into the room. "Please, come in. It is such a pleasure to be visited by one of the handsome Yen brothers. I will let my mistress know you are here,"

Jalan never understood how the woman packed so much enthusiasm into everything she said. Her greeting seemed unusually warm this time and she held his arm longer than necessary to guide him into the room. "Thank you," said Jalan not certain if he had expressed gratitude for showing him in or finally releasing his arm.

The small salon had several chairs and a love seat arranged against the walls. The center of the room remained clear and easily seen from any seat. Jalan recalled being forced to stand there as his mother and Mistress Treana inspected him and fussed over some detail of an article of clothing. He set aside his reminiscing when Mistress Treana entered through a doorway at the back of the room.

"Jalan!" she said with exuberance similar to her maid's. "Let me guess." Mistress Treana studied him as she tapped her lower lip with the index finger of her left hand. "You are looking for something in Blue and Tan? Perhaps with the insignia piping of a captain?"

Mistress Treana was a notorious gossip who was well informed about anything deemed to be public knowledge. She had a spotless reputation for never being the first to reveal anything about the family and had never tarnished the Yen reputation. But once someone else revealed anything, the seamstress learned of it very quickly. Jalan would not be surprised if Treana knew what he was thinking even before he did.

"You are very perceptive," said Jalan. His mother always gave that response when Mistress Treana was correct about something.

"Very good. Let me take your measurements. I am sure you have grown since I saw you last."

Mistress Treana worked with a knotted string that she stretched along or wrapped around various parts of his body. He held still until she began to measure the inside of his leg.

"Young man, please don't squirm," said the seamstress.

"Um, ah, sorry," was all Jalan managed to say and by then Mistress Treana had finished.

She wrote figures on a slate tablet using a bit of chalk. Jalan remembered she had several slates, one for every project. With the measuring completed, Mistress Treana asked Jalan to return in two days for a fitting. He thanked her and Brianne escorted him out of the salon.

"I look forward to seeing you in your new uniform," said Brianne. Then she winked at him.

Jalan felt the heat rise in his face and could not think of a thing to say. He made a quick bob of his head and fled.

"Good day, young Captain Jalan!" reverberated through the hallway as Brianne closed the door behind him.

Master Enmar would expect an explanation for Jalan's absence from training. Jalan started to jog along the empty hallway in order to reach Master Enmar faster, not because it carried him away from Brianne more quickly. Nor did he consider spending the next two days convincing Tomac to come with him to the fitting an act of cowardice.

CHAPTER XII

Master Enmar stood toe to toe with Master Chander outside the Training Hall. Both men looked flush and Jalan heard Enmar shout, "... in my training hall. I don't care where you put your supplies. This is not a warehouse!"

"We'll see about that!" shouted Master Chander in return before he spun around and stormed away.

Jalan had never seen Master Enmar or Master Chander angry before. It frightened him to think that those too could even become angry. Master Chander was either much braver than Jalan ever expected or he did not understand how dangerous Master Enmar truly was. And, nothing good could come from upsetting the Yen quartermaster. Master Enmar would be lucky to requisition a beating after that exchange.

"A madness has taken this place," grumbled Enmar as Jalan approached. "I suppose it has afflicted you as well, since I have not seen you all morning."

"Yes, sir. It has," agreed Jalan. "I was summoned by my sister who immediately sent me off to Major Erida..."

"Major Erida?" interrupted Enmar.

"Yes, sir. He's been promoted. At least Lady Darla told me that much. And, when I found the major, he promoted several lieutenants to captains and made me a captain too. I am to command a company of archers. And if Major Erida hadn't explained about the attacks I still wouldn't know why I am a captain."

"You refer to the attacks on the outposts, I presume?"

"Yes, sir. Major Erida was kind enough to explain that much."

"But, he didn't explain why you are a captain or why you will command archers?"

"Mounted archers actually, and he did explain. He said many lancers died in the attacks and they need everyone now." Jalan looked around to make sure no one else listened. Apparently the shouting had cleared the area. "He said I'm a prince and this is something princes do to learn to command men. And he told me I'll be in the reserve because they don't want me to get hurt. Although Major Erida was sure I will see battle eventually."

"How do you feel about being a captain?" asked Master Enmar.

"I've done what I thought I should. No one else asked any questions. They all seemed to know what to do," said Jalan. Only now did Jalan start to feel a little sorry for himself. It was his Name Day after all.

Master Enmar gave him an appraising look. "I'll wager you've done fine, but tell me what you have done and I'll see if I can think of any suggestions for you."

Jalan felt a sense of relief. Major Erida did not trust Master Enmar. But, Jalan trusted both men with his own life. He detailed his morning for Master Enmar.

"I'd say you've done well for your first morning as a new lancer captain," said the master. "It is true that mounted archers do not charge the enemy line and gain the glory of facing down an imminent death, but they can change the course of battle and be the key to victory. They are mobile and able to follow the flow of the fight. There is honor in being the captain of such men. If you are wise enough to use what you have been taught, it will be well with you and your men."

It reassured Jalan that Master Enmar seemed to approve of his commission. He was not sure what he should say. Jalan thought he might like to hug Master Enmar, but he had never done such a thing before and he did not believe it was what a captain would do. He settled on saying "Thank you, sir."

"I'll go to Lady Darla and volunteer to train your archers. I'm sure I will be needed for that and more as they cobble together this new army. I need to speak with her about the proper use of our Training Hall as well. You might consider assisting Major Erida's second officer. As I recall, that used to be Captain Burk. Without him to pick up after the major there may be some things that need doing. If I were you I'd be sure the list of promotions and appointments with your name on it makes it to the paymaster. It's my experience that they will remember to order you into battle long before they will remember to pay you."

Jalan smiled. He had not even thought about pay. "How much is a lancer captain paid?"

"I don't know," said Master Enmar "But, whatever it is you'll find that for every coin you earn there are ten ways to spend it. You might want to ask Lady Darla to hold at least half your pay in trust until you get used to having coin in your purse."

"Why?"

"Because something will come along and you will have the coin for it."

"Like what?"

"I don't know, but if you don't set some aside I do know you will wish you had. Why not talk to Lady Darla and see what she says?"

That made sense to Jalan. He would talk to Darla. "All right," he said.

"And don't forget about helping with support duties for Major Erida. You'll need good relations with your commanding officer."

"All right. I will try to help. I have to wait until Burk, Martus and Sert pick their men before I can pick mine. I guess if I can help them leave sooner then I'll get started sooner too."

"Good luck, captain," said Master Enmar.

"Good luck, master," said Captain Jalan with a laugh.

"And, good fortune on your Name Day."

Jalan and Enmar parted company. While Jalan jogged toward the barracks, he decided the world really had been turned on its head. It scared him and excited him.

Δ

Jalan spent the remainder of his first day as a captain helping Lieutenant Goss gather information on the condition of various workshops, and their craftsmen, apprentices and assistants. Goss, small for a lancer, barely topped Jalan in height. But with his head covered in a shock of reddish brown hair and his short beard that matched it, he stood out in a crowd. Jalan and Goss worked together to rate each crafter according to their ability to support both the ongoing civilian and military needs of House Yen. At first it seemed impossible to Jalan that anyone could do such a thing.

"It's not so bad," said Goss. "This is the sort of thing leaders always want to know and the last thing they want to take the time to figure out. All we have to do is ask the right questions. Over and over and over."

Jalan listened during the first two interviews and by the third, when Lieutenant Goss questioned Master Doon about the number of assistants he had and the current work he was doing, Jalan knew the next questions would be about any tasks Master Doon planned to undertake when his current projects were complete. The process soon became so predictable that Jalan wondered how Lieutenant Goss could continue to sound interested while asking the same series of questions again and again.

When Jalan asked, Goss said, "Work is work. How do you stay interested in the practice yard when you are covered with sweat and so tired you almost forget your own name?"

"I concentrate on doing whatever I am doing and I don't think about anything else," said Jalan.

"It's the same with this. You don't sharpen a saber with one stroke of the stone. And you don't stop until you've honed a fine edge and oiled the blade. We're only now finding the nicks that need extra care."

Assisting Goss exposed Jalan to other things he did not fully understand about Masters Ritka, Doon, Anton and Brunt. He thought of the boys and young men that worked with them as helpers. Many of them turned out to be apprentices who worked for each master in order to learn that master's specific craft. They were students in the same way Jalan was a student of Master Enmar. And, they were often not much older than Jalan. He started to wonder how many other things about the estate and House Yen he had ignored while focusing on his training and immediate family.

Goss might never be a great leader in battle. He was proficient in arms and had a saber strapped to his side like every lancer did since the attacks on the outposts. But he served best though his perseverance and attention to detail when dealing with people and numbers. Jalan knew full well that there were many lancers that could not do what Goss did. For some reason the image of the two servants that almost collided in the hallway that morning came to mind and Jalan wondered how much her really knew about what they did.

Goss and Jalan finished the report by lamplight that night. They moved quietly through Barracks One to the Command Room where they found Major Erida still reading. Two hanging lamps had been lit. A third sat on the table where the Major worked. Erida accepted their report and placed it on the bottom of a stack of other papers. Jalan noticed it was the same stack that Major Erida read from earlier. The stack had grown much shorter and a tall stack of papers sat next to it.

Major Erida rubbed his eyes for a moment and then said, "Lieutenant Goss, please take this pile of paper and organize it by outpost. These are copies of the monthly reports from each outpost commander. I'm afraid the originals were likely destroyed when Southway burned. The copies have all been stored together with no thought for organization. Lady Yen reviewed them, but I think she assumed we had been keeping up with them as well. I can tell you that we have not. We relied far too heavily on Major Jeckler to organize things for Southway and the other outposts. Since he is missing and presumed dead, I have taken on the task."

"Yes, sir," said Lieutenant Goss.

"Unfortunately, there is no standard report format. Some information is included one month and missing the next. You may even have to search the document for the name of the related outpost. Apparently each commander reported things his own way. That's something we are going to change. But, not until I've gotten some sleep. Once you get those reports sorted, get some rest. I'll need you early tomorrow."

"Yes, sir."

"Captain Yen, I'd like you to continue to assist Lieutenant Goss tomorrow. The other captains should be leaving and you can return to organizing your company after that."

"Yes, sir," said Jalan.

Major Erida stood. "The walk to my quarters will do me some good. I've been sitting in this chair too long. I'll see both of you tomorrow at first light."

"Yes, sir," said Goss and Jalan in unison.

Erida left. Jalan stayed and helped sort the reports. Together he and Goss performed the tedious and time consuming task of bringing order to what almost seemed intentional disorder. Why had the officers in charge of the outposts created reports in such a haphazard way?

Jalan wondered what Major Erida got out of reading all the reports except a headache. His eyes itched and he fought the desire to lie down and sleep on the Command Room floor as he and Lieutenant Goss doggedly sorted papers. They added a title page to each report that did not have one and called it a night. Lieutenant Goss produced a key that hung from a long fine chain about his neck and used it to lock the door of the Command Room when they left.

Δ

Jalan had to make certain he rose early. Before he went to bed he drank a lot of water because that would wake him. It turned out that waking early was not a problem. In addition to needing to relieve himself and the worries of being a new captain, someone started tolling the estate's bell. He pushed himself up and out of bed to look out his bedroom window. The sun had not risen but Jalan could see well enough that sunrise could not have been far off.

After a quick scrub of his face at the wash basin, he dressed in a fresh set of cloths and combed his hair. Then he went downstairs to the kitchens to see what he might find. There was some day old bread, butter and cheese along with apples in a bowl, all sitting on a table in the winter kitchen. Mistress Dahlia was there, but she didn't even bat an eye when Jalan helped himself to some bread with butter and an apple.

"If you'll be rising this early, young captain, I can have a little something ready for you each day," said Dahlia.

He stopped to consider her offer. It seemed likely that being a captain would continue to mean rising early. "Yes, please," said Jalan.

"Likely they intend to keep at that bell each morning. You come down right after and I'll have a breakfast ready for you."

"I will," said Jalan. "Thank you, Mistress." And then a question occurred to him. "If you didn't expect me this morning, why is the food set out?"

Mistress Dahlia shook her white scarfed head and said, "Do you think the servants don't eat?"

Jalan felt the heat rise in his face, "I suppose. I mean they must certainly. It's just not something I thought about."

The mistress wiped her hands on her stained apron and said, "Well I must, and certainly they do. There are two of them waiting outside the door right now."

"Waiting? Why?" said Jalan as he looked toward the doorway in time to catch a sliver of motion as someone disappeared out of sight.

"They defer to you young noble. There are many things servants do to spare the tender sensibilities of their betters."

Jalan said nothing more. Having done what he could for breakfast, he left the house through the kitchen's exit as he pondered how much he actually knew about the servants. The morning air was cool, especially compared to the heat from the kitchen's ovens where Dahlia was baking bread. Jalan ran to Barracks One, not because it was necessary to run, but because he wanted to run. There had been no time for exercise yesterday. His body seemed to miss it. He had to find a way to make exercise and practice part of his schedule now that he was a captain. It felt good to move.

As he neared the stables he saw a double column of riders forming up. The corral had a dozen horses in it. There were more men, both mounted and others standing next to their mounts, that had formed two loose groups. Captain Burk rode along the double column. As Jalan neared, he heard Burk checking that each man was ready. At the end of the column were two large wagons covered with canvas sheets. It was probably some of the locally woven sailcloth. House Yen grew flax that was used to make the cloth. And, under the cloth would be supplies needed for Burk's men.

127

Teams of four large draft horses were being hitched to four more wagons. No doubt the two groups of milling lancers were Captain Martus and Sert's men awaiting their turns to form up and ride out.

When Jalan arrived at the Command Room, Major Erida was the only one there. The major called him into the room and asked him to close the door.

"There was an order given by Lady Darla yesterday," said Major Erida. "She decided to send specific lancers to the five closest houses in order to convey her personal request for aid. It seemed that all five lancers happened to be some of our better mounted archers. I was tempted to countermand the order. Would you be interested in knowing why?"

Jalan got the feeling Major Erida was trying to tell him something. His mother, Lady Shara, had done the same thing several times. She spoke to him as if they were talking about someone else. Although he hesitated, Jalan said, "Yes, sir."

"First, I had ordered that Captains Burk, Martus and Sert select their companies from the available lancers. Had I wanted to remove any men from the choices available, I would have done so myself. Those three are even now deploying on missions critical to the safety of us all. Inhibiting their ability to carry out my orders is a serious offense. Such an action could be viewed as treason."

Major Erida studied Jalan as if he expected treasonous intent to burst forth at any moment.

"Second, it is unwise for an officer to allow anyone to bypass the chain of command. It undermines the officer's authority if people believe they can bypass him and go to someone above him to get what they want. That is not something I will tolerate. Ever."

"Yes, sir," said Jalan as he began to feel ill.

"You, captain, have managed to not only circumvent the chain of command but to undermine the effectiveness of the Yen Lancers at the same time. Not only did you do entirely the wrong thing, you did it with a level of efficiency I can only hope my officers exercise when carrying out my actual orders.

"Yes, sir," repeated Jalan as he felt forced to make some response when Major Erida paused. He worried that anything he said would only make things worse.

"I have been forced to reconsider the decision to make you a captain. You are very young and perhaps you are not entirely ready for the responsibility. However, our need for trained lancers is great and your demonstrated skills, should you have the opportunity, would be an asset in battle. After much thought I have decided to leave things are they are despite the fact that your offense could warrant a severe punishment."

"Yes, sir. Thank you, sir," said Jalan with sincere gratitude that the major had not seen fit to take his commission or impose whatever a more severe punishment might be. When he thought of a clever move while sparring, he used it. Clearly, clever command required much more thought.

"Consider what I have said. And, consider this conversation a warning. I will not allow you to play Lady Yen and me against each other in order to get what you want. Any further attempts to subvert my decisions will be dealt with harshly."

Jalan had gone to Darla knowing she would contact the neighboring lords. He thought he could solve his problem while Darla solved hers by asking her to send lancers he needed as her messengers. When those lancers where away from Yen Manor serving as messengers, the other captains would not be able to take them first. He would have a few good men to build his company around. He never considered how his clever solution might look to Major Erida. "I am sorry, major. I should have talked to you," said Jalan in the most earnest tone he could manage.

"Yes, you should have. But, I don't expect you to be perfect and to always know the best way to handle a situation. That is why I allowed your maneuver to go forward. Although I had good reasons to oppose this decision, it was not worth having a disagreement with Lady Yen over it. I will discuss the situation with her so that she also understands we cannot operate this way in the future."

"Yes, sir."

"I am glad we understand each other, captain. The fact that you only attempted to hold onto five good men and not the five best made your flawed plan more palatable. They will all be ordered to report to you and Sedic upon their return to Yen Manor. And, I've found one more lancer for you as well. I believe he will help you better understand the chain of command."

"Thank you, sir."

"If you want to thank me, use your men to train a company of mounted archers that the enemy will fear. Make them effective in battle. And, do it quickly. That's all the thanks I require," said Major Erida.

"Yes, sir. I will."

"For the rest of the day, work with Lieutenant Goss on registering all the new recruits and volunteers. Find someone who can read and write well enough to replace you, because tomorrow you start training your own men. Dismissed."

"Yes, sir," said Jalan following it with a nod of the head before he stood and retreated from the Command Room to look for Lieutenant Goss. For once he looked forward to burying himself in paperwork. Out of everything he needed to do, it posed the least risk of further aggravating Major Erida. Things should be easier with the help of the new lancer Erida had promised him.

CHAPTER XIII

Sedic and Jalan stood together at the practice field when the first of Jalan's mounted archers returned from his journey to one of the other landed houses. Lancer Serks was no taller than Jalan, but two years older. Serks volunteered for the lancers a year earlier. Before that he was one of the stable boys on the estate. Sedic probably knew more about Serks, but for Jalan it is enough that Serks rode well and shot well.

Sedic looked up as the breeze played with his shaggy hair and addressed the mounted new arrival, "Serks, you remember Captain Yen don't you?"

Serks arched an eyebrow and said to Jalan, "They told me at the gate to report to Captain Yen, but I never thought it was you. Ah, no disrespect, but I thought maybe some distant relative of your father."

"It surprised me too," said Jalan with a smile as he tried not to stare at Serks's crooked nose. Instead he looked   straight at the lancer's brown eyes. They almost matched the color of his hair. For that matter, Jalan noticed, they were nearly the same color as the dun bay he rode.

"Captain Yen's young, but he's solid," interjected Sedic. "You and me, we're part of his new company of mounted archers."

After a short pause, Serks nodded to Jalan and asked, "Where are the others, captain?"

"Coming," said Jalan. "Dost, Harna, Miltrip and Reest should all return today too. They were visiting other houses."

"And, we'll be adding recruits as they come in," said Sedic. "We billet in Barracks Three, Ground South. See to your mount, drop your gear and get back here."

"All right," said Serks. "Captain," he said to Jalan with another nod.

"And sergeant," cut in Sedic.

Serks raised his eyebrows questioningly.

"I know. I haven't had time to sew on the fool braid," said Sedic.

Serks rode off. Sedic's comment about sewing reminded Jalan that he needed to see Mistress Treana for his uniform fitting. It would probably make meeting the rest of his men easier if he were dressed properly. Jalan excused himself and went directly to Mistress Treana's salon. He had never spoken with Tomac and knew he would have to face Brianne alone. But, after surviving the dressing down by Major Erida, she seemed less formidable.

While at his fitting, Jalan recalled his need to speak with Darla about his lancer pay. If he wanted time to get anything done with his men he needed to see Darla right away.

He discovered Lady Darla set up in the Business Room right off the manor house parlor. Jalan arrived at the parlor hoping to drop in on his sister and quickly speak with her. When he walked into the room he found that it had been transformed from a comfortable meeting and entertaining room into a waiting room to see Lady Darla. The comfortable chairs were no long arranged around the fireplace. Instead they faced more toward the doorway of the Business Room. A desk sat next to the doorway. A young woman, maybe Darla's age with brown hair tied back by blue and tan ribbons, sat behind the desk. She looked up from the bound set of papers she read.

"May I be of service, young gentleman?" Her voice sounded very pleasant and she finished her words with a little smile. Jalan noticed that her eyes were dark like her long hair. Then he realized he was staring at her and hurried to explain himself.

"I am here to see my sister. Er, I mean, Lady Darla," said Jalan in a rush.

"Oh, you must be Captain Jalan. I am Jacey, Lady Darla's assistant. Might I ask about the nature of your visit? Perhaps there is something I can help you with?"

"Well, um, no. That is, I think, I think I would rather speak with Lady Darla, please." The room seemed suddenly warmer and he hoped he did not sound as much the fool as he felt his stammering made him.

Jacey frowned slightly and said, "Very well. The lady is meeting with someone now, but when they finish I will inquire if she wishes to see you next."

"Well, I suppose, that is, I imagine it would be all right to talk with you," said Jalan. He did not really want to, but would not mind seeing Jacey smile again.

She rewarded him with another little smile and said, "Please, tell me your concern."

"I'm a captain. Well, you know that. I mean because I'm a captain the lancers pay me." He stopped, uncertain what to say next and worried that he would only continue to muddle every sentence.

"Yes?" said Jacey with a clear sense of expectation in her voice.

"I don't know what to do with the money," he confided.

Jacey giggled.

She is laughing at me. Jalan felt his face flush which only intensified his embarrassment. Why should he care what some pretty girl thought about him, he told himself angrily?

"That is the best problem I have heard all day. That is a wonderful problem to have," said Jacey. "And, you were right. You do need to speak with my lady. You have a family issue and I cannot help with those."

"Why not?" said Jalan.

"Because, I am Lady Darla's assistant. I'm not family. There are some matters that should be private."

"Oh. But if you are working with Lady Darla, what difference does it make?"

Jacey seemed to consider her answer before saying, "Perhaps it is a matter of degree. What passes between you and my lady she will share with me as she sees fit and that is all I need to know."

"If only more people felt that way, I would not be plagued with questions," said Major Erida as he stepped out of the Business Room with Lieutenant Goss behind him.

Jalan automatically straightened his posture and focuses his attention on his commanding officer.

"Captain Jalan is there anything we might need to discuss before you see Lady Darla?" said Erida.

"No, sir. Just a family matter," said Jalan.

"Very good. As you were." Major Erida walked across the parlor and exited the room with Goss trailing behind him.

Some of Jalan's tension slipped away when the Major departed. He turned back to Jacey.

She rose from her seat behind the desk and said, "A moment. I will announce you." Then she stepped into the Business Room.

After a moment waiting, Jalan thought he should take a seat, but Jacey returned and escorted him into the Business Room where Lady Darla sat in a chair behind a large worktable covered with documents. Darla looked so busy that Jalan almost felt sorry to interrupt her until he recalled everything else he needed to do today. It seemed they were both very busy. He decided to be as brief as possible.

"I hope you're not going to ask me to assign tasks to any more lancers," said Lady Darla as she looked up from the papers laid out before her. Her smile told him she was teasing.

He smiled back and shook his head. "Never again. I need to speak with you about my lancer pay."

"Jacey indicated you had a concern about how to handle the money?"

"Yes, my lady."

She pauses and said, "Please, call me Darla. I'm not ready for my little brother to be so grown up. This war, if that is what it is, is making us older much too fast."

"Yes, Darla."

Darla laughed. It had been so long since he heard her do it that Jalan laughed too.

"All right," she said once her mirth subsided. "If you are going to make my name sound like that, you might as well call me lady. Now explain your concerns so that I can understand how I might help."

Jalan told Darla of the conversation he had with Master Enmar concerning saving a portion of his pay. And, he explained the items he was purchasing from Mistress Treana.

Darla brought up even more items Jalan would need including a field chest to carry his personal effects on campaign, provisions that he would be required to purchase for himself and any extra he might wish to share with his men. If he wanted something more than the common issue tent, as most captains did, he would have to buy it. Jalan's head began to swim with all the details, but Darla simply made a list containing each item they discussed and did not appear alarmed in the least by its ever increasing length. When she capped it off with 50 golds for a fine war horse, Jalan started to have trouble breathing.

"But, my pay is only two silvers a day," protested Jalan. "It would take..."

"500 days," said Darla

"What?"

"It would take 500 days for you to earn 50 gold," said Darla. She looked up from the list. Her eyes widened and in a voice of concern she said, "Jalan? What's wrong?"

"500 days," said Jalan. "That's, that's, well, almost two years!"

"Close to one and one half. But, why does that trouble you so?"

"How will I ever have enough money for all this?"

Darla sat back in her chair and blinked. "I see. Mother never discussed money with you did she?"

"No," said Jalan, mystified as to what his mother had to do with this.

"So you don't know anything about the house finances?"

"Ah, no. I though you and mother took care of it."

Lady Darla closed her eyes and began to massage her forehead with the fingertips of her left hand. It was a familiar gesture that Jalan remembered from several childhood lectures on behavior. The feeling that he was in trouble again settled over him, only he could not think of anything he had done wrong this time.

Darla set her hands in her lap, took a deep breath and slowly exhaled, and then opened her eyes. "I don't have time to explain it now, but you have the money. Anything you earn as a captain you can spend or set aside as you wish. I'll arrange to have your captain's pay held back in the family accounts. You need to take this list and speak to the quartermaster. Anything he cannot supply you will have to find. I suggest you trade with one of the crafters or any of the merchants that now frequent the estate. Have them apply to Jacey for payment. You may meet with her to verify the purchases. If you want to buy anything more expensive than the war horse, see me first."

That was definitely Darla's matter-of-fact behavior lecture voice, but Jalan felt relieved rather than chastised. It seemed foolish of him to never have considered money before. But, he had assumed that, as a child, his mother had seen to it. As a man, a caption of the lancers, it became his responsibility. No one had ever told him that he, Jalan, had money. Perhaps he should have asked sooner? However, the meeting took so long he had no time to ask now and Darla had no time to answer. He thanked her, took the list, and left wondering how he would ever acquire everything on it.

As he crosses the parlor on his way toward the hallway door he heard a man say, "Finally!" from somewhere behind him. "I can't believe I was kept waiting because of some boy."

Jalan turned around, uncertain if he felt upset or guilty. At the very least he wanted to see the man who spoke.

"That is Captain Jalan Yen, sir," said Jacey in a tone that gave up nothing to Darla's lecture voice. She stood and walked around the desk to place herself directly between the man and the door to the Business Room. "He is a lancer officer and a member of the Yen family. You will take this opportunity to apologize to him or we can reschedule your appointment with his sister for a time when you are more contrite."

Somebody's in trouble. He made a mental note not to upset Jacey. Jalan watched the man step back from her. He faced Jalan and straightened his short gray dress jacket before he ran a hand through his equally gray hair.

"I sincerely apologize for my outburst. I have allowed my impatience to get the better of me. I hope that a young gentleman of your obvious quality will grace a foolish merchant, for such I am, with, if not your forgiveness, then your forbearance. I am truly deeply sorry for any insult I have given you."

No one ever apologized to him like that. What choice was there but to accept? He started to when his mind settled on something the man had said.

"You're a merchant?" said Jalan with the hope that all the Name Day wishes for good fortune had finally caught up with him.

"Yes," said the gray man with a quizzical expression on his face. "What do you sell?"

"All number of things. I am here to offer my services as a supplier to the lancers, captain."

What do I have to lose? Holding out his list, Jalan asked, "Can you supply these things?"

The gray man took the paper and scanned it. "Why, yes. Our caravan has all this and more."

Throwing caution to the wind and knowing he had no idea how to properly negotiate with a merchant, Jalan said, "I need to buy those things."

"I am sure we can settle on a fair price, captain."

"Then I forgive you," said Jalan. He hoped his quick decision to seek the gray man's aid had not run him afoul of Captain Erida, Lady Darla or anyone else. He also hoped that he would not spend the rest of his life second guessing himself.

Δ

All five lancers had reported to Sergeant Sedic by the time Jalan returned. He finished the apple he had taken when he passed through the manor's kitchens. It filled the empty spaces left after the thick slice of bread and a small cheese wedge. All of which, he washed down with water he drank when he passed the well. Jalan felt refreshed and confident enough to inspect his men.

"Sergeant," said Jalan.

"Yes, captain," said Sedic.

"Have the men form a line for inspection."

"From up for inspection," called out Sedic.

Serks was the first in line. The lancers do not take anyone until they are 15. The former stable boy was 17. He knew how to care for his horse and tack, and showed precision with his longbow. Even without Darla's special assignment, Sedic thought Jalan would get Serks because the other captains would pick older more experienced lancers who did not have Serk's crooked nose and reputation for brawling. Serks, no taller than Jalan, was clearly more heavily built and more muscular.

Miltrip, the next man in line, stood head and shoulders taller than Serks and was four years his senior. Sedic claimed Miltrip was an all-around good lancer, equally skilled with the bow, sword and lance. Jalan hoped that Miltrip was a good leader and able to handle his own fist. He held that same hope for all five of his lancers. If he could assign four recruits to each of them it would give him more tactical and training options.

Harna stood next to Miltrip and at 5 feet 11 inches he was nearly as tall. At 20 he was a year younger than Miltrip. Lancer training had made them both strong. With similar straight black hair and blue eyes, they could easily be mistaken for brothers except that Harna's hooked nose and prominent brow ruined the imagined resemblance. Before joining the lancers, Harna did whatever work he could get in Falloak. Sedic praised Harna's ability with a knife. Jalan knew that made Harna a dangerous opponent in close quarters. Sedic and Harna should be able to assist anyone in Jalan's company that needed to improve their knife work.

Forth in line was Reest. Not as tall as Miltrip and Harna, he was still at least a head taller than Serks and six years older. Sedic told Jalan that Reest was the son of a lancer captain with House Olin. Reest did not talk about his father or family and had never explained why he volunteered with House Yen instead of being a lancer with House Olin. It did not matter to Jalan. Whatever secrets Reest kept underneath his shaved skull he was welcome to keep. Jalan had enough of his own. Like Miltrip, Reest was a balanced fighter with good skills. Sedic called him disciplined and said he got along well with the other men, even Serks.

Dost, tallest of all, was the last man in line. At 27, he was nearly as old as Sedic and looked every bit the veteran lancer. He stood straight and relaxed as though nothing else in the world needed doing except following the next order. Confidence seemed to surround him like a cloak. Jalan counted on Dost and Sedic to make up for the experience he lacked. He hoped to rely on their judgment to keep him out of trouble.

"Lancers!" said Jalan only to be interrupted by a familiar voice.

"Captain! Lieutenant Yen reporting as ordered," said Tomac as he jogged up and joined the line. Jalan notice the black braid of office had already been sown to his uniform.

Jalan forgot what he had been about to say. "Whose orders?" he said and added belatedly, "lieutenant."

Tomac smiled and said, "Major Erida's, sir. He said you would be expecting me."

"He said he'd found another lancer to help me... oh." Captain Erida's sense of humor seemed as biting as his reprimands. He sent Tomac as a junior officer under Jalan's command in order to help Jalan learn about the chain of command. Great. Now he had to maintain discipline with his older brother who already resented Jalan surpassing him and a company of men watching to see if Jalan favored his brother over them. Compared to this, Erida would have done him a favor by rescinding his commission.

Jalan took a long deep breath and tried to do what he did when sparring, ignore everything except the moment. He began again. "Lancers! I learned today that there are many items a soldier requires. Rather than drill during the daylight remaining, you will all spend the next hour sorting your belongings for inspection at Barracks Three. I do not know when we will be sent into the field, but it could be at any time. We are going to be ready. Any equipment that needs attention gets it. Anything we have to acquire will be found. You five, ah six, lancers are the experienced core of the company. When the recruits want to know how things are done, I expect you all to be their best example. Let's get squared away. Dismissed."

"Captain?" said Tomac.

"Yes," said Jalan.

"My equipment isn't at the barracks. It's over at the manor just like yours."

Jalan thought for a moment about what was fair and how the other officers were housed. Technically, he and Tomac were young bachelor lancers, exactly the kind of lancers that usually lived in the barracks. "Perhaps we should move into the barracks," said Jalan.

"Captain, I don't think you and the lieutenant need to barracks with us. Given your commissions and birth, I worry the men might chafe at your presence. No offense, but the regular lancer prefers some distance between himself and the officers."

"Let us not forget our place," said Tomac with a grin.

Sergeant Sedic, Jalan and Tomac went to the Officers' Workroom in Barracks Three. It was essentially a duplicate of the Command Room in Barracks One and the place where Jalan and Goss had finished their report on the estate's craftsmen two nights earlier. Jacey had made two copies of Jalan's equipment list before he left the parlor. She kept the original in order to negotiate prices with the gray haired merchant, Trader Grom. The trader took one copy and Jalan took the other. Jalan, Sedic and Tomac studied Jalan's copy and created a new list of standard items each lancer in the company must have. Some things never included in Jalan's original list, such as weapons, were added to the standard lancer equipment list and others were left off or modified as appropriate. They numbered each item on the list. At the end of the hour, they started the inspection.

Jalan began with the condition of uniforms, boots and small clothes. Weapons were next. Each man had a good curved saber for fighting from horseback. Dost also had a short sword, a longsword, two daggers and two stout recurved short bows. All the others were similar but each tended to have an item less or more. Each man's armor was checked to verify the condition of the metal, leather and bindings. After the larger items were inspected, Sedic and Jalan looked at mess kits, water skins, tinder boxes and bedding. Anything lacking was noted by writing the item's number from the master list next to the lancer's name on a new sheet of paper.

The inspection continued until Sedic declared, "We're done. That's everything from boots to bowstrings." Captain Jalan and his sergeant returned to the Officer's Workroom and compiled a written list of items Jalan would take to Quartermaster Chander tomorrow morning. Sedic would have the men prepare their horses and all related items for inspection. Once the equine inspection was over, the lancers would take their various items that require repair to the appropriate craftsmen. In the afternoon, Jalan planned to have the men drill at the practice field where he anticipated new recruits would begin to report for duty. With the schedule for tomorrow completed, Sedic headed for his pallet in the barracks and Jalan returned to his room in Yen Manor.

Once he lay down, Jalan's worries drove away any thought of sleep. How could he accomplish everything that needed to be done?

What kind of recruits could he expect? How would he make good on his promise to Captain Erida? Could he even build an effective company of mounted archers or had a terrible mistake been made when Captain Erida put him in charge? He tried to stop thinking about it, but that only made it worse as his mind galloped from one thing to the next like a runaway stallion. That allusion, a runaway horse, embodied every fear Jalan had about being a captain.

He sat up in the darkness of his room and rubbed his face to massage away the anxiety and frustration. Out his window, stars twinkled in the blue-black sky, scattered points of light beyond his reach. They called to him like the duties he must perform. Achievements beyond his grasp, like the sleep that eluded him. And yet, his mind kept reaching. He wished it could be still even as new thoughts rose to vie for his attention.

Jalan decided to ignore them. In his half-awake, half-asleep and completely disheartened state he gave up caring what his thoughts did. He lay down, closed his eyes and let the thoughts run. He felt himself to be something other than the images that streamed by. It was not him. It was water, a river he stopped standing in and, from the bank, watched flow past as he drifted off to sleep.

Δ

The next two days were a mix of sorting out issues with new recruits, chasing down supplies, working with Sedic, meeting with Lieutenant Goss and approving the prices of everything on Jalan's personal supply list. Jacey negotiated with Trader Grom. Jalan's approval was limited to Jacey telling him the prices. He was fine with whatever she agreed to pay. Jacey had taken care of one of his biggest concerns. And, it was pleasant to see her too.

On the morning of the third day he met with Darla who explained that Jalan had a personal account with House Yen. Although Jalan rarely gave it a thought, he was the heir apparent to the throne of Ojmara. His birth parents, whom he had never met, sent him an annual royal stipend.

"I still find it difficult to believe mother never told you. When I asked her why, she said the time was never right." Darla shrugged and said, "Apparently, the time is now right, though I judge it to be long past. I was seven when mother and father started teaching me about the accounts. It seemed so ordinary a thing. I never considered that any of the other children would not know."

Jalan had not known. He wondered what else his mother had not told him. She wanted to protect him, but how did withholding things from him protect him? Unsure what to say, Jalan asked the most obvious question. "How much is the annual stipend?"

"Over three times your pay as a lancer captain. 100 golds. A princely sum, in the most literal sense," said Darla with a little crooked smile.

"I'm 15. Does that mean I have 1500 golds?"

"More actually. There is your family stipend too, 10 golds. A much smaller amount, but more than the average man could hope to earn in a year," said Darla.

"I have 1650 golds?" said Jalan. He never expected to hear himself say such a thing. Was it possible he was dreaming or not understanding what Darla had told him?

Darla reached toward him and said, "I am sorry you did not know about this. At least it is a pleasant surprise, I trust."

Is it? Jalan was not sure and then it struck him that having the money certainly helped in his present situation. He never needed to worry about his uniforms and supplies. He even had extra that he could spend on his men. A new idea occurred to him. "May I have some of the coins?"

"You certainly may. However, you did ask for my help with your finances and I would like to discuss any expenditure you wish to make?"

"Expenditer?" asked Jalan as he tried to repeat the unfamiliar word.

"Any use of the money," said Darla. "Expenditure."

"I need a few coins to offer as prizes for my men. I want to have a competition. I think they will try harder if they can win a prize."

Darla looked puzzled. "What type of competition?"

"Horsemanship and archery."

"Oh. Hmm. I might try something like that myself."

"Really?"

"Well, not for horsemanship and archery, but for other things. It's just a thought." Darla waved a hand as if shooing the idea away and said, "You were asking about coins. Your account balance is something I think you should keep to yourself. However, all 1650 are not kept as coins. It is not even all coins. There are several letters of credit drawn on the royal treasury. In order to convert them to coin we would have to contract with a banker. That could be done if necessary. But, I doubt it will be. How much do you need for the competition?"

Jalan considered what he wanted to do. His company was split into five fists. Each fist would eventually have five members. Offering prizes to the first four fists seemed the way to do it. "I would like 10 silvers for first place, five for second, 50 coppers for third and 10 for forth."

"The man that wins 10 silvers should be extremely pleased," said Darla.

"It will be a fist. They will have to split it five ways. Do you think that will still be enough?"

"A fist?"

Now it was Jalan's turn to explain. That did not happen often when he spoke to Darla. She had never chided him for not knowing something and he decided not to tease her about it either. "A fist," he held up his fisted hand and then opened it, "has five fingers. A fighting fist is a team of five lancers that must work together as one." He closed his fist again to illustrate the five coming together as one.

Darla pursed her lips and nodded. "I see. It makes good sense now that you have explained it to me. Thank you."

Jalan smiled and said, "You are most welcome."

"I do think the prizes are large enough for a competition among your lancers. If it were a tournament attracting men from across the district and beyond it would call for more, but you have made a good choice."

Darla rose from her seat behind her worktable and withdrew a key from a pocket in her skirt. It surprised Jalan that Darla had a concealed pocket. As he watched, Darla went to a small wooden box bound with iron that sat in a back corner of the room. She bent down, inserted the key and opened it. She reached into the box and withdrew coins. A moment later she returned to her worktable with the coins and a small book she also took out of the strongbox. Then Darla closed and locked the strongbox before she moved to another wooden box on a shelf. This box looked much lighter than the first and was not bound in metal. It had no latch and Darla easily opened the lid. She removed a small piece of cloth and closed it. When she returned to the table, Jalan could see Darla had a coin pouch. She counted the various coins from the iron bound strongbox and had Jalan recount them. When they were both satisfied that all the prize coins were there, Darla had Jalan put them in the pouch and Darla wrote something in the small book.

"What are you writing?" said Jalan.

"I'm making an entry in the strongbox ledger. It keeps track of all the money that I put in or take out of the box."

"Why do you do that?"

"Are you serious?" said Darla.

"Yes. I really do want to know."

"I'm sorry. It is another thing I've been doing for so long that I forget others may not understand it. If we keep track of everything House Yen earns and where it comes from plus everything spent and on what it is spent, it helps predict future income and future expenses so that we have a better idea where things are going well and where things need more attention."

"I don't understand."

Darla said, "Give me a moment." She returned the ledger book to the strongbox and then settled back into her chair. "Why do you follow a game trail when you hunt?"

"Because that is where the animals are most likely to be," said Jalan.

"So you look for how the animals travel through an area in order to find them?"

"Sure."

"Money is like that too. It has paths that it tends to travel. There are certain things that we typically must spend our money on, for example, the outposts. Every year there are similar expenses that must be paid for each outpost. If we track the money spent, we have a better idea of how it is used and if we spent it wisely. In short, does the trail lead to the quarry we hoped to catch?

"I can't see how you found a trail, much less where it leads, given the state of those reports," said Jalan.

"What reports?" said Darla with a puzzled look.

"The outpost reports. I spend hours sorting them with Lieutenant Goss. They were completely disorganized. It's hard to imagine how lancer officers ever did work that poorly," said Jalan.

"Wait a moment. You sorted all the outpost reports? That pile of papers Major Erida had?" said Darla.

"Yes. And I hated every minute of it."

"Where are they now?" asked Darla with an uncharacteristic look of excitement.

"I guess Erida still has them," said Jalan.

Darla looked as though she would say something more when the estate's bell began to ring. Instead of tolling the time of day, it rang repeatedly.

Jalan leapt to his feet. "That's the alarm!" he said as he stared at the wall in the general direction of the bell while he tried to imagine what was wrong.

"You had better go," said Darla.

Jalan ran from the room without another word and moved as quickly as he could through the parlor, down the hall and out the front door of the manor. He ran around the Manor House and toward Barracks One where Major Erida expected him to report. Sedic would be rounding up the company. The lancers should all be armored and on horseback by the time Jalan reached them after he received orders from the Major.

CHAPTER XIV

Major Erida was pacing back and forth when Jalan sprinted into the Command Room. Lieutenants Goss and Jalt were standing near Erida's favorite worktable along with a captain Jalan did not recognize. Lieutenants Book and Larkin came through the door close behind Jalan.

Erida turned to them and said, "Close the door." Lieutenant Larkin pulled it shut. "The Southway Company commanded by Lieutenant Burk has been attacked. Burk sent a messenger with a report. He was forced to fall back to Midland. We have to assume any work done to restore Southway has been lost. Burk's report states that the attackers were Polnue and the force was at least twice the size of his. Half his men were lost in the fighting and the retreat to Midland. The number of enemy casualties is unknown, but it is likely to be far lower as Burk was hard pressed to simply maintain an orderly retreat. Questions?"

"Did the enemy attack Midland?" This question came from the captain Jalan did not know.

"There is no report of an attack yet. However, I think it likely there will be one given that the enemy has attacked all the outposts once and then Southway a second time. The outposts seem to be their targets."

"Have we heard anything from Pass or word of enemy activity anywhere else?" said Lieutenant Goss

"This morning's report from Pass said all is well with them. Merchant traffic was almost at a normal level," said Major Erida.

"What are your orders, sir?" said Lieutenant Larkin.

"Given the second attack at Southway, the enemy seems determined to destroy our ability to operate in that area. I think it gives them freedom to move along our southern border and we have to expect that the main force of the enemy is there. Midland is the next outpost to the north of Southway. It is closest to Greenhills River Bridge. That is the easiest place for troops to cross from Polnue into Yen land. The fact that Midland has not been the enemy's primary target makes me think they have found another place to ford the Greenhills, somewhere further south and closer to Southway Outpost. With the enemy south of us, our main concerns have to be Midland Outpost and Yen Estate. I am sure that the king's forces have been alerted. They can watch the way to Lavembra and fortify the Sand Hills. If this is another Chalmar War then there is nothing we can do to help them except locate the enemy's new river crossing and stop more enemy soldiers from reinforcing those already on the march. If we are very fortunate, we can flank the force now on this side of the river and take them from behind while the king's army attacks the van. However, the very first thing we must do is find the enemy. None of this matters if we cannot located their men or where they are crossing the river. Now that you know my mind, here are my orders. Captain Niksus will lead the defense of Yen Estate under my direction." Erida indicated the captain Jalan did not recognize. "Lieutenants Jalt and Larkin," said the Major as he made sure to catch each man's eye, "you two will lead two teams of scouts and find the enemy positions and the ford they are using to cross the river."

"Yes, sir," say Jalt and Larkin almost in unison.

"Captain Yen, you will take your mounted archers and 10 lancers to reinforce Midland. You will transfer the 10 lancers to Lieutenant Burk's command when you arrive. You, Burk and Martus will work with Midland's commander, Lieutenant Caser, to defend the outpost and to take control of the Greenhills River Bridge. We have to prevent the enemy from using the bridge for their own purposes."

"Yes, sir," said Jalan.

"Questions?" Major Erida waited a moment as he scanned the face of each lancer. When no one spoke up he said, "Dismissed."

Lieutenant Goss caught up with Jalan just outside Barracks One. "You'll be escorting a supply train to Midland," said the lieutenant. "If you can tell me how much space your company will require I can have one or two additional wagons added."

"Thank you," said Jalan. Then he considers for a moment. He would like to talk with Sedic, but he knew it was more important to make a fast decision and not keep Goss waiting. "Two wagons will do." He believed that would be enough to move all his and his men's belongings from Yen Estate to Midland. There should be room in the Midland barracks, but the company will be out in the field too and there is no way to know if anything can be brought from the estate later.

"Two it is," said Goss as he made a notation on one page in a bound set of papers. "Stop by here after morning bell and I will have a copy of your orders and a manifest for the supplies ready for you."

"Yes, lieutenant."

"I'm sorry there aren't more lancers to send with you. You'll have 20 wagons to watch over."

"Why so many?" said Jalan. He expected four or five, something similar to what had gone with the other captains.

"Major Erida is worried about opportunities to safely transport supplies. We're sending double the usual shipment. There are merchants and craftsmen making the trip as well. They have their own wagons. Along with the two for your company that makes 20. The merchants have five of their own guards. I suppose that's something if you run into trouble."

Jalan could tell that Lieutenant Goss was not convinced the guards would be any real help. Despite men like Sedic, who was the son of a merchant and trained as a guard before joining the lancers at 17, the reputation of most merchant guards was little better than the brigands they were supposed to protect against. "We are servants of the king," said Jalan. The words felt like the right response to him though he could not say why.

Lieutenant Goss's eyes grew wide. "Who taught you that?" he asked.

"Major Erida said it to Master Enmar the day he arrived."

Goss looked thoughtful and said, "Ah, yes. I remember now." His voice and demeanor took on a serious note of warning as he then said, "A lancer says that when accepting a duty that could mean his death."

"Then why did the major say it to Master Enmar?"

The lieutenant shrugged but his eyes dart around as if checking their surroundings. Then he leaned in and spoke in a low voice, "You'd have to ask Erida, but I don't think that would be wise. He's not comfortable with Enmar. Doesn't seem to trust him. There's a story there. It's just none of our business."

Jalan nodded. If either man ever wanted him to know, they would tell him. "I'll see you in the morning," he said. Jalan left to find Sedic and share the company's assignment with him.

Δ

Sedic was not surprised when Jalan shared the company's orders with him. It turned out that the rumor of another attack on Southway had reached every corner of Yen Estate. The company was already mustered. Jalan and Sedic ordered the lancers to begin packing. Jalan walks out of the barracks room used by his company on his way to the manor house where he would pack his gear. His brother Tomac was just entering the building through the main door.

"Master Enmar said you might need some help packing," said Tomac. "He also mentioned that you had probably not seen to your horses."

"Horses!" said Jalan with a rising sense of panic and a sick feeling in the pit of his stomach. "I've been so busy I completely forgot. This is terrible."

"Some lancer captain you are," said Tomac as he laughed so hard he barely finished speaking.

Tomac's mirth drove a spike of failure deep into Jalan. He fought against the anxieties that roiled within him, the worries and duties that seemed beyond his ability. A rage welled up and engulfed them. It boiled forth as he yelled, "It is not funny!"

Tomac's eyes popped open wide. He staggered back and doubled over holding his stomach.

Jalan felt tired, as if he had spent the last few hours in hard training. A new panic rose in him. It had nothing to do with horses or any ordinary mistake. His mind brought forth the image of a hallway where Vee, her face ashen, leaned against a wall and Tomac knelt down on one knee. *No, not that.* "Tomac? Are you all right?" Jalan reached out his hand to help steady his brother.

Tomac knocked it away. "You didn't have to hit me," he said, hurt and anger intertwined with his words.

"I didn't mean to," said Jalan before Tomac's words registered.

Tomac eased himself up straight. "I didn't even see you swing. Did you kick me or something?"

"No. No I didn't kick you." Jalan tried to push his panic away and think. The fog of sudden fatigue hindered him. "I got upset when you laughed."

Some of the anger faded from Tomac's eyes. "I don't even know why I laughed. You had that look on your face. It seemed funny at first, but not anymore. Especially not after you hit me."

"I'm sorry. I don't even know what happened. I just did it."

Tomac looked almost back to normal. He said, "Master Enmar can deliver your horses next time. I'd like to see what happens if you try to hit him."

The notion of anything close to this happening with Master Enmar almost started Jalan panicking again until he realized Tomac said something about delivering horses. "What horses?"

"The horses I just brought you. Master Enmar knew you would be too busy so he found horses for you, a palfrey and a couple of fine chargers."

"Three horses? I worked so hard trying to make certain each of my men have two. I forgot to even find one for myself."

"And you took it out on me," said Tomac.

"I really am sorry," said Jalan. *More sorry that I can say.*

"Not as sorry as you will be next time we spar."

Tomac's sounded serious but his smile showed he had nearly forgiven Jalan. He would let Tomac past his guard once or twice the next time they sparred, a small price to pay for accidentally using the Ability on him a second time. Jalan breathed a sigh of relief in gratitude that no one else saw what happened and that Tomac thought Jalan punched him.

"Thank you," said Jalan not certain if he meant his deliverance from anyone discovering his curse or his elation at having horses. Jalan could feel the big smile on his face. *I have the best brother.* "Let's go see the horses," he said.

They walked to the rope corral erected to one side of Barracks Three. There were plans to build corrals near each of the barracks, but the lancers made due with the simpler temporary structures. Tomac pointed out Jalan's three horses among the couple of dozen in the corral.

"That grey one is Stone. The black with the white flecks over there is Axe and the smaller fellow here," said Tomac as he pointed at a brown and white horse standing near them, "is Bottle."

Captain Erida, a skilled horseman himself, had insisted Jalan learn not only to ride but to tend to the needs of his mounts. A lancer, especially one of Erida's officers, was expected to know horses and how to care for them. Master Enmar had chosen very well. Jalan, amazed at his good fortune, did not know what to say.

"So did you need help packing or are the horses enough?" said Tomac?

"You'd rather go back and train some more?" said Jalan.

"No. I'd rather see if Mistress Dahlia left anything lying around. Master Enmar's not expecting me anyway. He knows I have my own gear to tend to," said Tomac.

Jalan smiled. A trip to the kitchens sounded good and it was on the way to his sleeping chamber and equipment. His thoughts of food and packing were interrupted when Sedic walked around the corner of the barracks and waved to call him over.

"Captain, the men have some questions and you and I need to talk, sir," said Sedic as Jalan and Tomac drew near.

"Guess you'll have to give your respects to Mistress Dahlia without me," said Jalan to Tomac.

Tomac shrugged and said, "I'll see you later then." He turned and jogged away in the direction of the manor house.

"And, thank Master Enmar too!" called Jalan after him.

"I will!" shouted Tomac over his shoulder.

Jalan stole one more look at his horses mixed in among the others in the corral. He was part of something bigger and he had better get on with it. He still had to go to the manor house and pack his own gear. But, he felt ready to face whatever the next challenge might be. "Let's go," he said to Sedic.

Δ

Night settled over the estate when Jalan made his way into the Winter Kitchen where he found a taper that he lit from the embers of the oven fire. Using its light he climbed the servants' stairs. With a sense of relief, he made his way through the little storage room and out into the hallway without having to stop and wait for his vision to adjust to the darkness. When he reached his room, Jalan lit the new oil lamp he relied upon due to the late hours he had been keeping. It filled his room with a warm glow and he blew out the taper.

Like his men, he had checked his own armor and dealt with a few minor issues. He would be wearing it in the morning which eliminated a need to figure out how to transport it. His saber hung at his hip. He unstrapped the swordbelt and hung it from the tree stand that held his armor. The weight of it reminded him of when he started training and could not even lift a real blade. In the corner behind the base of the tree stand leaned a stick with a worn rouge edge. Not his first training sword, that one had broken long ago. But it was one he had used and decided to keep, although he could not explain why.

He looked around his chamber. His new field chest sat against the wall just inside the door. It stopped the door form fully opening but there was no other place for it in the small room. His dresser with the pitcher and wash basin stood beside the field chest, next to a little table where the oil lamp stood with his chamber pot tucked beneath it. His bed rested in its corner. The length of the bed ran along the wall below the single window. A wooden storage chest sat on the floor at the foot of the bed. Its flat top was hinged and easy to open, although Jalan rarely opened it.

Jalan decided to start with the storage chest. An inventory of his boyhood treasures would not take long, but if he left for an extended time he felt he should have a look in case it contained something he wanted to take with him. He carefully removed what he found, feathers he had collected from around the grounds, interestingly shaped or colored stones and some roughly animal shaped chunks of wood he had carved as part of learning to handle and care for knives. He recalled that one of the stones was the first rock he ever threw to kill a bird, but he no longer knew which one. Further searching brought out woven leather cords and bits of line tied with various knots Jalan had learned.

Finished clearing the chest of its obvious contents, Jalan paused. For a time, he simply looked into the empty cavity and debated his next step. *Should I open the hidden compartment?* Perhaps, after so long, he would not remember how. But his traitorous fingers sill knew the way of it. He removed the false bottom before he could stop himself. There, despite his best efforts to forget them, lay the two things he least wanted. He reached in and picked up the letter. Its wax seal was cracked but still in place. Jalan had seen one other seal like it. He turned it over. In a graceful script was written one word, Jalan. He sat the unopened letter aside. Next came the final item in the chest, a necklace. It was a loop of intricately woven fine black strings, an orange stone in a silver setting hung on it.

After Jalan had finally admitted to Lady Shara that he knew who his birth parents were, she showed him the false bottom and the hidden compartment. She said that the letter and necklace were part of his heritage. He remembered the word and that when she said it he did not know what heritage meant.

"These are gifts from your parents," said Lady Shara.

"I don't want them," said Jalan flatly.

"I understand, but these things came with you when you were brought to us. No matter how we feel about them today, you may want them, or even need them later."

She placed the letter and the necklace back into their hiding place and set the false bottom over them. "Forget about them if you like. You never have to look at them again. Just let them stay here in their secret place."

At first Jalan could not forget them. He would remove the false bottom of the chest and think that maybe this time they would be gone. They never were. Eventually, as his training continued and a few years pasted he did nearly forget. He had long ago stopped checking on the letter and necklace. He had covered them with the mementos of his life at Yen Manor. But now he had opened the compartment again and they were still there.

HIDDEN ABILITY

He took the necklace and slipped it over his head and under his tunic. He lifted the letter and for a moment he nearly touched it to the flame of the lamp. Then he clenched his jaw, turned to his new field chest and laid the letter in it. He returned everything else to the storage chest. When he came back, it would all be there. He closed the lid and turned his back upon his childhood as he moved about the room collecting garments and weapons to place on top the letter.

Δ

By midmorning the caravan of 20 wagons, 30 lancers, various merchants, crafters, teamsters, five merchant guards and 50 additional horses moved loosely west in a line strung out over half a mile of road. Jalan had lancers in the lead and at the tail of the column. Men from his company drove eight of the wagons. It was cool when they left Yen Estate. The day turned warmer, almost hot, as the sun reached toward its zenith. The road ran mostly through farmland with an occasional stand of trees that provided brief periods of shade.

Jalan rode Axe. The long-necked wide-chested horse quickly responded to cues. Jalan eased back on the more forceful directions he normally gave other mounts. He groomed and saddled the horse that morning in order to spend what time he could bonding. But the ride provided the real opportunity for horse and rider to learn about each other. Based on Sedic's suggestion, Jalan ordered all the lancers to wear full armor. They could meet their unknown enemy at any time. It would be too late to don armor then.

Jalan had not worn his plate armor regularly. The added encumbrance took some getting used to. Practice leathers were stiff heavy and hot. His steel plate was all that and even heavier. Of course he had drilled in it, all lancers did. But none of them wore armor regularly. Sedic pointed out the men needed time to grow accustomed to it.

Metal covered almost every part of Jalan's body. A cuirass over his chest and a backplate across his back added the greatest weight to the burden he carried. Much of the weight rested on his hips where it slowly bored into him as he rode despite the quilted padded gambeson jacket beneath the armor. With the padded hood topped

155

by the open faced helmet on his head, his armor felt like his own personal oven as the day warmed.

Axe seemed less bothered by the additional weight. The warhorse had not only an armored Jalan, but his own padded barding to carry and still he walked or trotted, tail held high, with no sign of weariness.

Moving up and down the line of wagons, Jalan wished he could see everything at once. The terrain moved slowly past and the wind blew out of the northeast. It cut across the road and carried the dust away from the caravan making the journey both cooler and more pleasant. As Jalan watched the dust fly he noticed a mounted lancer on a hilltop to the south. The lancer rode down the back side of the hill. Jalan wondered if the scout had seen anything.

"Captain," called out Sergeant Sedic as he rode down the side of the road toward Jalan. "The scouts are back and ready to report."

"Coming," called Jalan as he turned Axe toward the front of the procession and with little more than a thought had him trotting forward.

Sedic wheeled his mount and led the way past several wagons to where the four scouts rode slowly keeping pace just ahead of the first wagon in line and behind the lead lancers.

"Scouts, report!" said the sergeant just as Jalan moved up beside them.

Miltrip responded, "Sergeant, we ranged out at least a half league on either side of the road. The farm lanes and activity along them looked normal. No sign of outsiders or hostile forces. No gathering of men of any sort."

"Did you see any other lancers? I noticed a rider to our south a few minutes ago." said Jalan.

Another scout spoke up, a new recruit Jalan thought was named Hamel, "I saw a lancer I thought was Glen south of the road, but by the time I made my way to where I caught a glimpse of him he had moved on."

"Where abouts?" said another scout.

"Near that copse of trees a bit north of Kenta. The one with the creek that feeds into Sweetwater."

"I wasn't over that way," replied the scout that must have been Glen. "Didn't leave the road until I'd fallen back a good quarter league and then I swept close on our back trail. Never went far enough south or west to see those woods."

Major Erida had spent considerable time teaching Jalan tactics based on battles from the Chalmar Wars. Master Enmar had continued instructing him, but with a more general set of principles. Ideas from both drifted through his thoughts. *War is about deception.* What did the enemy want him to believe? The lone lancer roaming through the hills south of the road bothered Jalan. Where was he based? It was possible one of his own lancers had wandered off, but no one had reported that and only the scouts had duty out of sight of the wagons.

"I want to find that lancer. Something does not add up. We should be the only lancers in this area. If he is one of our men, then why has he not announced himself?" said Jalan.

"The afternoon scouts are ready for their orders. We could have them search," said Sedic.

"Let's send two additional men south to look for this mystery lancer," said Jalan.

"Miltrip, tell Reest to pick two more men from the ten new lancers assigned to us. He's to pair them with two of his other men and have the pairs scout along the south side of the road. Their priority is to find the lancer both Ninus and Captain Jalan saw and bring the man back to the caravan to answer a few questions."

"Aye, sergeant," said Miltrip before riding over to Reest's group that had formed up a short distance away.

"Sergeant, this ground is fairly open and we have good visibility, but I can't help feeling exposed. The wagons are strung out along the road further than I like. Is there a way to have them move in a tighter procession?"

"I know of a way, captain," volunteered Glen.

"Let's hear it," said Jalan.

"It's an old way to have a group move as fast as possible. It also helps keep down gaps in a line. You put the slowest up front. No one is slower than the slowest wagon so no one falls behind. And everyone can maintain the slowest pace so nobody falls farther behind the wagon ahead of them."

Jalan pursed his lips in thought. "What do you think, sergeant?"

Sergeant Sedic shrugged as he shifted in his saddle. "Never going to move faster than the slowest wagon anyway. Not sure what we get by having it in front, but it can't slow us down any. We could give it a try."

"Let's look for the slowest wagon," said Jalan to Sedic.

They rode the length of the caravan and spotted three different wagons that looked slower than all the rest.

"What do we do now? I don't know which ones slowest," said Jalan.

"If we move 'em all to the front, one is bound to be the slowest," said Sedic.

Jalan called out the order to halt. Sedic echoed him and it was passed up and down the line. Once the caravan stopped, Jalan rode to the first of the three slowest wagons while Sedic trotted his mount to the second of the three.

"Good day," said Jalan as he rode near the driver seated on the slow wagon.

"Is there a problem?" said the driver from beneath the wide brimmed felt hat he wore.

"I need you to drive your wagon to the head of the line," said Jalan.

"I'd rather not, uh, lieutenant," said the man with a frown on his creased sun-darkened face.

"Captain, Captain Jalan Yen." He pointed to the white gorget that protruded up from beneath his cuirass. The metal ring protected his neck and the enameled color indicated his commission as a captain. "What would be the problem with moving up?"

"I like it here. Up front there's always a hue and cry to pick up the pace. I got no need to hurry."

"We don't expect you to go faster."

"Well then, I can just stay right here and go at my one pace as I have been," the driver said in a self-evident manner.

"No, you don't understand. We need you, moving at your own pace, at the head of the line," said Jalan trying not to sound annoyed.

"But, I'd slow down the entire line," said the man evidently certain Jalan had missed this critical point. "Nothing against you young captain, but is there someone a little older I can speak to about this?"

Jalan shouted, "Lieutenant Yen to the captain!"

He heard the shout repeated up and down the caravan as he sat on Axe and smiled politely. Less than a minute later, Tomac came at a gallop and reined up next to Jalan.

"Captain?" said Tomac.

"May I ask your name, driver?" said Jalan.

"Rostin, captain," said the driver as he rose a little straighter on his seat.

"Rostin, this is Lieutenant Tomac Yen, my brother. He is a little older than I, just as you requested. You have two minutes to discuss moving your wagon with him. After that, if you have not proceeded to your new place at the head of the line, I am ordering him to commandeer your wagon and have a lancer drive it to the front for you. Either way, in two minutes, this wagon will take up its new place. Have a pleasant conversation with my older brother."

Jalan rode to the next slow wagon in the fervent hope that Tomac could convince Rostin to move up before time ran out. Ultimately, Rostin did and so did the two others after similar discussions that managed not to end with threats to commandeer their wagons. Twenty minutes and one more halt that moved the true slowest wagon to the head of the line left the caravan stretched out only a quarter of a mile from end to end. Glen, it appeared, had been right.

"Something on your mind, captain?" said Sedic as they rode together near the head of the line.

"No," said Jalan and then he thought better off it. He needed to talk to someone even if it happened to be that Sedic was part of the problem. "Well, yes. I requested three wagons change position and they baulked. What happens if real trouble starts?"

"Don't let it bother you, captain," Sedic told Jalan.

"I shouldn't be bothered when they are quicker to listen to my sergeant than to me?" Jalan said.

"'Tis the price of success at a young age, sir," said Sedic with a wry smile.

Jalan certainly felt young even if he did not feel particularly successful.

CHAPTER XV

There were times an empty road stretched before them and other times when a farmer's cart or wagon pulled to the side to let the caravan pass. The people waiting watched the procession of lancers and merchants pass by them and often smiled or waved when they saw Jalan and his men. But as the day wore away toward evening, their fellow travelers tended to be on foot rather than in a wagon or on horseback. They kept their eyes lowered and did not meet Jalan's gaze. Several of them carried bundles and walked with children. Others were elderly and had difficulty walking at all. Jalan got a bad feeling about the condition of the people the caravan passed.

Sergeant Sedic rode up beside him and said, "Sir, we're encountering a number of refugees along the road. Perhaps you would like to have us stop for the night while enough daylight remains to select a good spot? It would also give us time to erect some temporary defenses."

Now it made a sad kind of sense to Jalan. The people carrying bundles, pushing handcarts, walking along with children or elderly were fleeing something. "What has happened to these people?" he said.

"I can't say exactly, but fighting has pushed them out of their homes and off their lands. The scouts will return soon and may know more. Some of the men are from this area and have had a little luck getting answers from the people along the roadside. But, mostly they are scared and do not wish to talk to us."

"What story do they tell?"

"They say hamlets and farms to the south have been burned. People have been killed. They are fleeing the fighting, hoping to save their lives and whatever they can carry."

"Where are they going?" said Jalan.

"Anywhere they can, sir." Sedic had a look on his face Jalan knew well. It was the same look Sedic gave him the first time he showed Jalan how to throw a knife. How to hold the blade, how to stand, how to whip his arm forward and follow through. That look said, "This is how it's done. Until you understand this, there is nothing more I can teach you."

Jalan looked about for a moment. Seeing a rise that plateaued in a patch of open ground, he pointed toward it and said, "What do you think of that rise? It's on the north side of the road and should give us a good view of it."

"Good choice, captain."

"Give the order then, sergeant."

Sergeant Sedic called out, "Wagons halt!" The command echoed along the line of vehicles. They came to a stop more or less at the same time as those who walked and rode along side, in front and behind. The extra mounts on stringers tied to wagons pulled at their leads. A few dug at the dirt of the road with their hooves.

Sedic and Jalan rode to the front of the caravan and directed two of the leading lancers to scout the ground between the road and the plateau to determine the best route for the heavy wagons. As those two moved off, the first rider of the afternoon scouts returned.

"Report!" ordered Sedic as Palst, one of the new recruits, rode up the road toward Sedic and Jalan.

"Sergeant, captain," said Palst as he drew near, "I traveled west along the road and ranged north of it as ordered. I saw signs of people and horses heading north. Not large groups, maybe six to a dozen together at most. There were also ruts left by the passage of wagons."

"How many wagons, lancer?" said Sedic.

"Can't say for certain. They traveled in a line. Definitely more than one, but not likely to be more than half a dozen."

"How long ago would you say they passed by?"

"The tracks were made in damp ground. There hasn't been any rain as we've traveled along this last day and I've seen none ahead of us. I would have to guess at least two days if not more," said Palst.

"How far ahead are these wagon tracks?" said Jalan.

"Maybe an hour's easy ride, captain."

"What are you thinking, captain?" said Sedic.

"Not sure," said Jalan.

"The other scouts should report soon. Perhaps we'll learn more then," said Sedic.

Tomac rode up, "Halting for the night, captain?"

Jalan nodded, "Let's set up camp. Then we'll call a meeting of the fist leaders."

"Yes, sir", said Tomac.

The only other scouts to see anything, Lancers Reest and Brax, spotted a lancer during their southern sweep of the road. They pursued him and although he got away, the two scouts found a campsite where at least five men had stayed. Banked coals in the fire pit, a few items left scattered around and fresh horse manure indicated the site had been abandoned recently and quickly. The camp had been so active that the two lancers could not determine in which direction the occupants had fled. When further questioned, the scouts reported that more men might have been based there within the last week. They found signs of a picket line and depressions made by wagon wheels. Because few other tracks crisscrossed the wheel marks, Reest felt strongly that the wagons only left in the last couple of days.

The sun dropped level with the horizon by the time the caravan set up camp on the raised plateau. Everyone shaped spikes from large sticks, small branches and saplings and planted them in the ground at an angle to form a bristling barrier around much of the camp's perimeter.

"It seems like a lot of work for one night," said Tomac.

"Refugees on the road, fresh signs of enemy riders and wagons nearby, if I have to dig, I'd rather plant spikes than lancers," said Sedic.

"I'd have been satisfied with the watch fires and sentries, sergeant. But I can't argue your point," said Tomac.

Jalan studied the defensive ring. Even hastily constructed, it should stop a cavalry charge. Night's full darkness would have the same effect, but enough light remained yet to support an attack, plus the opportunity morning would bring. He stifled a yawn and said to Sedic, "Send the fist leaders to my tent. We need to discuss our plans for tomorrow."

"Sir," said Sedic as an acknowledgment and he moved off toward the double row of the lancers' canvas tents.

"Tell them they can finish eating first," called Jalan as an afterthought. Now that the camp seemed settled he felt his own fatigue and hunger push past his other worries.

"Let's eat," he said to Tomac.

"Best decision you've made all day, captain," said Tomac.

They went to the cook fires and got hot bowls of stew and mugs of watered ale. Jalan led the way back to his command tent.

Δ

Jalan stepped through the open flap of the command tent, *his* command tent. The disbelief that he should be in command eight days after turning 15 hounded his every decision. All right, he was a prince. But, he could hardly believe that either. In his heart, he would always be the son of Hallis and Shara Yen. Once his fist leaders arrived, they would make a plan. So far Jalan's only plan was do what seemed most obvious and trust to Providence that it all worked out. Surely Sedic knew to warn him if he proposed anything too foolish. He would have slumped into his folding chair under the weight of everyone's expectations if Tomac had not been there to witness it.

Tomac did slump. The luxury of being only a lieutenant, Jalan supposed. They sat across from each other at a small table. Above it hung a lit oil lamp. By the light of the lamp, he watched Tomac take a large spoonful of hot stew, blow vigorously on it and put it in his mouth. Tomac's eyes widened, he grabbed up his mug and took a drink. He swallowed the barely chewed mixture of hot stew and warm ale and made a sour face.

Jalan stopped blowing on his own spoonful and said, "Surely the stew is not that bad."

"What's this?" said Tomac as he held up his mug.

"Watered ale," said Jalan. He raised his own mug and took a sniff. "It does have a certain..."

"Odor," said Tomac.

"Just so," said Jalan as he ate his first spoonful of stew. It was still quite warm and he too took a sip of ale to help cool his mouth.

"I see you like it as well as I do," said Tomac.

Jalan shrugged. Hungry and tired he would have taken almost anything and the stew, at least, was not bad. He kept blowing on spoonfuls and wolfing them down with ale until his bowl was empty. Tomac made no further comments as he did the same.

Jalan drained the last of his ale from the mug as Sergeant Sedic stepped through the opening created by the tied back tent flap.

"I hope you're not making that face because of me, sir," said Sedic.

"No, nothing like that. It's the ale. Tastes bitter," said Jalan.

"Like the life of a lancer they say," commented Sedic.

Tomac barked a laugh.

"If the ale's the worst of it then I am much relieved," said Jalan.

"Merely the sauce we are cooked in, captain," said Sedic.

"And we won't know the worst until the cook lights the fire, captain," said Dost as he entered the tent with his head bent low to clear the canvas ceiling.

Sedic grinned.

"We'd always had water on patrol. Why the watered ale now?" said Tomac.

"They say the alcohol keeps the water good longer. But, some say it's the other way round," said Sedic.

Serks, Harna, Miltrip and Reest filed in. The press of bodies urged Jalan to stand, fold up his chair and set it on top his field chest which sat against a canvas wall. Tomac passed his chair over and Jalan placed it on top his own.

"Miltrip, Dost, sorry about the headroom," said Jalan.

"Think nothing of it, captain. We crawl in and out of our tents," said Miltrip.

"We'd never get all of us in one either," said Tomac.

"Though we don't have to avoid a hanging oil lamp either," said Dost.

Not excited to make the crowding worse, but with no other recourse, Jalan swallowed and said, "Gather around the table as best you can." He concentrated on picking up the map case that lay on the edge of the small table and spreading the map out. He used four stones he found to weigh down the corners and keep the map flat.

Looking up he asked, "Does anyone know where we are?"

The men chuckled and Jalan smiled before he pointed to a spot on the map and said, "All right, as you all know, we are here. Reest, can you show us where the camp you and Brax found is?"

Reest squeezed himself closer to the table with apologies to Harna and Miltrip. He studied the map for a moment and then touched a spot saying, "About here, captain."

Jalan nodded and then indicated a new spot on the map before saying, "Palst said the wagon tracks he found are about here." He looked around and asked, "Anyone have some string or cord?"

Sedic reached two fingers into a small pouch hung from his belt and fished out a bowstring. He handed it to Jalan.

"Thanks, Sedic. This should do." Jalan stretched out a section of the bowstring and then laid it across the location of the discovered campsite and the wagon tracks. The bowstring formed a line that ran generally from the southeast edge of the map to the northwest edge. Along the line's northern run, it almost touched Pass Outpost. Jalan got a queasy feeling in the pit of his stomach that he could not blame on the ale. The string ran near nothing else noteworthy. But the path made no sense. Why drive heavy wagons across farm fields and rough country instead of using the road? According to the map, the men and wagons that appeared to be headed toward Pass Outpost did not come from anywhere within Yen land. Midland and Southway outposts sat too far west, more directly south of Pass. And from the last report, Southway no longer exited. Everyone left was at Midland. They would not be traveling across country to Pass.

"I think we've found the enemy," said Miltrip.

Jalan felt excited, satisfied and worried. They had found something the enemy tried to hide. Now that they knew, what should they do about it? He let the bowstring go slack and left it lying across the map. His first instinct was to mount up and give chase. There was so much more to take care of than a hunt for those wagons, but the wagons might be the most important thing, more important than the caravan. The lancers crowding around him reminded Jalan that he had help. "Does anyone have a suggestion?"

"I want to go after them," said Serks. "Look at the refugees along the road. They're out there causing trouble and we need to stop them."

A couple of the other men made sounds of agreement.

"What about our orders?" said Sedic. "We're to go to Midland. We can't abandon the caravan, especially if the enemy is active in this area."

"We could send scouts to locate the wagons," suggested Miltrip.

"What will the scouts do when they find them?" said Dost.

"Hmm. I see what you mean. By the time they get word back to us or Midland Outpost it could be too late," said Miltrip.

"Then we should send enough men to engage the enemy when we find them," said Serks.

"What do you think, captain?" said Sedic

"Serks is right. We need to send enough lancers to make a fight of it if we find those wagons. But, Sedic is right too. We can't abandon the caravan. The resupply wagons and merchants need to make it safely to Midland. Here are my thoughts. With luck, we take the enemy from behind. If we can capture those wagons we'll gain useful vehicles and whatever they contain. If we cannot capture them then we can destroy them. Either way, the wagons are traveling across country and even with a couple of days head start we have a chance to catch them with a day's hard riding."

Anticipation coursed through the room. Jalan wished to be tested in battle and knew Tomac felt the same. And even though the rest were more experienced, they had never faced more than bandits. These could be Polnue troops from Ankena, the kingdom's old enemy. House Yen lancers knew they represented the legacy of Lord Hallis Yen, the last great general of the kingdom, the man credited with having led Ojmara to victory over Ankena in the last Chalmar War.

"Let me lead the chase, sir. I'll find those wagons," said Reest.

All the men except Sedic immediately made the same request, each tried to speak over the other. Jalan held up a hand for silence and shouted, "Hold!" He tried to make his voice sound like Major Erida because everybody listened to him. Silence fell, even Tomac held his tongue. Before anyone else interrupted Jalan said, in the calmest most self-assured voice he could manage, "Thank you for your ideas. I will consider your requests. Dismissed." He met the eye of each man one by one, challenging them to say anything more.

Harna and Reest both look angry, but neither spoke. Miltrip and Dost acted a little embarrassed. Serks's face gave nothing away. Dost, head still bent to avoid the ceiling, shrugged before he turned to leave. Sedic simply nodded and moved to leave along with everyone else.

"Sergeant, Lieutenant," said Jalan

"Sir?" said Tomac.

"Yes, sir?" said Sedic as he paused and half turned back to look at Jalan.

"Stay for a moment."

"Yes, sir." Sedic turned fully back around and waited. Tomac nodded, still standing where he had been during the entire meeting.

Jalan grasped his hands behind his back and tried to let some of the tension flow out of him. "Who do you think should lead the hunt for the wagons?"

"You, captain," said Sedic without hesitation.

Tomac clenched his jaw and nodded in agreement. "I won't lie. I wanted it to be me, but Sedic's right."

"Why?"

"You're the captain."

At the moment, nothing seemed worse to Jalan than being the captain. No matter what he did, someone would be unhappy about it. He decided to give the biggest disappointment to the person he trusted most.

"Brother..." he said.

"Stop right there," Tomac said as he held up a hand to forestall Jalan. "You never call me that unless it's something bad. I'm not going on the hunt, am I?" He gave Jalan a skeptical look that bordered on angry.

Jalan shook his head and said, "No. I need the person I trust most to see that the caravan makes it to Midland."

"Well, since you put it that way, I still hate it," said Tomac.

"I could order you to go."

"Do it then," said Tomac, his chin jutting out and his voice full of defiance.

"Lieutenant Tomac, you are ordered to take charge of the caravan and see it safely to Midland Output."

"Aye, captain," said Tomac. He nodded in angry acknowledgment and marched out of the tent.

Sedic stood at attention during the entire exchange. Jalan met his expectant gaze and said, "Sedic, keep him out of trouble."

"Aye, captain," said Sedic without the rancor of Tomac's response. He then nodded and left as well.

Δ

Ultimately, Jalan called all the fist leaders back to his tent. He had them draw straws because he had no reason to prefer one over another. Serks, Harna and Reest pulled long straws. They and their three fists won a place in the hunt. Jalan would lead all 15 men. Miltrip and one lancer from his fist were given the task to deliver a report from Jalan to Lieutenant Caser, the commander of Midland Outpost. Miltrip left immediately to travel through the night and reach Midland as soon as he could. The hunters would leave at dawn. They needed light to be sure they did not miss anything important as they tracked the wagons.

Jalan woke at the end of the first night watch.

"End of watch. All secure," called four voices in loose unison.

"Start of watch. All secure," responded the relief watchers.

He woke again at second watch and forced himself to remain on his cot. Drawing long slow breaths, Jalan practiced letting his body relax. Sleep settled over him once more. Jalan rose when third watch, the last of the night, began. The fire ring closest to his tent still held hot coals from last night's banked fire. He knelt at the uneven circle of stones and earth which surrounded the shallow pit, and blew on the coals until they glowed hot enough to light a taper. The candle burned brightly. Jalan used it to light the small lantern that hung from the central roof poll of his tent and blew the taper out. By lantern light, Jalan donned his armor. Sergeant Sedic arrived to help Jalan check over his armor, ensuring everything was in place and fastened properly. Jalan did the same for the sergeant.

In the predawn gloom, the white flecks on Axe's black coat stood out as Jalan walked to the picket line. Axe performed well yesterday. Each lancer would take two horses on the hunt. Stone looked magnificent. Jalan looked forward to riding him. He groomed and saddled Stone, taking care not to irritate the large barrel chested warhorse. There were enough things to worry about without getting bitten or kicked by his mount.

He patted Axe and said, "You'll get your turn today too." He fastened a long lead to Axe's halter and tied the other end to a ring affixed to the back of Stone's saddle. The other lancers formed up on the road. Each of them had their spare horse on a lead as well.

When the hunters were ready, Palst led as they chased their long shadows down the road, the newly risen sun at their backs. The riders slowed their horses to a walk and continued to follow Palst when he turned north off the road and crossed open ground. When Palst halted, Jalan called the riders to a halt as well and dismounted to examine the tracks. Palst pointed out the clear signs of wagon ruts, horses' hooves and booted feet.

Jalan had contemplated what to do next during the ride. He hesitated only as long as it took to wish Sedic was within earshot instead of back with the caravan. This order would be the first he gave without his trusted sergeant present to support him.

"Serks!" called Jalan as he stood from examining the tracks.

"Sir!" said Serks from horseback a few yards away.

"You and Palst scout ahead along the most likely course the wagons took. Once we verify their direction of travel, we'll ride fast to gain on them. When it is time to switch mounts, we'll scout again to make sure we're still on the trail."

Jalan knew that his men could easily cover in one morning the same distance the wagons traveled in a day. He had to be careful and certain the hunters stayed on the trail. Riding hard in the wrong direction would be a foolish waste of effort. He still did not know what to expect when they found the wagons. Hopefully, an opportunity would present itself.

"Sir, what will we do when we find the wagons?" said Reest.

Jalan answered the way he thought Major Erida would. "If they are friends we'll help them. If they are enemies, hurt them." He shrugged and added, "We'll figure out how when we find them."

He addressed all the lancers in a louder voice, "We need information. If we run afoul of anyone, capture them if you can or kill them if you must. We can't have anyone escape and spread the alarm."

The lancers nodded in acknowledgment of the orders. Harna and Reest both said, "Yes, sir."

The full impact of what he said only hit Jalan after the words left his mouth. He had ordered men to kill and he had never even drawn an enemy's blood. These were not pells or archery targets they hunted. It further bothered Jalan that he and his men had to sneak through Yen territory like criminals avoiding capture. The wagons they followed took the least populated route they could find. They hid and Jalan wanted to know why. In order to find out, he must hide too. Again, he missed Sedic's reassuring agreement or correcting suggestion.

Jalan led the lancers forward in the same direction taken by his two scouts. The hunters moved at a walk when they must and a trot when the terrain allowed. Once Serks and Palst returned near midmorning, the direction of the chase was set and the mounted men moved faster by taking their horses to a gallop over open ground. Two lancers acted as outriders and scouted to the left and right of the hunters in order to minimize the chance of riding past signs of their quarry or being surprised by an enemy.

Near midday, they arrived at a stream that ran past a stand of brush and trees. Jalan twisted in the saddle to pull a strip of dried meat from his saddlebag. Stone took the opportunity to walk under a low branch that might have unseated the young captain had he not noticed in time and bent low against the horse's back. Jalan took it as a sign to let Stone graze and drink from the stream. They had traveled since first light and rarely been within sight of a hamlet or cottage. Jalan wondered if the wagon drivers knew the land well enough to avoid all habitation or if they had help from a guide more familiar with the area.

The men ate their dried meat, dried fruit and hard bread rations as horses were watered and grazed. The sun shown down from overhead. Jalan moved his saddle to Axe and put Stone on a lead. His men switched mounts as well and refreshed, they continued the hunt.

Jalan concentrated on his riding, the reports from the scouts and the needs of his men in order to keep his mind off wondering how far ahead the wagons truly were. With three days of travel they could have reached Pass Outpost. Should he have taken the road and ridden hard to arrive their first? What if that wasn't where the wagons went and he didn't follow them? How would he ever know who he hunted? But, if Pass were under attack, could Jalan have warned them? His jaw clenched tight again. If this was being in command, Jalan was not certain he was ready for it.

"Captain! Captain!" cried a scout galloping toward him.

Jalan shook himself. His pulse quickened and his heart pounded. "Report!" he yelled.

"We've spotted a wagon!"

CHAPTER XVI

Lady Darla and her sister, Lady Guri, sat in the parlor of Yen Manor laughing and reminiscing with their mother, Lady Shara.

"I am so glad that Master Enmar offered to give Juin a tour of the grounds. He would never say it, but I know he is feeling out of place in a house run by women," said Lady Guri.

"It is too bad Tomac and Jalan are not here. They would love to see you. And, they would keep Lord Juin occupied," said Lady Darla.

"It's only one more day and then we will be heading back home."

"So soon," said Lady Shara. "Can you not stay another day and help me with plans for the wedding?"

"Surely Darla has been some help," said Guri.

"As she can. But, you have no idea how busy your sister is. I'm afraid the current troubles have left her little time for her dear mother's wedding," said Shara.

"Mother," chided Darla, "you make it sound as if I've done nothing."

Lady Shara looked carefully at Darla and said, "On no, dear one, you have done a great deal. It is only that Guri, as our guest, has an abundance of time to assist me. Something that would also lighten the burden I'm placing on you."

"Oh yes, that and you two could happily spend hours in the company of Mistress Treana," observed Darla.

"You wound me," responded Lady Shara in an overly dramatic tone.

Guri and Darla laughed and Shara joined them.

"Very well, I will speak with Juin and see if he can bear another day or two. He does enjoy it here. He simply feels at a loss as to how he can make himself useful."

"Don't worry. If Major Erida sees him, he is likely to have your husband leading a company of men on patrol before Juin can form two words of protest," said Darla.

Lady Guri hesitated and then said, "You don't think there is a real chance of that do you?"

"Of course not dear sister, your husband is perfectly safe. It was a jest. The Major would never dream of forcing such an imposition on Lord Juin," said Darla. *At least I don't think he would.*

As her sister settled back into place and looked less like a bird about to take flight, Darla's thoughts turned to her newest concern. Despite the pleasant distraction and real enjoyment of Guri's visit, the trip was not about mother and Lord Brace. As Guri had warned in her letter, Guri and her husband had brought a formal proposal for Darla to marry Juin's cousin, Lord Merk Shrift.

Perhaps her mother picked up on the turn of thought or it was simple coincidence when Lady Shara said, "Guri, dear, your help with my preparations would be marvelous. And, good practice should your sister accept Lord Merk's offer."

"Oh yes, there is indeed a lot to consider," said Lady Guri brightening considerably. "It will be such a wonderful wedding."

"You have me matroned already, but I do not find it so easily done," said Darla. "There are so many concerns before me each day. It is difficult to imagine having time for a wedding, much less a husband and new family."

"It was certainly unsettling for me at first," said Guri. "Leaving father and mother, you and my other siblings and moving into a new home and new life. I had looked forward to marriage, but it was very difficult those first few months. Juin was so patient with me. Now I would find it even harder to leave Shrift Manor. My family is there. My husband. My children. As much as I love the old, I never guessed how deep my ties to the new would be. I want you to have that, to not be afraid of losing the past and to discover the same joy I have in your own future."

Guri's words and enthusiasm were a flame beginning to light the fire of Darla's own hopes. *If only it were so simple.* "Guri, I am so happy for you and just a bit jealous as well," said Darla with a smile. "But, I am the head of House Yen just as Lord Merk is the head of his house. I am not willing to leave that behind or simply pass it over to a husband."

"Merk has made it clear he wishes to combine both houses. How could there be less to do then or less need of your talents? Surely, there will be a place for you in the administration of the joined houses if you wish it."

Darla did not know what to say. She felt selfish and foolish. How could she tell Guri that she did not want a husband to take over the leadership of House Yen? She wanted to lead House Yen as she already did, not take a lesser role even if that role were part of a greater house. Her father's legacy and her own ability would be buried, hidden beneath the Shrift name and legacy. *But, would that really be so bad? Am I too proud to take help?*

Darla spoke, uncertain of what she would say or even what she wanted. "I am not just Darla. I am House Yen. If I wed, then I wed the fate of my house to another as well. If I take a diminished role then House Yen is also diminished. And if I reject Lord Shrift's proposal and his offer of funds and armsmen, House Yen might not only be diminished but very possibly destroyed. Taking the offer does not save House Yen either. The lands will still exist and the people will be saved, but our father's legacy will become only a part of another house. I don't know if I can do that to our people, or to Father's memory."

"But Merk doesn't want House Yen. He has said as much by suggesting you turn over the manor to Tomac," said Guri.

"The manor is only a small part of our holdings. What Merk asks for is the greater share of Yen arable land in exchange for saving a small portion for Tomac."

Guri wore an apologetic frown as she said, "But Juin read the entire proposal to me. I don't recall anything like that in it."

"Contracts, agreements, merchants' deals are all rarely what they appear to be on the surface. You are correct. The document does not state the resulting division as clearly as I did. I would not have seen it even a week ago."

Lady Shara, perhaps sensing a rising tension between her daughters or because of her own curiosity, asked, "Seen what, dear?"

"The long term impact of the terms of the marriage proposal," said Darla. "I started a new project to find ways to increase the house income. Over the last several days I have analyzed crop yield patterns, growth of habitations and changes in travel and trade patterns."

Now Guri looked truly perplexed. "What does that have to do with Lord Shrifts offer?"

"I have to admit that I am equally in the dark," said Shara.

"My research and projections are not complete, but given the patterns I am seeing the land Lord Shrift proposes to leave under Tomac's control is in every case land that has a lesser future potential to produce an income. For example, Tomac stands to maintain control of some prime farmland. However, most of it will lie fallow for two years whereas land ready for renewed planting will be given over to Merk's control. He will gain two seasons of production while Tomac gains nothing."

"I do remember that provision," said Guri. "It seems fair that for taking the poorer land Lord Shrift might have the benefit of planting sooner."

"That alone does appear fair. It might truly be fair except when combined with the other provisions. Lord Shrift also comes out ahead when examining the villages and hamlets he gains. Tomac is left with some of the largest populations, but Lord Shrift gains developing areas that already show signs of being favored by crafters, factors and traders. After two years of crops that are an addition to what Merk Shrift already has and two years of increasing trade and taxes, the good Lord gains much advantage over the state in which Tomac has been left. Tomac becomes Lord Yen through a loss of land and income which he will never have the opportunity to overcome. If someone else deals with Tomac as sharply as Lord Shrift appears to be dealing with me, then there will be no House Yen in a very few years more."

"Crows," said Lady Shara in a whisper just loud enough for the other two women to hear it.

"Yes, mother. That is precisely what I fear it is," said Darla.

"What do you mean?" said Guri. "What do birds have to do with any of this?"

Darla turned to her sister. "It's something mother said to me when I became lady. Father had just passed. I was scared and full of doubt. Mother tried to reassure me. But, she also warned me that if I was not strong enough the crows would tear House Yen apart."

"What crows? I still do not understand." Guri looked less confused but more anxious with her hands clasped tightly together as if pleading for insight and a look of concerned concentration on her face.

"The crows are the enemies of House Yen, the people who exploit our weakness for their own gain," said Shara.

"Merk is a crow?" asked Guri. Her voice is tentative in a way that made Darla think her sister was asking for confirmation rather than for an answer.

"Yes, Guri," said Darla. "Given the terms of his proposal and the timing, he is whether he intends it or not." Darla tried to sound calm and reasonable. She thought her sister was on the edge of a realization which she might share if Darla listened patiently and gave Guri time to think. She desperately hoped their mother remained quiet, but she dared not even glance away from Guri for fear of breaking the tenuous connection she felt forming.

"He's not a crow," said Guri. Her words were firm as if stating a fact. "He is a vulture. That is what I heard Juin call him once and now I know why." Guri looked straight at Darla and reached out taking both Darla's hands in her own. "Please forgive me. I have been trying to make you a bad match. I am so sorry. So very sorry." As she spoke the last words, silent tears begin to fall down her cheeks.

Δ

Jalan moved through the trees on foot. He whispered, "Show me the wagon."

The scout crept ahead to crouch behind a thicket and waved Jalan forward. Jalan signaled the men behind him to hold. He wanted to see the enemy before he deployed them. Slowly he moved up beside the scout, careful to keep low.

Through the thicket he saw the side of a heavy wagon among the trees several yards ahead. He listened for voices, horses, any sign of the enemy but heard only the wind in the trees. Silently he used more hand signals to send two men to the left and two more to the right. They would flank the wagon's position. He felt himself sweating from creeping through the woods in full armor and he winced whenever one of his advancing men inadvertently made a sound, which was often because they were in full armor as well. After he allowed sufficient time for his first four men to reach their positions, he signaled the rest of the men to advance. Six men could not help but make noise and they did not try for stealth but jogged forward and found whatever cover they could with bows ready and eyes searching for enemy targets.

Nothing happened.

Slowly Jalan moved forward. Those near him did the same. After he advanced a couple of yards, Jalan saw the wagon leaned badly and the bed appeared to be empty. He listened and watched for another moment before he gave up and called out, "Does anyone see anything besides the wagon?"

No one spoke.

Jalan stood up and walked the rest of the way. The back axle had broken and the wagon had been abandoned.

"At least we know we're still on their trail," said Reest

Jalan looked up at him, not ready to be gracious. "Back to the horses. We're losing ground," he shouted.

Δ

On the afternoon of the second day, Jalan's scouts returned. The trail led to an encampment. The hunters reined up within a large grove of trees and dismounted to hear a full report from the scouts. After *The Battle of the Broken Wagon* as some of the men now called yesterday's discovery, Jalan intended to be certain this time before attempting to engage the enemy.

Palst used a stick to scratch out a rough outline of the enemy camp on a small patch of open ground. Jalan and the three fist

178

leaders, Harna, Reest and Serks were crouched down examining Palst's sketch. According to both Palst and a second scout, their opponents had felled trees and used them along with earthen mounds to build low walls. There was only one opening through the walls, large enough to allow one of their big wagons to pass. The camp proper was populated by tents. One slightly larger tent sat pitched near the center. There were five large wagons. Three inside the walls and two more next to a rope corral set up outside the walls near the entrance.

"How many men?" said Jalan.

"Could be 50. Maybe more. I counted tents and the rope corral has at least 30 horses in it."

"And they're close?"

"A short ride, captain. They're on a hill. Far side of the next ridge over." Palst pointed in a northerly direction to indicate the way.

"It's lucky we didn't ride right into them," said Jalan.

"Not luck, sir. Good scouting," said Serks.

Jalan nodded in agreement and said, "Thank you, Palst. You and Oatin have done well." Then he spoke out in general to the fist leaders, "Any questions?"

"What colors are the snakes wearing?" said Harna.

Palst glanced at the other men who had begun to gather around and said, "Two sets, ours and Nakra's."

"What?" said Harna, sounding angry.

Others within the rough circle of listeners beyond Jalan, the fist leaders and the scouts began to mutter and exclaim.

Jalan stood and held up a closed fist. Most of his men fell silent. The remaining few were quickly elbowed or prodded until they paid attention to Jalan's signal. Once everyone quieted, Jalan ordered Harna to set his men watching their perimeter. "Come back after you set the watch," said Jalan.

"Yes, captain," said Harna as he signaled his men to follow him.

"Lancers! See to your mounts!" called out Jalan in a loud clear voice. Then less loudly, "Scouts and fist leaders with me." He led the other four lancers a short distance further into the trees to give them a little separation from the main body of men and horses. When Jalan stopped he turned to the men following him and said, "We've chased these wagons and now we've found them in a camp that appears to be both Yen lancers and Nakra soldiers. Is that an accurate overview?"

"There were other men as well, but they wore no colors," said Oatin.

"Then how many were Yen, how many Nakra and how many of them unknown?"

"Perhaps 10 to 20 of each, captain," said Palst.

"Did either of you recognize any of them? Anyone in that camp that you might have seen somewhere before?" said Jalan to the two scouts.

"I don't think so, sir," said Palst.

"We were too far from them to see faces clearly, sir," said Oatin.

It had been a dim hope that either man would be able to identify any individual in the enemy camp. They were both new recruits and were unlikely to know many lancers. But, Jalan had felt compelled to ask.

Neither scout had anything more to add to their report. Jalan dismissed them to see to their horses. As the scouts left, Harna arrived and Jalan briefly restated what Harna missed since he left to set the watch.

"Does anyone have an opinion about who these men might be?" asked Jalan.

"Deserters perhaps," said Serks.

"Traitors more like," said Reest.

"Is it really possible there would be 10 or 20 deserters from House Yen?" asked Jalan.

"There are always some, but 20? Most of the lancers are looking for a chance to make someone pay for what's been done to us, not trying to run away from the fight," said Serks.

"I can't see it being deserters at all. Where would they have run off from? I don't recall talk of deserters," said Harna. "It means they had to run when the fighting started. How would they have time to find this encampment and join with the enemy that set them running in the first place? I can't see it."

"They're traitors then. Lancers that allied with the Nakra before the fighting started." The words tasted bad as Jalan spoke them, but he did not know what else to think.

"Or men pretending to be House Yen," said Dost.

Reest turned his head and spat. "That and worse for them, whoever they are," he said.

They caught their quarry, but what would keep the quarry from turning on the hunters? The camp had Jalan's lancers outnumbered three or four to one. Many of his men were inexperienced recruits barely adequate with their bows. His lancers were light cavalry at best. They can't charge the enemy. They can't even afford to stand and fight. Jalan tried to imagine fighting the men he grew up knowing, not for training or fun, but for blood and to the death. The idea disturbed him; he felt a little sick. If they were traitors, Jalan would know some of them, perhaps all of them. They were lancers that Jalan and his men would have willing fought beside and trusted. He felt his anger and disgust rising to join with his sense of violation. No wonder the punishment for treason was death.

"They outnumber us," he told the fist leaders. "We cannot make a direct assault. We need to study the enemy, discover when and where they send out scouts or patrols. If we could capture one or two of their men we might be able to learn something useful. But, whatever we do, we need to be certain we only fight when we have superior numbers."

No sooner did Jalan finish speaking then a panicked voice shouted, "To arms! To arms! The enemy! To arms!"

Jalan spun toward the shout but could only see his men straining to look past each other and their horses for a glimpse of the trouble. "Fist leaders, rally your men on me!" he cried and sprinted toward Axe. Jalan leapt up and vaulted over the rear of his horse to land in the saddle as he sent a silent thank you to Master Enmar for every frog hop he ever endured. He snatched up the reins and began to calm his mount. Axe must have been well trained; the gelding barely protested Jalan's sudden weight falling into place on his back. Letting the reins hang loose across Axe's long neck, Jalan pulled his bow from its scabbard and strung it almost without thinking, one more task he had learned to do on horseback.

With his bow held firmly in his gloved left hand and the reins grasped in his right, Jalan spurred Axe forward and swung him sharply toward the area from whence the warning shout came. Harna, Reest and Serks were all mounted. Several others were on horseback or mounting now that the fist leaders were back among them and chivying them to action. The tumult of mounted and mounting men being coerced into organized fists made it impossible to hear anything else. Jalan held his bow horizontally above his head and the fist leaders looked at him. He pointed the tip of the bow at Serks and swung it to his right. Then he pointed the tip at Reest and swung it to his left. Finally, he pointed the bow tip at Harna and swung the tip up to hold the bow vertically. Serks already had his fist moving among the trees toward a position on Jalan's right. Reest's fist moved toward Jalan's left. Harna took up his place next to Jalan as the din of mounting died down to be replaced by stern commands from the fist leaders that guided them into place, made certain they were armed, and told them to keep quite.

Jalan strained to see as he began to walk the line forward, desperate to know the fate of Harna's fist. He never imagined how difficult it would be to maintain an even advance while his heart pounded and the fate of his own men played out just beyond his sight. Around him every hoof thudded agonizingly slowly, caught in frozen moments of perception where he felt as though he saw and heard everything except that which he most desired. He watched the smooth flow of his arm as he pulled an arrow from the quiver strapped to his back.

Two lancers on horseback burst into the grove at precisely the instant Jalan called out, "Hold! Ready bows!"

A third rider, twisted around in his saddle, crashed through the brush and into the grove as he shot an arrow at an unseen target behind him. Each fist leader repeated Jalan's order to ready bows while all three incoming riders pulled back on the reins and threaded their way between trees and the somewhat ragged line of Jalan's company.

Jalan noched his arrow and raised his bow. Arrows loosed from beyond the edge of the trees pursued the three riders. They ripped through leaves, deflected off branches and stuck fast in tree trunks. A breath behind the volley at least a half of a dozen mounted men charged into the grove screaming mayhem and murder for those they chased.

"Loose at will!" shouted Jalan. A flash flew through his peripheral vision as he heard the sound of Harna's bow. Jalan studied his aim and released. He forced himself to hold position for a heartbeat more, then pulled, noched and loosed his second arrow almost as fast as thought.

His mounted archers picked their own targets and the trees interfered with the choices. Three of the enemy suffered multiple hits, and toppled from their saddles, feathered by two or more shafts. The remaining fought to turn their mounts and save themselves.

"Lancers! Advance walk, loose at will. Begin!" bellowed Jalan intent on being heard over the cacophony of battle.

Harna took up the cry and Jalan believed he heard Serks and Reest shout out the order too.

The company's line became a broken wave as the green lancers attempted to steer their mounts with their knees, advance around obstacles and feather the enemy with arrows. Their aim suffered more than the enemy. A few arrows struck the mark more by chance than skill.

Time no longer flowed like cold honey for Jalan. No matter how quickly he raised his bow, he feared it could never be fast enough. His third arrow flew true, striking down a fleeing rider that had taken a wild shaft in the arm as well. For his fourth, Jalan noched the arrow and raised his bow seeking an escaping rider who had nearly reached freedom beyond the trees. He saw arrows go wide or be hindered and deflected by foliage. At the moment he meant to release his bowstring, it felt wrong. A triangle of light brightened in his vision and the certainty gripped him that he must send his arrow there or lose his chance. His arrow point swung to the triangle as if anchored to it and he let fly. Jalan perceived what happened next through the sensitivity he experienced only with the longbow. His arrow would never strike the rider. It collided with another arrow in flight, altered that projectile's course and sent it plunging through an opening in the fleeing man's armor. The dead man slid from his mount at the moment the horse reached open ground.

Jalan pulled a fifth arrow and had it noched before he knew no enemies remained. It seemed as if his hands needed little conscious guidance as they performed the task while he searched in vain for a target. Seeing none he called out ",Bows down!" It surprised him when his throat felt a bit raw.

Harna, still by Jalan's side, said, "I request permission to see to my men, captain."

"Go," was all Jalan could say and all Harna needed to hear. He turned his mount toward his three men who had been on watch and had fled back to the company when the attack began.

After he put the arrow back into his quiver, unstrung his bow and slipped it back into its scabbard, Jalan dismounted and led Axe a little bit apart from the battle line. He waited there, knowing the fist leaders would soon come to him. The silence of the grove seemed predominant now and the voices that broke it were a mixture of raucous and subdued. When Harna, Serks and Reest walked over, Jalan listened to their reports.

Four enemies died. Two were badly wounded and likely to die. One might live. The last had fallen victim to a strange form of luck, uninjured expect for the bruises he suffered when his horse tripped and threw him. One of Harna's fist, Cail, was killed when the enemy riders spotted him and attacked. Cail had called the warning. The other watchers, overwhelmed by the number of enemy riders, could not save him before being forced to flee into the grove.

With his fist leaders, Jalan inspected the enemy dead and captured. He tried to make himself hard so that the bodies and blood did not affect him. He did his duty. His men did their duty. They fought as they must and killed the enemy as they must. But when he came to Cail's body and looked upon the dead face of one of his own men, he did not feel hard. He did not feel like a lancer captain. He felt like a boy. He felt like he had the first time he had seen a farm animal slaughtered. He remembered the knife and the killing stroke, the smell of blood and the struggle of the goat as it weakened and died.

He turned from Cail's body and walked a few steps as his own guts twisted and his stomach roiled. Jalan steadied himself by placing his hand on a nearby tree and forced himself to take slow deep breaths hoping the queasy sick feeling in his belly passed soon.

"Don't worry, captain. The others will be done soon," said Reest. "It's hard to hold your stomach when half the men around you lose theirs."

The comment confused Jalan at first. Then he realizes many of his men were scattered among the trees retching. That sound alone was almost enough to push his stomach over the edge, so many others with the same problem. It was so absurd. The horror of the dead and wounded mingled with the sickening sound and smell of vomit was so unexpected that Jalan almost started to laugh. And then he did bend over and lose the contents of his stomach.

"Ah, well there it is," said Reest in an aside to no one in particular. He followed his quite comment with a question. "Captain, may I ask you something?"

"Ungh," said Jalan. Then he spat to try to clean some remnants from his mouth and eased himself upright, feeling a little dizzy and a little better at the same time.

Reest seemed to assume Jalan's grunt meant yes when he continued by asking "Is this the first time you've killed a man?" The question was pitched quiet, hardly louder than Reest's earlier side comment.

Images flashed in swift succession through Jalan's mind. Taking aim. The arrow loosed. The first target is struck in the neck. The second target was in the underarm as he appeared to be raising his arm and shouting to his companions. The third was well armored. Jalan could see his arrow strike. The rider was hit with three shafts at almost the same time. A fourth arrow struck the enemy's mount. It could be that none of the three arrows pierced the rider's armor, but when the horse was hit in the front leg the limb buckled and the animal tumbled and threw the rider beneath the weight of the rolling horse. His fourth, the last fleeing rider, a miracle of death. A bow shot that might haunt him for life even if others, had they known about it, might celebrate it. Four targets. Four dead men.

Jalan shook with little tremors that moved through his muscles. His throat burned and the taste in his mouth was sour and foul. He pushed away the memories and took a trembling step toward his horse. The next step was easier. After a few more he was almost walking normally. When he reached Axe he took a short pull from his water skin to rinse out his mouth and then a longer drink.

Reest was not where Jalan left him. The older man was checking on the members of his fist now. Both Harna and Serks had their men mounted and formed up. Harna eased his dark gelding toward Jalan and said, "Captain, the men tell me those were not the only enemy riders. Two more turned back when those eight attacked. It's likely they've gone to warn the others."

Looking up at Harna, Jalan considered protesting that the fist leader should have told him sooner. But with his water skin still in his hand and his insides barely feeling regular again, he understood why it might have been pointless to report it sooner. "Remind your men of the importance of reporting what they observe promptly no matter what else is occurring."

"Yes, captain. I'll make certain there is no delay in the future."

The delay was possibly Harna's own choice. All Jalan's men were older than their captain. Reest tried to help Jalan through the shock and fatigue following Jalan's first battle. Now Harna may have given his captain time to recover before delivering bad news. If his lancers kept playing father to him they might protect him right into an early grave.

CHAPTER XVII

Jalan steeled his expression and moved toward the prisoner with a controlled confident walk. *Don't trip. Don't do anything foolish that might appear weak.* Beyond that advice to himself he had no idea what to do or say. But, Reest did.

The fist leader walked up to the prone captive. The man, bound hand and foot, lay on his side on the root entwined ground. One side of the captive's face purpled. The opposite eye wore a darkening bruise and blood trickled from his lower lip. Nothing about the man's oval face seemed familiar to Jalan despite the fact the stranger wore the House Yen Blue and Tan. Reest kicked the bound man in the stomach. Before the fellow could hope to recover, Reest grabbed him and roughly sat the prisoner up against a nearby tree trunk. The man gasped in short shallow breaths.

Glancing up from the captive, Reest called to another lancer, "Shrim!" Reest jerked his head toward the captive while drawing his own belt knife. Shrim drew his saber and quickly placed the sharp tip of the weapon against the captive's throat. Using his knife, Reest cut the rope tied around the enemy's wrists. He moved behind the captive and pulled the man's arms back around the tree trunk, retying them with a set of leather laces. The captive held his head back against the tree trunk. His eyes darted about but settled back onto Shrim's sword. Once Reest finished, he nodded to Shrim. Shrim removed the sword tip from the prisoner's neck.

Reest moved around in front of the prisoner and crouched down, putting him somewhat eye to eye with the bound man. Without looking away from the prisoner Reest said, "Shrim, I'm thirsty. Would you get my water skin?"

Shrim retrieved the water skin from Reest's horse and Reest took a long drink. Then he offered some to the prisoner. The captive stared at him without responding. Reest shrugged and handed the water skin back to Shrim.

"I'm Reest. What's your name?"

Again, the man did not respond.

"I've been a lancer with House Yen for a few years now. I know a lot of people. But, oddly, I don't know you."

Jalan saw the man's mouth twitch as if he might have started to smile or speak.

"Harna, does this fellow look familiar to you?" said Reest to his fellow fist leader.

Harna rubbed the stubble on his chin as he looked at the unknown lancer. "No. I don't recall ever seeing him before."

"Don't ask," said Serks before Reest could query him. "I don't know him."

"That's unfortunate," said Reest. He stood up from his crouch. "Very unfortunate. As I'm sure you know, wearing the colors of a house means you are in service to that house. But, we don't seem to know you. It's very difficult to imagine that you are truly a Yen lancer. That leaves us only a few possibilities." Reest began to count using the fingers on his left hand. "One, you are not a Yen lancer but you are wearing Yen colors. The punishment for impersonating a lancer is severe, but you'd probably live. However, you are wearing a captain's braids and the punishment for impersonating an officer is death." Reest raised a second finger and said, "Two, you really are a Yen lancer and somehow we have never met you, in which case you are welcome among us. Except, you were fighting against us and that would mean you are a traitor. Again, the punishment is death." Reest paused for a moment and then dropped his left hand to his sword scabbard and reached across his body to grasp the hilt with his right. "Which leaves only one option," said Reest as he drew his saber in a measured and deliberate manner. "We have to kill you."

The prisoner remained silent during the entire time Reest spoke. When the sharp edge of the saber came completely free of Reest's scabbard the man protested with a mixture of anger and alarm, "But, I'm a captive. The Covenants prohibit the execution of prisoners!"

Reest sighed as he examined the bared blade he held. "That is true. But you are not a captive. You are a traitor or a spy and The Covenants do not protect one who abandons his honor."

He took a two handed grip on his saber and moved into a stance that would allow him to swing the weapon in a smooth arc which would most likely pass through the captive's neck. Reest stopped with his blade partially raised and said, "Oh yes, I forgot, number three. There is that one way we can avoid execution. But, really, I just don't see how that could be possible." Then he raised his blade to strike.

"Wait! What way?" said the prisoner as he pushed himself harder against the tree trunk in a futile attempt to put distance between himself and Reest.

Making a slow practice swing, Reest allowed the blade to gentry touch the bound man's neck. It left a thin red line behind. "The only way we would not execute you is if you were our spy. That would explain why you were with the enemy. You would be wearing our colors in an effort to convince the enemy you are a deserter and can be trusted. It's a bold move. You could have been killed out of hand." Reest drew his saber back and set himself to swing in earnest.

"Wait!" shouted the man a second time. "I'm a spy. I'm your spy".

Still coiled to strike, Reest's eyebrows raised in a suggestion of shocked surprise. "Truly? Our spy?"

"Yes! Yes, your spy. I am a spy for House Yen."

Reest lowered his sword and stepped back. "Why did you not declare yourself sooner?"

"Um, well, when I was captured I did not see my contact among you. I could not be sure it was safe to tell you who I am."

"Who is your contact?"

"I, uh, I cannot tell you that." The man saw the expression on Reest's face and said, "But, ask me something else. I... I can tell you other things."

"Very well. Who are the men in the encampment a short ride from here? Why do they wear both our colors and Nakra's colors, and no colors at all? What is in those wagons inside the compound? How many men are there in total? What are their plans? Answer those questions and others and I am sure I can convince our captain that you are the man you claim to be."

At this point Jalan felt like a top spun too fast. He almost shouted an order for Reest to stop before the prisoner spoke first. All Jalan could think as he looked at the prisoner was that the captive must tell the truth. *He must!* And in a mere twinkling he felt something slip between himself and the prisoner. The bound man jerked and shook his head as if he had been slapped. Jalan felt momentarily dizzy, but this time he managed to hold back some of, well, whatever had gone between them. And in the tiny sliver of time where they were joined, something slipped from the prisoner to Jalan.

"They are mercenaries," drawled the bound man. He looked a bit woozy.

The lancers looking on began to murmur amongst themselves. Jalan could not tell if the captive's answer or his sudden change in behavior sparked the men's comments.

"What?" said Reest, who for the first time sounded genuinely surprised by what the prisoner said.

The bound man spoke slow and soft but finished loud and angry, "I said we're mercenaries. Now tell me what in the Four Corners of Damnation you've done to me!"

Jalan watched Reest's face darken as the lancer pointed his saber at the captive's nose and growled angrily, "What have we done to you? We've fought you when you attacked us. We bested you and now we're questioning you." He dropped the sword point away from the other man's face and leaned down. "We bloodied and bound you. A captive would expect no less. You have admitted to the false display of our colors, and now you tell us you are a sell-sword honorless dog who has taken up arms against House Yen. No house would let you live after a transgression like that and you have the nerve to ask what we have done to you?" Reest straightened and spat on the ground at the captive's feet. "I'll tell you what I'm going to do to you. I'm going to ask the captain for permission to separate your head from your shoulders." Reest looked toward Jalan and said, "Captain?"

HIDDEN ABILITY

All the lancers had fallen silent. Jalan felt their eyes upon him. The prisoner knew more and Jalan new some of it too. But, Jalan could not reveal what he learned through his curse. He could never explain how he learned it. Now that the captive believed they would likely kill him, he would never tell them more. If they were back at Yen Manor or one of the outposts, there would be time to question him or call for a tribunal. There would be time to think and the final decision would come from someone more experienced. Here, with everyone watching and the threat of a superior enemy force arriving at any time, Jalan felt he had no choice. If he delayed it would call into question his ability to lead and only give more time for the prisoner's companions to return with enough men to wipe out the company.

The prisoner's eyes moved back and forth between Reest and Jalan. Jalan sighed under the weight of the moment and started to announce his decision. The bound man interrupted him with a shout, "I demand a trial!"

Δ

A man with gray hair who wore a gray jacket entered the Business Room and waited quietly for Lady Darla to acknowledge him.

Darla marked her place in a ledger she examined and greeted the man, "Trader Grom, how are you today?" Darla did her best to sound pleasant. Jacey seemed to be a little suspicious of the man, but Grom had been a miracle worker when it came to finding supplies and equipment.

"I am fine, my lady. And I trust that all is well with you," said Grom.

"As well as may be," said Darla. "Please, be seated."

"Thank you, my lady," said the trader as he lowered himself onto a chair in front of Darla's worktable.

"Master Chander tells me that your assistance with supplies has been invaluable. He claims you have even done the impossible and persuaded Master Enmar to let you use part of his precious Training Hall as a warehouse."

"Master Enmar and I have an understanding built on mutual benefit that Master Chander was unable to establish. I do not mean to sound immodest, but I may possess some skills as a trader that other men lack. I am certain they exceed me in their areas of expertise."

"However you accomplished it, House Yen is grateful for your assistance. Now tell me why you requested to see me," said Lady Darla.

Trader Grom took a moment to look around the room before returning his gaze to Lady Darla. "The time has come for me to present a special letter of introduction."

Grom reached into an interior pocket of his gray jacket and extracted a sealed envelope. He passed the envelope to Lady Darla.

"This is the king's seal," said Darla.

"You are correct, lady. Please, read the letter and after I will answer any questions you wish to pose."

Darla broke the seal and removed the letter from the envelope. The letter was brief and Darla quickly read it. She read it a second time and then to be absolutely certain she read it a third time as well. The message was clear, surprising and yet oddly reasonable. Lady Darla looked up from the letter and asked, "Have you read this?"

"No, my lady," said Grom.

"The king says that you are the answer to House Yen's request for men and supplies," said Darla.

Trader Grom smiled and said, "That I am. I apologize for not being exactly what you expected, lady."

"There is no difficulty there," laughed Darla. "I have grown accustomed to answers I do not expect. The king further states that you can provide knowledge and council on a variety of subjects."

"I have a number of merchants that work for me throughout the kingdom and beyond. It is not uncommon for them to pass along information on matters that affect trade."

"You're a spy," said Darla.

"I am your spy," said Grom.

"Mine?"

"The king ordered me to offer my services to House Yen. King Tamaron said that your father was a great general and had proved himself a good Steward of the Land. But, the king seemed certain your father would not have woven a strong net for catching information. He was a man of specific interests whose accomplishments were enough to forestall his enemies. His presence alone gave them pause. Without him, it will take more for you, Lady Yen, to cast as long a shadow."

Darla understood precisely what Trader Grom was saying. She had been undervalued due to her youth and inexperience by many who dealt with her. She had even undervalued herself. Without Lady Shara stepping in to encourage and support her, Darla was certain she would have accepted the lessor life she once believed was her lot. She could never have been her father. But, she could be someone of whom Father would be proud.

"Why did you wait until now to present the king's letter?" said Darla.

"It pains me to admit this. I had to wait until I knew House Yen was worth saving."

Darla had no answer for that. It hurt that anyone, especially the king, would deny help to House Yen.

"What about Jalan? How could the king not aid his own son?"

Grom sat back in his chair, clearly thrown deep into his own thoughts. "So that is it," he said.

"You didn't know?" said Darla as a sense of alarm set her nerves on edge.

"Please, my lady, calm yourself. It is true. I did not know. I cannot say why the king did not tell me. There was no reason for me to know before I was sent here. Perhaps there was no time to tell me before I left. Tamaron is a very prudent ruler. I am certain he knew I would discover this eventually. Now that I think on it, I see why he could not have done otherwise."

Darla felt confused, "Why not? Why would he not tell you?"

"It is part of the pattern, my lady. Why did the king not send lancers? Why did he not begin moving the levers of war in order to prepare for hostilities with Ankena?"

"Levers of war?" said Darla.

"I'm sorry. It is an expression for all the things a country does when making ready for war. They might increase taxes and raise additional troops. Emissaries are sent to the houses and contact is made with the potential enemy to look for a political solution. Those can be difficult tasks, much as prying large boulders up and getting them to roll where you wish is a difficult task. It requires the right lever and strength just to start each bolder moving."

"You're saying the king is not doing those things?"

"Not on a noticeable scale, my lady," said Grom. "And, there may be several reasons for that. First, there is no indication of hostilities except around the border between House Yen and Ankena's Principality of Polnue. Second, although a border skirmish can eventually lead to all-out war, there is no indication that Polnue has been planning for war. It would be unwise for the king to overreact to your situation. He would not wish to draw excess attention to it and cause Ankena to believe Ojmara is preparing for war. He sent me to assist you. But, he did not tell me that the prince was here. That allowed me to believe this is a serious situation, but that it is not vital to save House Yen. It did not cause anyone observing me to think my actions were out of the ordinary. My actions fit in with the king dealing with your situation as indirectly and quietly as possible."

"So Tamaron gave you the option of not helping us?" said Darla.

"No, my lady. The king only gave the appearance that I could choose to not help you. He had to know I would discover the presence of the prince and realize that the heir and his safe hiding place are in danger. It leaves me with no choice." Trader Grom spread his hands wide as if to indicate how obvious the intricacies of his position had become.

"But you said you decided to help House Yen before you learned about Jalan," said Darla.

"Sadly, I did not discover the prince was here as quickly as our liege may have assumed I would. I do feel badly about that. Happily, I have already determined to help you on your own merits regardless of Jalan's presence. This speaks well of you and House Yen, my lady."

Lady Darla was only certain about two things. Trader Grom's explanation of the king's machinations gave her a headache. And, Trader Grom had already been useful to House Yen even before declaring his commitment to help.

"I take your judgment of House Yen as a compliment. Now, please, tell me how you will help more than you already have?" said Darla.

"Have you rejected Lord Shrift's proposal yet?"

"How did you know about that?" Darla heard her indignation in the question, but she was too upset to care.

"My lady, I am sorry to upset you. I only ask because Lord Shrift's offer is a part of the attacks on House Yen."

"Again, I must ask how you could know that? I only began to suspect such was true recently and no one outside my family has seen the document. I demand you explain yourself!"

"My lady, please forgive me for upsetting you. I have not invaded your privacy, at least not specifically. The nature of my true work for our sovereign, and now for House Yen, is to gather information. As I mentioned, others watch my actions and learn things from what I choose to do, and I also watch the patterns of what others do. Your sister's visits are special occasions. It does not take long for rumors of why Lady Shrift and her Lord husband are here to circulate throughout the estate. Add the likely reason for their visit to other information gathered pertaining to Lord Merk Shrift's activities and a dark pattern begins to emerge."

Trader Grom's tone seemed both conciliatory and frank. Darla's curiosity overcame her displeasure.

"Of what activities do you speak? Surely, you refer to something more than his proposal to me?"

"Assuredly I do, lady. Lord Shrift has built a sizable force of lancers over the last two years, at least double the forces you command."

"He has offered to send a large contingent of his lancers to aid us in our fight," said Darla.

"As part of his marriage proposal, no doubt?" said Grom

"True. It is contingent on my agreement to marry him," said Darla.

The trader nodded thoughtfully and said, "I imagine that would make it easier for him."

"What are you implying?" said Darla.

"I will explain, but allow me to ask a question first. How is it that Lord Shrift can afford to keep so large a force of lancers?"

"I imagine the yields from his lands are sufficient."

"I ask you to accept my word that they are not and assure you that I can prove it so."

Grom's assertion puzzled Darla. How could Lord Merk have all those lancers if he could not afford the cost? "That does not make sense. He has all those lancers. Surely, he must be paying for them. Even if he defers the men's pay, there are still uniforms, weapons, housing and a number of other expenses that must be paid."

"As best as I am able to determine, the Lord is covering the cost, yet his income is insufficient, he has sold no personal goods or holdings and he has not borrowed the funds," said Trader Grom.

"Wealth is not magic. It does not flow from nothing. You ask me how Lord Shrift pays for his lancers, but you tell me at every turn he cannot be paying for his lancers. Are you saying that he does not truly have those lancers or are you accusing him of purloining the funds?"

Grom's eyes opened wide and his posture stiffened, "I would never dream of accusing a lord of a crime. I am merely a master trader without standing from which to make such a charge. What I have said is offered under my role as adviser in order that my lady may come to her own conclusions."

The sound of Grom's voice and the way he posed himself as he spoke reminded Darla of a troupe of play actors that once performed at Yen Manor. He presented his protest as though it were rehearsed and delivered it in a way that strengthened her suspicion. Although Trader Grom denied it, Darla was certain he accused Lord Merk Shrift of stealing the money. But, from whom would he have stolen it?

Darla felt warmth flood her cheeks as understanding and embarrassment arrived hand in hand. In a rush she saw the connections, the pattern Grom had been trying to show her. Merk's lancers and the odd regularity of the accounts for the outposts were related. When she had spoken with Captain Niksus he explained that Major Jeckler, the former commander of Southway, reviewed and approved all the financial reports. Jeckler received the reports from Midland and Pass and compiled the official report for all three outposts. It was Jeckler's report that was sent on to Yen Manor. Jalan told her of the ordeal he and Lieutenant Goss struggled through to bring even a modicum of order to them. Darla had never seen the original outpost reports until Captain Niksus showed her the records he had been ordered to bring back from Pass Outpost.

HIDDEN ABILITY

The Pass Outpost records showed that tariffs had been increasing steadily for the past three years while the traffic through the outpost also grew. The three outposts might have collected a far greater sum than Major Jeckler reported or sent on to Yen Manor. Jeckler obfuscated his reports and kept an unknown portion of the tariffs for his own use. Now it seemed he had allied himself with Lord Merk Shrift and House Yen paid for Lord Shrift's extra lancers. Jeckler had betrayed House Yen.

The final realization of Lord Shrift's duplicity in the matter rapidly converted Darla's embarrassment to anger. "The dirty two-faced scoundrel," was all Darla managed to stammer out as the enormity of the betrayal hit her. She was not even certain her insult was meant for Merk Shrift, Major Jeckler or both. "Our tariffs! He's using our tariffs for his lancers."

"My thinking exactly, my lady," acknowledged Grom.

Darla's anger grew stronger. For a moment she could not summon any rational thought. She wished only to lash out at Lord Shrift, to harm him, to extract retribution. When she overcame her rage Darla started a list of the actions she intended to take in order to hold Merk Shrift accountable. "I will submit a complaint with the other houses. I will take this before the court and king. I will not stand for this! I will..."

"Those are reasonable but lengthy steps, lady," interrupted Trader Grom. "You may not have time for them to work."

Her anger subsided to a level where reason became possible. Grom was right. Politics took too long. The threat to House Yen was imminent. She could go to the other families and the king with her story and the little proof she had, but even if they decided in her favor it would take months or maybe years. In the meantime, Merk Shrift would deny her aid. Most likely he would actively begin to work against her and deploy his ill-gotten lancers to harass House Yen in ways that would not draw the direct attention of the other houses or the monarch.

A new and equally unpleasant thought sprang forth in Darla's mind. Lord Shrift might already be doing exactly that. "This is horrible. What am I to do?" Misery and doubt made her question sound like a plea and Darla could feel how close she was to being overwhelmed by hopelessness.

Trader Grom smiled. "That is easy, my lady. Do that which your enemy least expects."

Δ

"You want a trial? I'll be happy to oblige you," said Reest, his knuckles were white upon the hilt of his saber and his entire bearing radiated anger like heat from a forge.

"Not you," spat the captive with anger of his own. "Him! Your captain," said the man with a thrust of his chin toward Jalan.

Reest's jaw clenched and then he said, "Think you'll have an easier time of it with the captain?"

"Don't you? He's a boy. No doubt a noble's son trained by some adequate and unimaginative arms master. You're just the warhorse he's using to ride me down. Look at you, chomping at the bit and afraid to stand aside and let your *captain* face his own fight."

Jalan stepped forward and placed a restraining hand on Reest's shoulder before the fist leader could respond to the provocation. "Hold. It's his right to face any able bodied opponent on the field. Moreover, although his colors are false, he wears a captain's braid. He may pretend to be of our house, but I doubt he pretends to his commission."

"And you," said Jalan turning to the captive. "You want to fight me as your trial? So be it. What will it be? Sabers, knives, clubs?"

"Your man's nearly killed me already. What guarantee do I have that I will be free to leave if I win?" said the captive.

"You will have to trust in the adequate sense of honor instilled in my men by their unimaginative training."

"I think I'll trust in my own skill instead. I'll face you man to man with no weapons. Then when I best you, you'll still be alive, which gives your warhorse here no call to trample me. You'll have to live with the shame of losing. But let's be honest, I'm a veteran and you are a boy. That should be some consolation. No one expects you to win."

"Then your loss will be even more humiliating," said Jalan. He held up his hand to silence the rough laughter and jeering remarks of some of his men. "But, besides your humiliation, what do I get if I win?"

"What do you mean? You've already taken me prisoner and you are likely to take my life. There is nothing more," said the bound man.

"I know you are a mercenary, but even you have a code. If I win, I will trade your life for your loyalty to me."

The mercenary tried to respond and Jalan gestured with his hand to indicate he had not finished. "Your loyalty and the loyalty of your men. That is what I get for giving you your life."

Jalan could see the gleam of speculation in the bound man's eyes. "And your men will not interfere? When I win, I take a horse and go unhindered?"

He doesn't believe he can lose. Jalan raised his voice so that everyone could hear him and said, "I will give the mercenary his trial. We will face each other hand to hand. The first one rendered unconscious loses. If the mercenary captain wins, give him a horse and let him go free. Those are my orders and anyone who disobeys them is a traitor to House Yen. Are we clear?"

Reest and a couple of nearby lancers said, "Aye, captain."

"I said, 'Are we clear!'"

"Aye, captain!" came the unanimous reply.

"Satisfied?" said Jalan as he watched for the captive's reaction.

The bound man gave him a small crooked smile and said, "Aye, captain," in a mocking imitation of Jalan's lancers.

"Get him up. Check him one more time for weapons. Cut his bonds and remove his armor." As Jalan gave these orders he unbuckled his sword belt and laid the weapon aside. Then he undid the straps of his armor.

Reest put his saber back into its scabbard and drew his belt knife. He stepped around the tree and severed the laces that bound the man's wrists together. Shrim, Reest and a third lancer formed a rough triangle around the tree and the prisoner. They kept watch as the mercenary massaged his wrists then slowly rose to his knees and stood up.

Reest said from behind the man, "Remove your armor." But the mercenary had already started to imitate Jalan by undoing the buckles of the few pieces of armor he still wore.

"I'm sure I'll be faster as soon as the blood returns to my fingers," quipped the mercenary in response to Reest while he kept his eyes on Jalan.

Shrim and the third lancer, Imus, helped the captive mercenary. In a short time the man stood unarmored and unarmed.

"Clear a space!" shouted Reest. Lancers stepped out of the largest patch of nearby open ground and moved to stand beside their compatriots among the surrounding trees.

Jalan moved to one end of the cleared ground. The mercenary took up a position no more than five paces away at the other end. A wall of watching lancers and trees formed a barrier around Captain Jalan and the captive. If the mercenary tried to run, he would never get past Jalan's men. The mercenary ignored the surrounding men and kept watching Jalan.

He keeps trying to anger me. Is he looking for a sign that it's working? Jalan studied his opponent's reactions; it only made sense that the mercenary did the same by watching Jalan.

"Ready, boy?" said the mercenary.

Moving into a slight sideways crouch, Jalan took up his position with his loosely open hands raised in front of him. He started to say, "Ready," as the mercenary sprang forward and dove with outstretched arms.

Jalan leapt up and out of reach. The mercenary landed hard and slid across the uneven root covered ground with his empty outstretched arms before him. Jalan drove his booted feet down hard and slammed his full weight into the prone man's shoulder blades. The man choked off a shocked cry of pain and tried to roll onto his left side to spill Jalan off his back. The young captain dropped sideways and slipped down behind his twisting adversary as he delivered a sharp blow to the mercenary's ribs with his right palm. Jalan snaked his left arm around the mercenary's neck and choked him from behind.

Strong fingers dug for purchase on Jalan's arm as his enemy tried to grasp it and break free. Jalan grabbed his own left hand with his right and pulled as hard as he could to keep the prying fingers from tearing his arm away. The pain in his arm and the flailing he took from the prisoner's thrashing about did not matter. His men and what happened to Cail were all he cared about now.

Time passed slowly with his body in the full fever of combat. If he made a mistake, if he held too long, he lost any chance to prove the truth he had glimpsed in the prisoner's mind. The difference between unconscious and dead came in heartbeats. He had to win and he had to keep the captive alive. His count reached ten and he screamed to himself to release his hold.

The mercenary's head and shoulders weighed upon Jalan's left arm. The fingers no longer dug painfully into his forearm and all the thrashing had ceased. Jalan pulled away and rose to his knees, his opponent's motionless form lay on the clearing floor. Panic formed a stone in the pit of his stomach until he saw beyond any doubt the slow rise and fall of the man's chest. *Thank fortune.*

Only now did Jalan hear the pandemonium surrounding him. He swiveled his head about trying to look in every direction at once. The fear for his opponent's life replaced by the fear that the man's friends had returned in force. Reest stood beside Jalan and offered a hand to help him rise. As Jalan was pulled to his feet he realized the lancers were cheering and calling out praise for his victory. It was not battle, but celebration that surrounded him and he felt his smile grow upon his face.

"They won't be cheering when his old friends arrive," said Reest as he prodded the mercenary's body with his boot. "What do you want to do now?"

Jalan massaged his left arm as he said, "Master Enmar and Major Erida would never forgive me if I didn't know that answer after all their lectures. When faced with a superior force, we retreat."

"Did they happen to say where to?"

Jalan looked down and shook his head, "I'm hoping our new friend can help with that. Have a couple of your men take charge of him. Give him water when he wakes. Then get him on a horse." Jalan caught Reest's eye. "And, no more rough handling unless he starts something. He might be a scoundrel and a mercenary, but he's our scoundrel now."

"Aye, captain," said Reest with a quick nod of his head.

"Also, have the company prepare to move out. I'm worried we may have stayed here too long already."

"Aye, captain," repeated Reest as he acknowledged Jalan's additional order and perhaps agreed with his worry. The fist leader called out the names of two of his fist and waved them over. Captain Jalan collected his armor and weapons. His left arm was scratched and bruised. He limped because of a kick to his right leg from the heel of the mercenary's boot. While he walked along his body informed him of other more minor injuries. Donning his armor, he tried to brush off dirt and debris from his uniform and discovered at least two tears in the fabric that he would have to mend provided he lived long enough to have the opportunity.

In this one routine moment of strapping on his armor, the idea that he could die became real. Some men already had, both his and the enemies'. Jalan's fingers trembled as he buckled a vambrace onto his left forearm. The trees loomed above him like a dark shadow of doom and he sensed the formless spectral presence of death drifting in the air around him. He closed his eyes and thought of home. The images of family appeared to him, mother, Darla, Tomac, Vee and, surprisingly, Jacey too. Then a memory of his father, Hallis Yen, returned to him. The Lord stood before him and towered over Jalan's little boy self like the trees that loomed above him now. Lord Yen said, "Death rides with a man all his days. It is not something to be feared, but a companion worthy of respect and careful consideration. Death rides with us always, until the last, when we ride with it." The love and comforting presence of his father enfolded him.

He opened his eyes and said to the shadows, "Ride beside me as you must, but I will not carry your fear in my heart, for that is where my family dwells."

The End

Dangerous Ability
Book Two of the Crown Saga

Danger lies down every road.

Did you enjoy Jalan's adventures?
Want to read more?

Book Two is coming in 2016.
Check **aldusbaker.com** to learn more.

ABOUT THE AUTHOR

Aldus Baker lives and works in Kansas. He is a father and husband, writer and software developer who juggles priorities like a circus performer. His lifelong love of science fiction and fantasy pulled him into writing. Aldus advocates that anyone who loves writing and is willing to do the hard work required can create the stories hiding in their hearts and heads. He enjoys creating those stories and reading the ones created by others.

Connect with Aldus Baker --
Website: aldusbaker.com
Podcast: Aldus Baker Update

www.ingramcontent.com/pod-product-compliance
Lightning Source LLC
Chambersburg PA
CBHW070821120626
46556CB00002B/609